PRAISE I

"*Amber Wolf* is enjoyable as a narrative, edifying as history, and inspirational as a story of struggle, survival, and ethnic pride—the David of Lithuania is caught between the twin Goliaths of Russia and Germany. What can a young girl do? You'd be surprised."
—Steve O'Connor, author of *The Witch at Rivermouth* and *The Spy in the City of Books*

"Captivating. *Amber Wolf* is a compelling story of bold resistance in the face of insurmountable odds. Wong skillfully paints a portrait of the hidden and mostly forgotten people who struggled to survive behind the front lines of the cataclysm of World War II."
—Guntis Goncarovs, author of *Telmenu Saimnieks – The Lord of Telmeni* and *Convergence of Valor*

"*Amber Wolf* is a compelling story that captures the brutal truth along with fictitious elements of Lithuania in World War II. Before my parents passed, I listened to countless hours of stories just like this and the reasons why they fled their beloved homeland. Bravo to Ludmelia for never giving up!"
—Daina Irwin, daughter of Lithuanian survivors

"In *Amber Wolf*, Ursula Wong turns an unflinching yet sympathetic eye on a brutal slice of history. Compelling and engrossing, and almost impossible to put down."
—Leigh Perry, author of the *Family Skeleton Series*

"Ursula Wong takes on a heavy subject: the grass roots of World War II—not of large-scale mass destruction, but of hand-to-hand combat, villager against soldier, deep in the forests of Lithuania. Ludmelia Kudirka is a girl who must quickly grow up if she wants to survive and ultimately fight for her people, her land, and her freedom. In *Amber Wolf*, Wong gives us a story complexly woven, yet easy to follow, and impossible to forget."
—Stacey Longo, Pushcart Prize-nominated author of *Ordinary Boy*

"*Amber Wolf* is a trek into territory that, seventy years after the dramatic events enacted there, still remains largely unexplored. Ursula Wong, using new source material and careful research, has crafted a harrowing, heroic, and at times poetic, tale of people caught up in the cataclysms of war."
—David Daniel, author of *The Skelly Man* and *The Marble Kite*

Books by Ursula Wong

Amber Wolf (The Amber War Series Book 1)

Amber War (The Amber War Series Book 2)

Amber Widow (The Amber War Series Book 3)

Black Amber (The Amber War Series Book 4)

Gypsy Amber (The Amber War Series Book 5)

Purple Trees

The Baby Who Fell From the Sky

Finding my Father: A Story of Vietnam

Ursula is available for speaking events and lectures on writing and publishing. For more information, contact her at urslwng@gmail.com and sign up for her popular Reaching Readers newsletter at http://ursulawong.wordpress.com.

Black Amber

Ursula Wong

Genretarium Publishing ~ Chelmsford, MA

Copyright © 2019 Ursula Sinkewicz

Genretarium Publishing, Chelmsford, MA
www.genretarium.com
For ordering information contact: info@genretarium.com

Cover Design by Jack Sinkus

Cover Photography courtesy pixabay.com

Map courtesy pixabay.com

ISBN: 9781695611290

All rights reserved. This work may not be reproduced, transmitted, or stored in whole or in part by any means without the consent of the publisher, except for brief quotes in articles and reviews.

This is a work of fiction. Names, characters, places, and incidents are used fictitiously. Any resemblance to actual persons, living or dead, or events is coincidental.

For more information about the author and her works, go to:

http://ursulawong.wordpress.com

First printing, November, 2019
1 3 5 7 9 10 8 6 4 2

To John

Energy security will be one of the main challenges of foreign policy.

—Daniel Yergin, Pulitzer Prize winning author of *The Prize: The Epic Quest for Oil, Money & Power*

ACKNOWLEDGMENTS

I'd like to thank all the people who graciously supported this project: Dale T. Phillips, Susan Fleet, Winona W. Wendth, Joyce Derenas, Sally Cragin, Ray Slater, Paula Castner, and Stacey Longo. For their subject matter expertise, I'd like to thank Michael Beck, Timothy Lawrence Champlin, Maria Egle Calabrese, and Esther Czekalski. I'd also like to thank the following organizations for their support and kindness: LABAS of Nashua, NH, the South Boston Lithuanian Club, the Corpus Christi Parish in Lawrence, MA, the Charles Zylonis Trust, Maironis Park in Shrewsbury, MA, and the St. Peter Lithuanian Parish in South Boston. I'd also like to thank the New Hampshire Writers' Project, the Seven Bridge Writers' Collaborative, and my friends at The StorySide.

A special thanks to Genretarium Publishing for support from their small but exquisite staff. A special thanks to Melinda Phillips for her kindness and expertise.

Finally, my deepest thanks to my husband Steve and my daughter Steph for everything they do, and all they tolerate. Unfortunately for them, I'm already working on another book.

Ursula Sinkewicz Wong
October, 2019
Chelmsford, Massachusetts

PREFACE

Set generally in 2020, *Black Amber* is the fourth in a series of novels about the relationship between Lithuania and Russia. It follows the history of the earlier books with a fictional story that reflects today's Lithuania, and in particular her political scenario with Russia. In *Black Amber*, Russian President Putin is out of office. His successor is Igor Fedov, who Vera Koslova deposes in a coup that takes place in book three, *Amber Widow*.

Black Amber addresses the question of whether Russia can be trusted as a major fuel supplier to Europe and China, or whether she will revert to a tactic she's used before in Ukraine—threatening to cut off fuel to exert influence. In the Ukrainian situation, the influence was for payment of debt. In supplying fuel to the EU, I contend there could be a set of political circumstances where Russia might ransom the fuel supply to force pro-Russia decisions in NATO or the EU.

I find that most questions involving Russia have many answers. I attempt to codify the German point of view for the pipeline as a necessary business collaboration with Russia. I express the concern the Baltics, Poland, and other Eastern European countries have voiced about Russian territorial aggression. I speculate about longer-term Russian interests (i.e. China).

The new Baltic pipeline that is cornerstone to *Black Amber* is a fictional pipeline modeled after Nord Stream 2, a real pipeline that goes from Russia to Germany through the Baltic Sea. Nord Stream 2 doubles the amount of gas flowing into Europe under the Baltic, complimenting Nord Stream, the subsea pipeline built in 2011.

Nord Stream 2 is due to be operational late in 2019.

The political issues surrounding the new Baltic pipeline are the same ones that affect Nord Stream 2, and are an important part of *Black Amber*.

The locations used in *Black Amber* are the same used by Nord Stream 2. Landfall locations for the fictional and real pipelines are the same: Lubmin, Germany, and near Narva Bay in the Kingisepp district of the Leningrad region in Russia. The control station in Zug and the Slavanskaya compression station are also real.

The holding company used in the novel, the Baltic Pipeline AG, is modeled after the holding company Nord Stream 2 AG. Both the real and fictional companies are headquartered in Zug.

The cyberattacks behind the Ukraine power grid outage in 2015 and the NotPetya attack in 2018 on their financial systems actually occurred. There is a surprising amount of information on the internet about hacking into pipelines and preventing cyberattacks. All cyberevents mentioned in the book, save the one relevant to the new Baltic pipeline, are real.

The novel starts with a scene in the KGB Museum in Vilnius, also known as the Museum of Occupations and Freedom Fights. During the occupation, the building housing the museum served as KGB headquarters. Visitors can go inside the cells in the basement and into the execution room described in Chapter 1. I was deeply affected by my visit there, and could only remember basics, such as thick walls containing divots and dots of a rust colored substance. I believe there was sand on the original floor visible now only through glass panels. It is a startling place.

Upstairs, the surveillance equipment used during the Cold War is on display—file cabinets containing information collected from informants and examples of more sophisticated electronic techniques.

On the ground floor between the basement cells and the upstairs surveillance rooms, there is a collection of artifacts from the Lithuanian partisans who opposed the Russian occupation. *Amber Wolf* and *Amber War* discuss the partisans in vivid scenes of historical fiction. Many items mentioned in the books such as partisan newsletters, bunkers, weaponry, and home-sewn winter camouflage gear are on display.

Baltic Watch is a fictional organization. ARAS, the Lithuanian Police Anti-terrorist Operations Unit, is real.

The towns and cities in *Black Amber* are real. The estates in Russia exist and many are currently owned by President Putin. Names of cities, towns, people and all non-English words adhere to the guidelines in the *Chicago Manual of Style* which calls for the omission of ligatures and diacritics. This makes the reading experience smoother for English speakers while keeping some flavor of the Lithuanian language.

All surnames have been "Americanized" in that the names of married and unmarried women don't adhere to the Lithuanian language. For example, in the novel, Lena's mother has a surname ending indicating she's either married or a widow—Markiene. Her husband's surname is Markus. Lena's surname is Markute in Lithuanian, as she's unmarried. English-speaking readers might assume these women aren't related as their last names are different. Therefore, I ignore suffixes in the interest of clarity in a book that already has a long list of characters.

Any mistakes are mine alone. Please contact me with any comments and corrections at urslwng@gmail.com. I'd be grateful for the feedback.

For those who wish to read more on topics covered in the novel, I've included a biography at the back of the book, along with a list of *Black Amber* characters. A map provides the general area where the *Black Amber* story takes place and the path of the Nord Stream pipelines.

MAP OF THE NORD STREAM 2 ROUTE

CHAPTER 1

KGB Headquarters, Vilnius, Lithuania—1946

Peter Landus flinched at the metallic bang of a cell door slamming. His head pounded. He was terribly thirsty and shivering from the cold. Rays of light coming in from around the dark cloth nailed over the window told Peter it was daytime. He didn't know whether it was morning or afternoon, not that it mattered. He considered getting up to pull away the covering so he could look out, but that would require getting out of bed and that was too much to bear. Besides, he knew what was out there and what the building looked like. He knew it was a short distance from Old Town. He knew the name of the street. There was an oak tree on the corner. Years ago, as a boy, he had played in the park nearby, when he and his mother had come to visit. Those were happy times. But then the Soviets came. There was no joy in Vilnius now. Perhaps there was happiness in the rest of the world as it healed from WWII, but not here. He pictured his mother's face rimmed by the kerchief she always wore, and her wrinkles gained from a lifetime of worry. But she wasn't worrying anymore—she had died in 1944. How he missed her.

He glanced at the dull green walls, wondering when his Soviet jailers would be back for him, and how long he'd last, for few left the prison alive.

Peter rolled onto his right side and winced, the throb in his shoulder worse than before. He felt every wooden slat beneath him, and imagined all the other prisoners who had lain here. Peter was certain they had avenged those who had died at the hands of the

Soviet invaders, just as he had done. Eventually, someone would avenge him, too. Of that, Peter was certain. But even amid the memory of all the souls who had passed through this cell and the people who loved them, he felt utterly isolated.

The raid had been two nights ago—or had it been longer? Peter and his friends had destroyed the communications lines to this very building, interrupting their interminable surveillance. The Soviets were always listening and watching. The upstairs rooms were filled with file cabinets jammed with information about the smallest things—a conversation with a friend, a nod to an acquaintance—blown into significance for no good reason. Peter had wanted to burn the files, but he hadn't the time and it would have been too dangerous. Now he didn't have a match, and the only things combustible here in the basement cells were people, and that damned rag over the window.

His friends who had joined him for the mission had escaped into the forest. Peter had stayed behind, believing the Soviets would never look for him hiding in an abandoned home right under their noses. But they had. The worst was that he couldn't get word to his friends that the house where he had hidden had been compromised. Someone had talked—perhaps a neighbor. He wasn't sure. When he didn't return, they'd know.

By their questions, Peter realized his captors suspected he had a great deal of information about the resistance–the partisans–Freedom Fighters–Brothers of the Forest–still stubbornly fighting the occupation, opposing the Soviets in any way possible. They had asked him the location of the next raid, whom the partisans were planning to assassinate, where they met, what they were going to blow up, information about other cells, and their plans to disrupt the voting that was to be held this spring, as if anyone's vote truly mattered. They suspected the skinny prisoner in this putrid cell was concealing a wealth of information. But Peter had told them he was merely a vagrant spending the night in an abandoned house. He had acted indignant, as if they were making a big deal out of nothing. It was his only hope. *Piss on them all!*

He stared up at the ceiling, thinking that everything he cherished and had ever done had come to this moment. This place and time were the culmination of his life. All he had to do was to survive the next torture. He had worked all his life for this test. If he passed, he'd save his friends. If he failed—well, he couldn't fail. He wouldn't. Having only one thing left to do to have lived a good life gave him an odd sensation of freedom. All he had left to do was to keep his mouth shut. One small thing.

Another noise—the scrape of metal against metal, probably someone looking in from the peephole. The guards were always watching. At the clang of a bolt sliding, the door swung open. Peter breathed in and stifled a moan.

Two guards entered the cell. One gestured for Peter to get up, but Peter was too slow for them. The other guard grabbed Peter's arm and pulled. It felt like a knife digging into his shoulder, and he cried out. He let his body go limp. The guard let go and Peter fell to the floor with a painful thud. They ordered him up. Peter lay still. One guard kicked him in the side. Peter closed his eyes and saw red. The color reminded him of the kite he had played with in the park as a boy.

The guards reached under his arms and lifted. He was half-dragged out into the corridor. They took him up a set of stairs, his bare feet bruising against the wood. They stopped at a landing and turned into a room.

The guards propped him up, gripping his arms. A single lightbulb in the ceiling shone over heavily plastered walls spattered with swatches and dots of reddish-brown. Peter didn't want to consider what they might be. Even the ceiling appeared to be of the same heavy plaster. The air smelled bad, like old earth and something else. There were deep gouges in the walls. There were no windows and no furniture—no chair and table for the Russian bastards who had attended his previous sessions. One had winced at the blood and teeth Peter had spat onto the floor yesterday. Peter had laughed out loud. Or had he? Had it only been earlier today? Or had he imagined it? His head hurt so badly he couldn't think. *My God, what if I said something and don't even remember?* Peter's heart raced. He felt panic rise to his throat. He had never been taken here before, but had heard of the place. They called it the execution room.

A man in a khaki uniform stood in the middle of the room, holding a revolver. He shrugged, as if fate absolved him from what he was about to do.

Peter spat at him, but the little saliva he could muster dripped harmlessly down his chin.

"Bastard!" muttered Peter as he stared into the man's eyes taunting him, daring him. Peter pretended control when he had none.

The guards forced Peter to his knees. Bending his arms back, the guards awkwardly stepped away from his body. The man brought the gun to Peter's forehead with a touch of cold metal.

It had all been for nothing and yet, maybe for everything. He would be avenged sometime, somehow, probably by someone he didn't even know. It's all that mattered.

The gun barrel pressed firmly against his head.

"I'm coming, Mama."

CHAPTER 2

The Kremlin, Moscow—2015

Vera Koslova looked up from the computer screen resting on her monstrously large desk. The surface was strewn with papers and red file folders, most of them from Vladimir Vladimirovich Putin. All were marked confidential. She glanced at her watch—silver with a small face surrounded by diamonds. It was part of the collection she was amassing. Like many Russians, she loved timepieces.

Yuri Rozoff, a Russian businessman, was due in ten minutes, and she had to be ready. She ran her fingers through hair that was turning white—the changed texture made it feel even fuller—and put the folders and papers in a drawer. She couldn't risk Rozoff noticing any confidential papers on the desk, or reading them upside down. Vera always thought it best to assume her visitors were as clever as she.

Two chairs stood in front of the desk—wooden with upholstered seats. Behind her were dim walls of old plaster and harsh lighting that fell upon a large portrait of Vladimir Vladimirovich. She would have preferred Catherine the Great, but Putin would do for now. A large table and chairs took up some space, but not enough to look significant. The office was the size of a mausoleum, and just as depressing.

The only item of beauty was the samovar she'd inherited from her grandmother, a family treasure Babushka had scrimped and saved to buy. Standing on a small tea table in the corner, it was all the inspiration Vera needed to tolerate this office and her boss, Igor Fedov. Assistant to President Putin, Fedov was a man of tedious ways. If anything happened to the great Vladimir Vladimirovich, Fedov would undoubtedly step in to fill his shoes. Then she would make her move, and both Fedov and this damn office would be a memory. The thought gave Vera a pleasurable chill.

A decade as Fedov's aide, confidant, and occasional bed partner had gotten her here. It had also given her an uncanny understanding of the entanglements of Russian politics and business, whose interests were remarkably the same. She had also learned the Russian ways, the old and very effective ways of getting things done.

She had just turned off her computer when a knock sounded at the door. "Come."

Yuri Rozoff walked in. He was a good-looking man, impeccably dressed, although every time she saw him, he seemed a little heavier, and his clothes a little tighter. She suspected he dyed his hair, because flawless black was unusual for a man of his age.

Rozoff looked around the office, as if sizing it up. He smiled and offered her his hand.

"Yuri, this isn't necessary," said Vera, remembering his old-world manners.

"Indulge an admirer."

Vera placed her hand in his. He lowered his head and kissed it. His lips were soft.

She smiled as she opened the bottom drawer of her desk, bringing out a bottle of Khortytsa vodka and two glasses. She had begun offering her guests a drink several years ago. She had found that the presence of alcohol changed the dynamics. It helped them relax and feel that the meeting wasn't going to be bad. Often it was, but rarely for her. She poured out a measure in each glass and handed one to Rozoff.

"To your health," said Vera. She took a sip.

He drank it down in a single gulp. She refilled his glass.

"How are things at the Baltic Pipeline AG?" said Vera.

"It doesn't seem right that the Germans own the company that manages the Baltic pipeline project, after all we Russians are the main investors. It should be us, but that's just one man's opinion. The CEO, Katharina Becker, has settled in nicely. As a German, a renowned chemist, and a woman, she lends credibility. Just as you had intended. No one's going to forget that there are Russians on the management team, but it becomes less of an issue with Katharina running things and Joe Day, the CEO of Britain-Energy, also on the team."

"Give Katharina as much positive visibility in the press as you can. My assistant, Nina Ditlova, can help you with that. By the time it's widely known that Katharina's husband was in the East German Secret Police, the Stasi, she needs to have such a strong reputation that his past won't matter."

"Certainly, Vera. I know you and Katharina are old friends."

Vera swirled the liquid in her glass, admiring how it caught the light. "I actually met Katharina's husband first. I was on a trip to Germany just when the KGB had reorganized into the FSB. He introduced me to Katharina at a reception in the Russian embassy. We became friends immediately. She taught Nina and me how to ski."

Rozoff gave her a tight smile. "We've done substantial work on the pipeline already, but there's an issue. We're getting opposition from our business associates in Russia. Some say there's no need for a second pipeline under the Baltic Sea. The one we built in 2011 has the capacity to supply fifty-five billion cubic meters of gas to Europe—enough to heat twenty-six million homes for a year. The cost of doing a second pipeline is very high. We even need to select a different route from the first one because of safety distance needs between high-pressure pipelines. They're asking, why do you want to build it? Why do you want to double the capacity? How much gas do you think Europe needs?"

Vera smiled. "The North Sea fields are depleting—Dutch gas isn't going to last forever, even with reduced consumption. The likeliest fuel alternative for Europe is shale gas LNG—liquefied natural gas imported from the Americans. Europe has an LNG terminal in Rotterdam, another is the Bacton terminal in the UK, but are there enough? Besides, the cost to liquify the gas to make it safe for transport, and then turn it back into a gaseous state again for consumption is very high. Russian gas will always be cheaper because our gas goes to Europe through pipelines. There are no liquification and regassification costs. I think we can convince Europe that buying our gas through the Baltic pipeline will be much cheaper, more reliable, safer, and better."

Rozoff cleared his throat.

Vera smiled. "Once the gas from the second Baltic pipeline is available at a good price, you think Europe won't buy it?"

Rozoff shrugged.

Vera said, "I need Nina Ditlova appointed to the management team at Baltic Pipeline AG."

"But she's your assistant."

"And I want her to be your equal on the management team."

He puffed out his chest. "We already have two Russians there—accountant Krum and me. I don't see the need for another Russian. What do you expect Nina to contribute? The staff from the first Baltic pipeline is still working. The environmental impact studies are done. Surveying the seabed is almost complete—it was a nightmare avoiding munitions that had been tossed into the sea during WWII. Our Russian company, EnergyLine, has a plan for laying the pipeline. We have initial agreements with other companies to assist. We've done all the preparation necessary to grant contracts and start the work. I have everything under control. Besides, the board is fully staffed. I'm not sure I can add anyone else."

Vera scowled. "Do whatever's necessary to convince them to appoint Nina. Remember my promise. That should be enough incentive for you."

"Vera, I do things for you because I like you, and you're the smartest woman I've ever met. I can't lie. I'll make a lot of money if the second pipeline is completed, but asserting your influence to make me prime minister is something that I doubt even you can do. Fedov will get the presidency when our beloved Vladimir Vladimirovich either steps down or, God forbid, meets his maker. Fedov will appoint Grinsky as prime minister. And Grinsky's no fool—once he's in, you can bet he has friends who will keep him there no matter what you do."

Why do men always underestimate me? "We all hope that Vladimir Vladimirovich lives forever, but things change, especially here in Russia. It may not happen the way you expect, and it may take years, but you'll be prime minister. First, we need to build that second Baltic pipeline."

Rozoff looked nervous.

Why is everything so hard for this man? "It's imperative that more Russians are on the Baltic Pipeline AG management team, because they will ensure that our company, EnergyLine, gets the pipeline contract."

Rozoff leaned forward. "We have to allow open bidding. I have confidence that EnergyLine will win, but there are no guarantees. Especially not in this business."

Vera's face grew rigid. "Once EnergyLine gets the contract, I want them to be directed by the management team to augment the pipeline with the most sophisticated military-grade acoustic and visual sensors available. Put them along the entire pipeline. The management team must see to it. The accountants—even Krum—are sure to argue against it from a financial perspective. I need both you and Nina to sway the decision. Tell them that the visual and acoustic sensors will appease the environmentalists who are worried about leakage. Tell them it's for better security. I don't care what you tell them. But I want the best sensors available because the information they provide may be useful to us."

"Those sensors are cutting edge. They're going to cost us a fortune. The engineers will say that the pressure valves will tell us if there's a leak and that should be good enough. As to security, who would have the resources to bomb a subsea pipeline?"

Vera stared at him. He looked worried. She liked that. "My old KGB contacts will give you all the help you need to convince the management team to do as I ask. Shall I get them involved?"

Rozoff tugged at the collar of his shirt. "I don't think you need to involve your friends. We're already exploring the use of acoustic sensors to detect outages. Undersea, it's the most reliable means. We just haven't reached a decision yet."

"Be sure to reach the right one." Vera watched him. "We need to assume terrorists will attack the pipeline." She waited for the words to sink in. *Two things in this world make men nervous: smart women and bombs.* "We need to be prepared for a strike as it's being built. We need to screen every person, every inch of every supply ship, and every scrap of material. Security needs to be an absolute priority. As soon as pipe is put in place on the seabed, I want it monitored. I want to show a strong presence so that subversive groups won't even think of interrupting the work. Once gas is flowing into Lubmin, Germany, we need to constantly monitor for an attack and be prepared to bring in our military if necessary."

"Who ever knew that there'd be such fuss over a little Russian gas?"

"If anything happens to my pipeline, I will hold you personally responsible." *That should get his attention.*

Rozoff took another swallow of his drink.

Vera waited for him to put down the glass before speaking. "I also want EnergyLine to own 50% of the pipeline."

"That's a lot of money. Accountant Krum expects the pipeline cost to exceed eight hundred billion rubles—thirteen billion US dollars. We'll need investors."

She clenched her jaw. "As long as we own half, you can bring in whatever other investors you like—Germany, France, the UK, and others."

Rozoff's expression finally showed a glimmer of understanding. "Germany wants that pipeline badly and is our ally on this. The EU investors could try to assert themselves, but without Germany's support, they won't be able to. Then owning that much pipeline and the gas running through it gives us reason to operate and maintain it. If we see any threat, we can take military action." He sat back. "That puts us in a very powerful position."

Vera suppressed a smile. "Exactly. And after the pipeline is complete, EnergyLine will have access to the sensors and the fiber cable. Putin himself wants this."

Rozoff glanced down at the floor. "Unfortunately, there's more—political backlash against the pipeline."

"I expect the Baltic countries to continue to complain—they hate us. The Americans still think the Cold War is raging, so they're against it. Eastern Europe, well, they don't like us either, but I expect that to change once they see our gas prices. Everyone loves cheap gas."

Rozoff nodded. "We have other concerns. Eastern Europe is claiming that years ago Russia denied Ukraine access to gas to influence a political situation and that we might do it again. But this time, they're saying we'd deny gas to Europe."

"We turned off the supply of gas to Ukraine because they weren't paying off their debt. Besides, without our gas, Europe faces hard times. Germany knows this and are supporting us to ensure their energy future. I expect them to counter any objections—even from the Americans. The Germans will say they can buy gas anywhere they damn well please."

Rozoff grimaced.

"Don't look so concerned, Yuri. The Americans may threaten sanctions against any company working on the pipeline, but the Germans will stand up to them. I think the Americans will either back down or limit sanctions."

Rozoff looked unconvinced. "We're expecting an objection on behalf of Ukraine, too."

Vera sighed.

Rozoff continued. "The EU is complaining that with the second Baltic pipeline, Ukraine will no longer be getting two billion dollars in transit fees from our gas flowing over Ukrainian territory. Why the EU cares so much about Ukraine, I can't say. They're much quieter about other countries like Poland and Belarus who also charge us transit fees."

"Avoiding the gas transit fees in Ukraine saves us money. If we're forced to make financial restitution, make sure they phase out within a year or two at the most. The two billion we save will weaken the Ukrainian economy, and that's good for us."

Rozoff tossed back his drink. He still looked worried.

Vera continued. "Cheer up, Yuri. In a few years, you'll be in your villa in Sochi with your next wife, wondering whether to spend Christmas in London or Paris, and people will be addressing you as Prime Minister Rozoff. Everything will be chocolate. Just keep up the pretense with Grinsky. He can't know about your involvement in this or what we've planned. As far as he's concerned, you and I don't get along. At all. Keep away from Grinsky as much as you can without alerting him. It'll be easier that way."

Smiling, Vera picked up the bottle of vodka and reached over the desk to refill his glass.

FIVE YEARS LATER

CHAPTER 3

Vilnius, Lithuania—December

Matas Nortas wasn't a priest anymore. Life had blunted his spiritual side long ago. But once inside the entryway of the church of St. Peter and St. Paul, he instinctively touched his fingers to the stoup, moistening them with the holy water and blessing himself.

He unbuttoned his dark overcoat and reached into his pocket for a handkerchief. He held it to his nose and blew. No one used handkerchiefs anymore. Another sign of his age. He wasn't old, just under fifty, but felt like he was. He was still thin, straight, and fit. His hair was a deep brown and he had all of it, although some had turned white at his temples. His skin was very pale, a trait shared with many people from this part of the world. Women had always admired his strong features and dark eyes. He was surprised that they still considered him attractive. He rarely reciprocated their advances. For a long time, he hadn't even looked at a woman, for it returned him to memories he couldn't bear to revisit. His good looks had been a problem in his previous occupation. Now he just didn't care. If he had energy enough for the job he was about to be offered, that's all that mattered.

There was no woman in his life, but he had friends. The two most important were Rina and Simona Kleptys from Alytus, Lithuania. They snatched luxury vehicles and other high-end consumer goods like TVs and computer equipment from homes in the Netherlands and sold them in Eastern Europe. While the women made their money illegally, they were smart, knew how to take orders, and could run a job. Above all, he trusted them. If he needed more people, he should be able to hire them, no matter the work. God knows, there were enough people in Eastern Europe looking for work. The problem was that the specialists he sometimes needed were strangers. Matas didn't like working with strangers, but often, he didn't have a choice.

Matas ducked his head as he crossed the threshold, another old habit from hitting it too many times on low doorjambs in old churches. In his youth, it had felt like he was entering an elevated plane of existence. Today, he was just going into a building.

His mother had always wanted him to become a priest. As a boy, he didn't know what it meant to be a holy man. Soviet-forced atheism had prevented any true knowledge of the church. He remembered thinking he had to die and become an angel before becoming holy.

He thought back to the event that had turned him toward the church. He'd been sixteen years old and had gotten home from school early. He'd gone right to his room, not even calling out to his mother that he was back. He assumed she was in her bedroom, praying as usual. He hadn't wanted to disturb her. He'd fallen asleep. Voices had awoken him. He'd opened the door a crack, giving him a view into the kitchen. Papa was home.

"You're here early." Mama glanced at the door to her bedroom. Matas assumed she'd forgotten to put away her prayer book—her most cherished possession. More than once, Papa had threatened to throw it into the fire, so she hid it from him.

Papa lifted the lid off the pot on the stove and sniffed. He tore the end off the loaf of bread, and dipped it into the broth. He took a bite. Then he reached into his pocket and pulled out a handful of rubles that he threw on the table. "How about this, eh?"

"Where did you get it?" Mama gazed down at the money.

"A family moved here from Kaunas and came into the administrative office complaining they had no heat. I told them it normally takes a month. There's paperwork that needs to be filed. Things need to be done. The woman said they had a baby. I told her there are people in line in front of them with babies, too."

Matas dreaded what was coming next. He tried to remember Papa laughing and playing with him as child—a far cry from the man Papa had become.

"The woman cried," said Papa. "But I've seen it all before. Tears don't affect me. I've seen plenty of women turn it on and off like water coming out of a faucet. But the man, he understood. He shook my hand—he had rubles folded up neatly in his palm. He pressed them into my hand. No one saw. No one knew."

"So, the woman and her baby have heat?" Mama pressed her hands together.

"Hell no. They have to wait just like everyone else. When they come in next time, if there's another handshake, then they'll have heat."

"But the baby . . . Why do you do this?"

"Because everyone does it. It's expected. It's how the system works. Besides, it got you all this." He waved his hand at the peeling wallpaper, scratched furniture, and floors that looked dirty, no matter how much Mama scrubbed them.

Mama crossed herself. She shouldn't have done that.

"What, you're praying again? How many times do I have to tell you? If they find out, it'll be the end of me. No more job. No more rubles. No more extras."

"I don't care. I'd rather you dig ditches for a living. At least it's honest work."

Papa scoffed. "There is no honest work anymore. Besides that, you're ruining the boy. Religion isn't tolerated here. The Soviets say God is dead."

"Matas is almost a man. He can decide his faith for himself."

"It doesn't matter. He'll sign up for the Communist party, and join the Soviet Army. That's his future. After that, if he comes home, I can get him a good job, just like mine."

Mama spoke. "You mean if he survives. I don't want Matas to join the party or the army. He wants to go into the church. I want him to become a priest."

"Stop filling his head with useless dreams. The churches are closed. He couldn't become a priest even if he wanted to."

"How do you know his dreams? You barely say anything to the boy."

Papa banged his fist on the table. "I won't have you talking to me this way. He'll join the party, like I did. Like you should. It's the only way."

"You're wrong. I told you things are changing. The Soviets are losing control. Just wait and see. Matas will have a choice. He won't have to do what they say."

"Religion has no place here. You have to change too, or you'll die."

"My prayers bring me comfort. God will save me."

"I want this talk of the church to stop. You're ruining Matas. There's no life here for a priest."

Mama let loose a sob.

"Woman, you make me sick. You're just like all the others." Papa picked up the money and put it in his pocket. "I'm going out for a drink. I'll see you when I get back."

Mama clutched a hand to her breast as the door slammed. She went into her bedroom.

Matas quietly closed the door. Leaning against it, he slid down to the floor, and rested his forehead against his knees. "Please, God. Pray for us all."

That evening, Matas had transformed his mother's wish for him to enter the priesthood into resolve, foolishly thinking it would make Mama happy and help his father reject the corrupt system that was driving him to drink. Matas believed the church would save them all.

~~

Inside the church of St. Peter and St. Paul, Matas let out a long breath as the memory faded. His decision to enter the priesthood, made when he was merely a teenager, had ruined his life. It hadn't saved him or his parents. He gazed at the altar and magnificent bas relief along the walls and ceiling as the old familiar feeling of peace and serenity returned.

He shook it off and got down to business. Churches were for fools.

No one was here, but in his line of work, it paid to be thorough. He pulled out the mobile phone from his pocket. While the device was convenient, Matas was leery of the mobile phone company's ability to track a person's location. He turned his phone off, took out the battery, and put it back in his pocket. He got some peace of mind from using burner phones. He had no permanent number. When he changed phones, which was often, he gave his new number to the few people he trusted.

He turned left and walked the length of the church, past magnificent white frescos on white walls, paintings, statues, and angels. Near the altar, he went to the door to the sacristy and listened; silence. Entering, he found himself in a room where robes and vestments hung from a rack. He looked into a bathroom, then a kitchen. He checked that the back door leading outside was locked. Pausing at a desk, he ran his finger along the cool wood, noting the prayer book and the Bible, allowing himself a moment to remember the ceremony of donning the vestments and the excitement of Sunday service. He opened the door a crack and looked out before returning to the main part of the church.

Matas crossed in front of the altar, blessing himself before he was aware he had done it. He paused at St. Augustine's chapel. Then he moved into the shadow cast by a column supporting the massive arches over the marble checkerboard floor and waited.

After a few minutes, the outside door opened with a groan that echoed off the high ceiling. Then came the clack of steps and the tap of a cane. Matas stepped farther back where he could see without being seen.

An old man came down the corridor, wearing a cashmere coat and a fedora. He was well-groomed and trim. Matas thought he must be at least eighty years old. The old man proceeded directly to the chapel. Matas stayed in the shadows. It paid to be cautious.

The old man made the sign of the cross, and stood there as though waiting for something or someone. After watching him for a few minutes, Matas came into the light.

The man glanced back at Matas. "I chose this particular church because my great uncle was named Peter. The Russians executed him in 1946. We still talk about him. In my family, the dead are very much alive."

The old man sat down in the nearest pew.

Matas sat beside him. "I'm here only because I owed our mutual friend a favor. State your business. I'm very busy."

"I got out after the Soviets left in the '90s. I had a good life in the United States and became rich. I found a wife and had a son. It's my curse to have outlived them both. Leukemia took my boy. A parent should never have to bury their child." He pulled out a handkerchief from his coat pocket and wiped his eyes. "But I have friends here and visit often. Their ancestors ran in the same circles as my uncle once did. And you, too, have someone like our Peter in your family?"

Matas made no reply.

The man shrugged. "It's said that you turned to creative enterprises to make a living some years after the Soviets left. You have a reputation for being smart, getting things done, and keeping your mouth shut. If the work is illegal, it doesn't seem to bother you."

"I don't know what you're talking about." Matas glanced over his shoulder.

"I need your silence and your friends—connections who will help you do what I want. Over two hundred and fifty thousand of us were deported during the occupation—stricken from our homeland. Now we wait like sheep for the Russians to return. I left for the West when I could, but perhaps I should have stayed. This is my amends for having left, and my revenge for Uncle Peter. I can't say I regret the life I led, but now I need to leave something behind—a legacy. Besides, what's an old man with no family and a lot of money going to do?"

He held out a thick envelope. "Startup money. For immediate expenses. The rest will be deposited when the job's done, into the account number your friend gave me." He held up a scrap of paper. Matas glanced at it and nodded. He took the envelope and slipped it into the inside pocket of his coat without bothering to count it.

The old man continued. "Do anything you can to stir up trouble for them. I want them to regret having built the Baltic pipelines. When they finished the first one, I thought it wouldn't amount to much. But a few years later they wanted another one. The Russians always want more. I want you to mess up their plans."

"There's nothing I can do about the new Baltic pipeline. It's a multinational project with billions of euros already invested. It's going to happen no matter what we do. If we blow it up, they'll repair it. Security will be tight. An overt attack could trigger an investigation that may point back to us. Then, the Russians will take their revenge, just like they did during the occupation."

"It was a terrible time," said the old man.

"Various political groups have already tried to stir up trouble for the governments involved. Political protests. Demonstrations. A writing campaign to the United States Congress warning what would happen if the pipeline is built. Nothing has worked. Even sanctions threatened by the Americans have had no effect. The Russians are going to build it, so you may as well get used to it. There's nothing we can do." Reluctantly, Matas reached inside his coat for the envelope.

The old man put his hand on Matas's arm, stopping him. "Having Russia as a wealthy neighbor is dangerous for us. They'll be here again. It's inevitable. They only understand one thing, something that hits them in the wallet. I'm not talking about your average Russian who wants to feed his family and send his kids to school. I'm talking about the people with real power."

"You're speaking nonsense. No one gets close to the real power in Russia. There's no point in trying." As much as he would enjoy doing something significant to hurt Russia, Matas stood up to leave. There was nothing more to discuss.

"A minute. Just give me a minute."

Matas sat back down. The old man took a few deep breaths and continued. "I want you to show Europe and everyone else that Russia can't be trusted. I want you to show them Russia isn't a good business partner, that they only care about themselves, and that Vera Koslova plans on using the pipeline for political purposes."

"I'm not a miracle worker, old man. How do you expect me to do this?"

"When the pipeline is done, stop the flow." The old man coughed into his handkerchief.

"I told you we can't blow it up. It won't do any good."

"Organize a big demonstration—one that is noticed in the press. Then stop the gas from flowing. Everything's computer controlled. Break into one of their computers. Make it look like the Russians did it in retaliation for the protests."

"I don't even know if it's possible. If we stop the gas, they'll just start the flow again."

The old man stood. "All we need is for the Germans to notice."

Matas paused to absorb this. It was an ingenious idea.

Continuing, the old man said, "The world needs to remember how Russia controlled us in the past, and worry that they could control us again. Don't underestimate the power of a small and dedicated team. It's part of our history. The partisans had nothing, but they worked together. They were effective because they shared a common goal: freedom. That's what all this is about, even today. I'll be in touch. By the way, the partisans used to use code names to hide their identities from the Soviets. My Uncle Peter's codename was Badger. Today, it sounds silly. You can call me Peter in homage to him."

Matas got to his feet to let Peter pass by.

"For our next meeting, if there is one, no more churches," said Matas.

Peter paused with his hand on the back of the pew. "Make sure the world remembers what Russia is capable of."

The clack of Peter's shoes and cane echoed in the church as he made his way to the door.

Matas leaned back in the pew. How ironic that he was being asked to be the hero. He might perpetrate the greatest ruse since WWII when the allies tricked Hitler into believing the allied invasion would be in Calais instead of Normandy. Matas might very well save his country and all of Europe from the Russians—if he could figure this out. He'd never been asked to do something so important.

The chance to embarrass Russia was rare. The opportunity to remind his country and others that Russia could never be trusted was vital. It might save Lithuania from another occupation. Who knows? Matas thought of his father and how the Soviets had twisted his mind. Maybe it sometimes took a criminal to do a heroic act. Of course, the payday would be very good, too.

He got to his feet. He didn't have time to think about being a damn hero. He had a job to do, and it was the most significant and dangerous one of his life. He left the church wondering what in hell he had gotten himself into.

CHAPTER 4

Moscow—January

President Vera Koslova stood inside the dark arched foyer, surveying the room. Delicacies on dishes of fine china covered the table—herring, pickled beets, and blinis. Next to the little pancakes on the end lay a bowl of caviar on ice. Dim light fell upon the burnished woodwork, and light conversation filled the room. The air smelled of salted fish and cigarette smoke. Wind blowing in from Siberia shook the windows.

Her escort for tonight stood beside her—Colonel Orlov, invited to remind everyone that the newly promoted director of the FSB, the famed police organization she had once headed, was her close personal friend. He was tall, gaunt, and aloof as always. She remembered the moon-shaped scar on his back, and the last time they'd made love. Her husband had been away in Sochi. Happily, he preferred the milder temperatures. She looked forward to spending more time with Orlov, provided her responsibilities as president didn't keep her too busy.

Men stood at the bar, downing glasses of Stolksi, laughing in a guttural way. All wore expensive suits. Some glanced at their wrists and the designer watches. Vera mused that even one, if sold, could feed a village near Tomsk for a year. Not that anyone cared about the millions of labor camp graduates living in the middle of Asia. Since she grew up in that area, she had a special feeling for the people there. One day, she would help them.

Oversized bodyguards stood behind the men, their gazes on the arched entryway where Vera waited with her own security team. She glanced at their young faces and broad shoulders, repressing a sigh. *Even an older woman can dream.* They probably wondered why she didn't enter the room and join everyone else. But Vera was never on time to meetings. She liked it when people waited for her, and tonight was no exception.

Eventually, a few men at the bar noticed her, turning their heads in her direction. They stopped talking. The others followed suit like trained seals, although these men were anything but.

When the room was completely quiet, Vera strode in, her head held high, wearing a white suit trimmed in black Russian sable. She went to the head of the table and sat, her posture ramrod straight. She gestured toward the empty chairs with a hand. Voices murmured. They came in from the bar in groups of two and three, nodding to her before settling into the oversized chairs. Some glanced nervously at Orlov, who took a seat at Vera's side.

Rozoff and Prime Minister Grinsky put their glasses down on the bar and came to the table when all the others were seated, as if making a statement that the party could begin, although it didn't feel like a festive event. Faces were dour, and that worried Vera. It also worried her that Rozoff was drinking with Grinsky. She'd warned him to stay away from the prime minister. Perhaps it was nothing–perhaps it was something. She smiled, noting that the only other person with a pleasant expression on their face was the toothless oligarch named Zeitzev, the richest and oldest son of a bitch in the room.

Grinsky went to his chair, but Rozoff stepped up to Vera and held out his hand. Vera waited a few seconds–long enough for the others to wonder if she was going to slap him. She needed to keep up the appearance of tolerating Rozoff, but just barely. Frowning, she placed her fingers on his palm. Rozoff kept his gaze on her face as he bent down and kissed the back of her hand. The others released a collective moan. She couldn't tell whether they were regretting that they had not done the same thing, or chiding Rozoff for trying to provoke her.

With a sneer on his face, Grinsky coiled into his seat like a snake. After becoming president, Vera had allowed him to keep the position of prime minister because he was a familiar figure to the oligarchs and she wanted to keep a close eye on him. She hoped it wasn't a mistake.

Her gaze went from face to face. She knew most more by reputation than personal interaction. She was here because they held the real money and power in the country, inviting the president of the

Russian Federation to dine with them once a year in a long-standing tradition. Usually, it was to celebrate profits and new ventures for making even more money. Former President Fedov had told her about their riotously drunken parties. The ones for Putin had been notorious.

As Rozoff went to his place, Grinsky got to his feet, making a show of sipping some water and clearing his throat. "Madame President, I'm speaking for these esteemed businessmen at their request. They've asked me to express concern about our country's future. We're troubled about recovering costs from the second Baltic pipeline you're building." He glanced at Krum, the accountant with hands like a pianist. "Some are wondering why you're building it. The Americans claim our gas is a security risk to Europe. They've imposed sanctions on more of our EnergyLine directors, freezing their foreign bank accounts. The Americans have placed restrictions on the Yuzhno-Kirinskoye oil field, preventing any multinational company with US ties from investing, forcing us to increase the amount of our own money we must put into developing the field. Who knows where they'll place restrictions next?"

Thanks to creative accounting, sanctions were unlikely to affect anyone in this room. Already, Vera regretted allowing Grinsky to keep his role of prime minister.

Grinsky's arm darted out like a conductor raising a baton to an orchestra. "In addition, we've spent a tremendous amount of money over many years to extract gas in Arctic conditions at Shotkman, and the pipelines are costing us billions of rubles. What would you have us do?" He straightened his back, stretched out an arm and pointed a finger directly at Vera.

You ever point anything at me again, I'll cut it off.

Grinsky continued. "She has us put a ban on food imports from the Americans as if that will hurt them, and then she lays even more pipeline."

Grinsky's words lay in her stomach like day-old bread. They had invited Grinsky here tonight to claim her position, the presidency, as his own. Rozoff should have known this, and he should have warned her.

Vera laughed. "Sit down, Prime Minister." She stood, her knees shaking. She wanted to hold onto the edge of the table, but didn't dare. "I've always admired your straightforward thinking, however flawed. Please. Have another drink." She snapped her fingers at one of the waiters.

Zeitzev, the befuddled old man, lifted his glass. "Are we making a toast?"

Grinsky's face grew red. He remained on his feet. Vera stared at him. After a moment, he sat, trying to look as though it had been his intent all along.

She swept her gaze around the table. "I look forward to meeting with each of you individually, and I appreciate the kindness of your invitation tonight. Since Prime Minister Grinsky seems adamant to discuss business before we've eaten, I'd like to remind him of a few things."

She paused. "Opening the Shotkman field in the Arctic Circle and building the pipeline linking it to Volkhov makes even more natural gas available to Europe for their future needs, through our Baltic pipelines. Certainly, it has been expensive. And it will continue to be expensive because we must retain controlling interest. One day, we will find that useful."

She paused and looked around the room. All gazes were on her. "EnergyLine won't see a profit for some time. But once both pipelines are operational and Europe has more gas than they can imagine, they will want to believe Russia is acting as a good capitalist country. And we will be. They won't look to the Americans for LNG imports any longer, because any security and political concerns about Russia providing their energy will fade, and our Russian gas will always be cheaper than LNG. Even Eastern Europe will see that we can provide all the fuel they need to live and prosper, at a good price."

"I don't trust the Americans," said Zeitzev, waving his empty glass in the air. His skin looked brown and thin, the wrinkles like crumpled paper. He turned to the waiter. "More vodka!"

Vera continued. "We'll soon have the support of most countries in the EU, Germany in particular. I can assure you China will be watching. They'll see we've taken on the expense of building the Power of Siberia, the pipeline that will bring them all the gas they could want. And they will see we can be trusted to do business. Before the decade is out, we'll be one of China's largest providers of natural gas, and every one of you will be making more money than you ever imagined."

"But first, we must spend another three trillion rubles building the Power of Siberia," said Krum, the always dour accountant.

Grinsky spoke up. "China will *never* rely exclusively on Russia for fuel."

Vera ignored them both. "And with the fiber optic cable and acoustic surveillance we're installing alongside the pipelines, we'll have an underwater view of the Baltic, and an overland view of contentious areas giving us reason to send in our military to keep our pipelines secure."

Grinsky flushed. "But we don't own pipeline we install on foreign land. And the Americans have banned Chinese fiber-optic cable from Hong Kong."

"They haven't banned *our* fiber-optic cable. We just need to show how committed we are to the secure delivery of our fuel. When China sees how well we're doing in Europe, they'll be even more interested in buying our gas."

A voice. "How many people are in China?"

Vera let out a breath. "Almost one and a half billion."

Some faces looked distracted, no doubt doing mental sums on their bank accounts.

She continued. "Our gas is Europe's future, but more importantly, our gas is China's future. Right now, we need to provide as much fuel as Europe wants, as smoothly, quickly, and as reliably as possible." Vera waited, hoping her ideas would take hold. She wondered what the oligarchs had in mind for her. Killing by explosion was popular these days.

"How long do you expect it to take before things turn around?" said Krum.

Vera wanted to kiss him. She raised a glass and smiled. "To next year, gentlemen. May it be our best one yet." She stared at Rozoff, hoping a year would be enough.

CHAPTER 5

Riga, Latvia—February

Wearing a heavy, dark coat, Matas blended into the night as he walked along the street called Kalnciema iela, just outside the center of Riga. He passed prosperous-looking shops, well-kept houses, and a new hotel favored by tourists for its sumptuous buffet breakfast. He walked faster as he glanced across the street at the single holdout left from the Soviet occupation: a large rectangular wooden structure with shabby brown siding badly in need of paint. Several downstairs windows showed dim light through partially closed curtains.

The street was deserted, except for a few stragglers, as most people were probably home with their families. Passing the shabby building, Matas crossed the road, went to the nearest crosswalk, and turned left. He doubled back in the direction from which he had come, but not along the street. Instead, he cut through the parking lot reserved for patrons of the hotel, gated to dissuade locals from stealing their cars. While walking around an open patch of yard behind a house, he tripped over a child's toy frozen to the ground, and suppressed a painful groan. He held still, examining the brightly lit windows. People were inside, but no one appeared to have noticed him.

He went to the rear of the shabby building, and found the third window from the left, the only one in back that showed a light. He looked over his shoulder, and then rapped softly on the glass. The curtain moved. He went farther down the building to a door. After a moment, it opened, and he went inside. The door creaked as it closed behind him.

With a dull click, a light came on, although it wasn't very bright. There was nothing much to see other than faded wallpaper in some sort of flower pattern extending down a long hallway, and an old woman in a black skirt and white blouse. Matas and the woman shook hands. Then she proceeded down the hallway. He walked behind her. She stopped at a door and opened it, clicking the hallway light off using another switch. She went inside.

He followed her into a kitchen with a wooden counter and yellow cabinets. A fixture hanging over a table cast the only light. The room smelled of boiled cabbage. At the table sat a scruffy man and Matas's friends, Rina and Simona, who looked like they just stepped out of a Russian prison, tattoos and all.

Matas took off his coat and hung it over the back of an empty chair.

Everyone at the table stood. Matas greeted Rina first, kissing her on each cheek. She was athletic and had messy, short-cropped, white hair. Then he kissed Simona on her cheek. She wasn't as tall as her sister, and had long dark hair. Both women wore heavy eye makeup, and looked like they hadn't gotten a good night's sleep in weeks. Each bore ring tattoos on the fingers of their left hands.

The scruffy-looking man approached Matas. He had on thick glasses and wore a long-sleeved T-shirt under a tan vest.

"Matas, this is Arkady," said Rina.

The men shook hands, and then sat down in chairs across from each other at the table.

The old woman filled a plate with food from pots on the stove and placed it in front of Matas, handing him a fork. He ate with intensity. When he finished, she got up from her chair, took away his plate, placed it in the sink, and left the room.

"That's one creepy lady," said Arkady, adjusting his glasses.

"She was here during the war," said Matas. "Her father—killed by the NKVD. Her husband, by the KGB. That type of history makes us all creepy. You could learn a lot from her. She lets us use her house. She feeds us and keeps her mouth shut."

Arkady put his hands up as if he were surrendering.

Matas narrowed his eyes to slits. "Rina and Simona told me about you, and you're here because of them. Being from Belarus, you should understand people like her." He pointed to the empty chair where the old woman had sat. "But I think you spend too much time looking at your computer, and it's made you blind to what's happening around you."

"Look. I'm here to do a job. If you don't want me, I'm gone."

"Nobody's going anywhere," said Rina. She went to the refrigerator and took out four bottles of beer, putting one on the table in front of each person.

Matas twisted off the cap to one of the bottles and took a long swallow. According to Simona, Arkady was a capable hacker who made his living selling information he'd stolen using his computer. Before suggesting Arkady for the job, she'd explained that he had learned his craft from the great Russian hacker who went by the codename Volshebnik, or wizard. Arkady had been working at a coffee shop near Victory Park in Minsk. Volshebnik had a passion for double expressos and gaming, as did Arkady. Volshebnik took a liking to the awkward young man and began teaching him his craft. Under Volshebnik's guidance, Arkady was soon dividing his time between working in the coffee shop and trolling the internet for information that he sold to various organizations. Arkady became adept at breaking into web sites. Occasionally, he broke into corporate networks, where he'd found troves of national identity cards and credit card numbers. Occasionally, he and Volshebnik had worked together on larger jobs for "businessmen" from Ukraine and sometimes Russia. After a while, Arkady quit his job at the coffee shop and turned to hacking for a living.

"Tell me how you met Rina and Simona," said Matas.

Arkady adjusted his glasses again, obviously a nervous habit. "It was a few years ago. I needed a car, and didn't have a lot of money. My friend knew Rina and Simona and introduced us. They helped me out. When I needed some high-end computers and peripheral devices, I contacted Rina who found exactly what I wanted. After that, they supplied all my electrical equipment."

"That's it?" Matas gazed at the young man.

"Well, no. Over a bottle of vodka one night, we got drunk." Arkady chuckled. "I had a hangover for two days."

"But why should I trust you?" Matas leaned forward.

Simona spoke. "Arkady would be dead by now if he hacked and talked. We trust him."

Matas stared at the younger man, his expression rigid. "I don't know you, but Rina and Simona vouched for you, and I trust them. I have no choice but to rely on people with specific skills. I will agree to hire you, but under no circumstances are you to speak of this job to anyone. If I hear otherwise, I will come after you, and you'll wish you'd kept your mouth shut."

His eyes wide, Arkady nodded.

Matas took another swallow of beer. Besides a chance to get back at the Russians and help Lithuania, Matas had personal interest in seeing his little team succeed. His life as a priest had been a painful regret. Years in the underworld had provided a decent living, but he wanted something else. He wanted enough money to buy a place in the country and live quietly for the rest of his life. He was tired, sad, and yearned for peace. He was sick of deals and dark alleys, and watching over his shoulder for people waiting to club him, or rob him. He had never carried a gun, and didn't want to start. But the more jobs he took, the greater his chance of getting caught, hurt, or both. This job would give him the money he needed to get out before any of that happened. And he would get out in an honorable way, by doing something that helped his country. He couldn't imagine a better ending.

Matas took out a packet of cigarettes from his jacket and offered them to the women. Rina took one. He offered them to Arkady, who shook his head. Matas dropped the packet on the table and took out a cheap butane lighter, flicking the flame to life. Rina leaned in, cigarette in her mouth. Her pale features and white hair made Matas think of a moth going to a flame.

"So, what's the job?" said Arkady.

"We're going to stop the new Baltic pipeline." Matas blew out the flame.

"That's insane," said Arkady. "They're going to finish it no matter what we do. If we blow it up, they'll fix it. If we blow it up again, they'll fix it again. End of story."

Matas took a long drag of the cigarette and tapped the ash into the receptacle on the table, trying to control his annoyance at the younger man. He wanted answers, not excuses. "I never suggested blowing up the pipeline, unless you're a weapons expert and have been hiding that from me. Besides, security is so tight we couldn't even get close."

"So, what do you expect me to do?"

Watching the young hacker, Matas spoke. "The student protests last year did nothing to stop the pipeline from going forward. The Germans are resolved to get the gas they need, and to see that it gets to the rest of Europe. They don't care that it's Russian gas, and I don't expect that to change."

"Exactly," said Arkady.

Matas continued. "Even if we cause the pipeline completion to be delayed, it'll only be temporary. It may give the Americans more time to threaten sanctions, claiming Russian gas is a security risk, but I expect Germany will stand up to them."

"That's what I mean," Arkady said. He seemed to relax a little. He reached for the packet of cigarettes and held his hand out for the lighter. Matas tossed it to him.

"The pipeline is too big to stop." Arkady looked nervously at Matas. "We're done, aren't we?"

Matas scoffed. "We're just getting started! I want you to wait for the pipeline to be finished, and use your impressive computer skills to stop the gas from flowing."

"But what would that accomplish?" Arkady shook his head. "They'll just assume a blockage, or some issue with the monitoring equipment, and go fix it. Then the gas will flow again."

"It doesn't have to last for long. Just long enough for them to realize it was a cyberattack, Word will get out, which is what we want." Matas pressed his lips together.

Arkady looked confused. "You want me to hack into the computers controlling the gas flow? It won't be easy. To even consider it, I'd need information I don't have."

Matas reached into his inner pocket for a sheet of paper and handed it to Arkady. "That's the list of all the companies involved in the Baltic pipeline project, and most of the equipment they're using including computers and satellite systems. Some of it's public information. Some isn't, but I have a few friends who were able to put this together. It's accurate."

Arkady examined the sheet of paper, looking as if he had just won the Latvian lottery. "This is great. I can work with this."

Rina and Simona smiled at each other.

Matas pointed at the paper. "There's a surveying company, plus twenty or so ships laying pipeline. There are transport and supply ships, dredgers that dig trenches under the sea in shallow areas where the pipeline must be buried, and companies providing raw materials. There are also communications companies, and companies supplying computers for the pipeline control rooms."

"The control rooms are in Germany and Russia?" said Arkady.

"There is monitoring and control where the pipe makes landfall in Germany and Russia. But there's a control room in Zug, Switzerland that manages the gas flow through Europe. Some control operations affect the pipeline through cable and satellite networks."

"I get it," said Arkady. "Each company has secure internet access from their headquarters all over the world into Switzerland. After all, the executives need to see real-time graphs and monitoring as assurances that the project is moving forward as expected. I can hack into their networks and get into the computers on the Russian side. Then I can adjust the monitoring so the control room assumes an emergency condition, and stops the gas from flowing. I don't have to stop it permanently, just long enough for the Germans or Swiss to notice."

"Simple," Matas said.

Arkady scratched his chin. "Many Russians honed their computer skills programming guidance systems for nuclear missiles decades ago, and they're still working for the Russian government. I wouldn't be surprised if some of them were on the pipeline project. I could try getting in from the Swiss side instead and install a virus on a few workstations."

Arkady fingered the piece of paper Matas had given him. "Engineers from the companies whose products are in the control room might need access in case there are problems. Once I figure out how they get in, I can do a lot."

Matas stubbed out his cigarette. Sometimes all it took was a suggestion. "Work it through and tell me exactly how you plan to do it. I review everything. Understood?"

Arkady looked confused. "Hacking is a complicated art. I'll tell you everything when I figure out what to do, but will you understand what I tell you?"

Matas pointed a finger at Arkady. "In the work I do, I have to know a lot about technology and even more about people. You'd be amazed at what I know. If you can't explain what you're doing so I understand it, I'll know you don't understand it either."

"How long do I have?"

Matas leaned back in his chair. "The Russians are saying the pipeline will be finished this year. They haven't announced an exact date. When I hear one, I'll let you know."

"Terrific," mumbled Arkady.

Matas gave him a dirty look. "We need a major demonstration before the pipeline becomes operational. I need the three of you to set it up using social media, but no one can know you're involved."

Simona glanced at Arkady. "We should be able to create fake accounts and get things organized online."

Matas continued. "Do a practice run in a few months in Klaipeda, near Lithuania's LNG terminal. Get people riled up with something like Lithuania is independent of Russian gas so the rest of the EU should be, too. Come up with a few ideas and we'll go over them. Keep yourselves invisible, but organize it and get people engaged. I want to see how many show up."

Simona's face brightened. "If the demonstration is vocal enough, people will assume the Russians stopped the gas in an act of retribution. That will remind people that Russia may use gas to influence European positions in the EU and NATO. People will get scared and force their governments to look at alternative fuel sources. It's brilliant, Matas."

Matas smiled. *At least the girls were sharp.*

Arkady leaned back in his chair and stared up at the ceiling.

"Talk," said Matas.

"I was thinking about a virus to track keystrokes for account names and passwords as well as network information. During the cyberattack on the pipeline in Ukraine a few years ago, the hackers embedded a virus in a resume sent to a hiring manager. Once he opened the resume, the virus was free to do whatever it needed on the internal network."

"Good, good," said Matas.

"We'll need to be shrewder than that," said Arkady. "The Russians are particularly keen on cybersecurity. We could try phishing. We find people who work for the pipeline companies through online databases, and send them email with a link to a website we infected with a virus. We have to be creative, because people are trained to be wary of links in email messages from people they don't know. But if they visit the bogus website, the virus will infect their laptop or workstation."

"You could send an email from a fake computer dating service that includes a link to a website with the virus," said Rina, smiling.

"What makes you think I use a dating service? I've never used a dating service," said Arkady.

"I'm not saying that," said Rina as she massaged her temples.

"I could do pharming, too," said Arkady. "It's harder that phishing, but I'm experienced enough to pull it off. Pharming is directing users to an infected website that mimics a real one. Several possibilities come to mind, and I have a ton of work to do."

Matas turned to the women. "Also arrange a protest in Lubmin, Germany, at the European terminus of the pipeline. Do it month or so before Vera Koslova is there for the dedication ceremony. I need it to be big and loud and very anti-Russia."

"Everyone will think we're young people without any real clout, merely expressing our political indignation," said Rina.

"That's right." This time, Matas actually did smile. The women were good soldiers. But Arkady was still an unknown despite assurances from Rina and Simona. Matas couldn't risk their efforts to a loose tongue, and unless they kept this an absolute secret, their plan would fail. He hoped that wouldn't be a problem.

Matas continued. "Once it's done, I'll need you to post a few pieces to social media blaming Russia for the whole thing. Have the fictitious event organizer write something that points a finger to Russia, and watch the responses. If you need to, do another piece to stir things up."

"From now until this is done," said Matas, "I need the three of you to stay together as much as possible. No bars. No restaurants. If you buy anything—food, gasoline, phones, use cash. You two need to go to the demonstrations."

Matas handed Rina some of the money he'd gotten from Peter. He nodded at Arkady. "And you need to stay put. Change houses often. Rina and Simona, you know where they are. You won't be seeing much of me, if at all. Arkady, we'll talk using Rina's phone. Remember, ladies: we'll change mobile phones every few weeks."

CHAPTER 6

Vilnius, Lithuania—March

Vit Partenkas leaned back in his chair and rested his feet on his office desk, while pondering his time in Lithuania over his third cup of morning coffee. As head of think-tank Baltic Watch, he was lucky to enjoy the benefits of a national visa from the Lithuanian government, allowing him to stay for an extended period of time. He was doing important work—the organization's mission was to monitor Russian events, analyze them, and report to the world. He had dedicated his energy and his own money to keeping Baltic Watch alive and improving a reputation that had been badly tarnished by former member, terrorist Darius Artis. Vit thought he had turned things around. Unfortunately, he'd been wrong.

He got up from his desk and stood by the window, looking down at the cobblestone streets of Old Town and the bustle of students hurrying to their next classes. Vit enjoyed the stimulus from working near a vibrant campus. It also gave him ready access to scores of experts in history and politics—an intellectual smorgasbord. They had helped hone his opinion, and that of his small team as they pondered the currently favorable public opinion in Europe toward President of the Russian Federation Vera Koslova. It was a phenomenon Vit had labeled *Koslovization*. God knows, he needed help figuring her out.

Vit believed in the value of Baltic Watch, and was happy to finance it, but subscriptions to the ezine-style newsletter were down. The electronic or digital magazine had stunning pictures, in depth reporting, and analysis. It was on a restricted area on the Baltic Watch website available only to subscribers. The public area on the website had a blog for news headlines and quick commentary. It was also a place where readers could leave comments that were usually quite blunt. The Baltic Watch social media site was where he posted updates about the company. But even the public area on the website and the social media site were seeing fewer and fewer readers. Money was becoming a problem. Even though Baltic Watch was a not-for-profit company, he still had to pay for computer hosting services, utilities, rent, and cover all the other expenses. He simply didn't have the funds to keep things going. He purposely did not allow companies to buy advertising space in the newsletter, because he wanted no hint of collusion, especially with Russia doing business with so many companies on the new Baltic pipeline. Without a scandal to report or significant news to dissect, people just weren't interested in what Baltic Watch had to say.

Recently, he had let both of his employees go, a man and woman from Latvia. He hated to do it, but couldn't afford to pay them any longer. Vit had never taken a salary, and was living on income from his investments, all garnered from selling his tech company, Sagus Corporation. The US Department of Homeland Security had bought the company, and had called him a tech-savant for creating Annie, a program that learned from her mistakes.

Vit didn't feel like a savant. He was just a computer savvy guy with a damn good idea, and the balls to see it through. Selling Sagus had made him plenty of money, but not enough to live on and support the needs of Baltic Watch.

The only other money he had coming in was from Peter Landus, an elderly Lithuanian from Boston who gave a sum each year to Baltic Watch. Peter liked to talk about his great uncle and namesake–a partisan who had been executed by the Soviets after the war.

Vit was looking forward to Peter's visit and putting some funds into the company checking account. Vit had already decided the money would pay an intern's salary, and he'd already selected someone. The two of them would spend a few months working on a final project focused on the state of energy in the Baltic countries. It would require some travel, but maybe their report would be significant and people would renew their subscriptions to the ezine. The way things were going, Vit wasn't so sure.

Except for a miracle, it would be Baltic Watch's last project. At just over forty years old, Vit had one successful company and one failing company to his name. He should have done better. Europe needed an organization like Baltic Watch and it was slipping through his fingers. Vit pondered his current near zero-sum balance, wondering if both he and his organization had become irrelevant.

He looked around his office. Even the minimalist furnishings added to his feeling of gloom. He had a large wooden desk, and two chairs for guests. His only extravagance was a beautiful mountain scene printed by M.K. Ciurlionis, paid for with his own money. He could always sell it if he got desperate, but he'd hate to part with it. Off the foyer outside his office, there were two more offices, a small conference room, and a kitchenette with a full-sized stove and refrigerator. Even the appliances were rented.

His funk deepened and his thoughts turned to Zuza Bartus, his only glimmer of brightness whenever things looked bad. Although he hadn't seen her for some time, he often pictured her thick brown hair and tall, trim body. She was an anti-terrorism agent with the ARAS branch of the Lithuanian Police, and the woman he loved.

Zuza had convinced him to take over Baltic Watch, because it had been left floundering after the Darius Artis episode when the then head of the organization had disappeared and was feared dead.

Zuza had insisted it was an organization whose opinion mattered. Vit's life was in transition after having sold Sagus. He had enough money to live comfortably for the rest of his life, but instead of taking the easy road traveling and enjoying himself, he settled down in Vilnius, rented office space for Baltic Watch, and hired two Latvian journalists to help him keep an eye on Russia.

After his intense affair with Zuza and his proposal of marriage, she'd broken it off, saying she couldn't keep a husband happy while fighting terrorists. Vit had had a taste of that life when they had hunted down Darius Artis. Vit still had frightful dreams of a Russian holding a gun to his head.

Vit and Zuza had an amicable parting, but over time, missing her grew into an incessant ache. He was reminded of her constantly in the places they'd visited and the things they'd done together. He had even considered going back to Boston, but loved the unusual and wonderful city of Vilnius and didn't want to leave Baltic Watch.

Thank God he had Annie to ground him and remind him of his past success. Annie was his artificial intelligence brain-child, a computer program that extracted data from social media sites, online databases, and anything else on the internet. Annie could tie a face from a social media site to the face captured on a security camera during a robbery. That feature alone was enough for Homeland Security, DHS, to buy exclusive rights. But Annie was also able to learn. By the time Vit sold the company, Annie had become adept at cracking low level security systems gaining her access to even more online information. He didn't know how far she could go, and ached to find out.

His DHS contact had been Mrs. Brown, an amazingly smart and demure woman. After a lot of convincing, she'd allowed Vit to keep an old, scaled-back version of Annie for personal use only on his office computer. Scaled-back Annie couldn't run on his phone, or the computer in his car like before. This Annie could only use certain public repositories, couldn't crack any encrypted data, and couldn't use any private databases. Scaled-back Annie couldn't be changed or enhanced in any way. Even so, Mrs. Brown must have suspected Vit would try something. She'd told him to refrain from improving Annie's capabilities and that she'd kick his ass if she ever found out he'd been tinkering.

But Vit had written a backdoor into Annie long ago that no one knew about except for him. He'd been overjoyed that DHS had missed it in the scaled-back version of Annie they had given him.

Even though Annie was protected by state-of-the-art security, including two forms of biometrics, the backdoor allowed him to enhance Annie. One enhancement was to allow other people to use her. Vit called it delegated access. He could use the backdoor to enhance Annie in other ways, making her more powerful, but hadn't had a need. Not yet, anyway.

Delegated access made Annie extremely useful in the office. His employees had used it often. Even the scaled-back version was quickly learning and regaining some of the capability the DHS team had disabled.

Vit's office computer was locked in a chassis welded to his desk, and his desk was bolted to the floor, because he knew the risk if Annie were to fall into the wrong hands. Someone with enough skill, patience, and curiosity might figure out how to enhance Annie and break into online banking systems, for instance. But she was simply too valuable not to use. There was no way Mrs. Brown could find out what he had done—she had no access to his computer and he certainly wasn't going to tell her anything. As a precaution, he'd added a self-destruct capability. With one command, Annie would disappear forever from his office computer. He hoped he'd never have to use it.

With a new intern coming in, Vit would be delegating access to a relative stranger. But it wasn't so bad. Annie had done an extensive background check on all of the top candidates. Their backgrounds were impeccable. As an added precaution, Vit resolved to keep a close eye on the newcomer.

"Good morning, Annie," said Vit, speaking into his computer.

"What can I do for you, Vit?"

How he loved that sultry voice. "When's the earliest the new intern can arrive?"

"Late this month, assuming it would be at least two weeks after getting an offer letter."

Sometimes Annie felt like a friend. He missed having other people in the office. He missed hearing voices in the kitchen, being interrupted at any hour of the day, and having sounding boards for his ideas. He was looking forward to the new intern arriving. It would be good to have someone besides Annie around, even if it was temporary. Still, it felt like the best days at Baltic Watch were over.

"Got a minute?"

Vit turned to an old man standing in his doorway, leaning on a cane, and wearing a cashmere coat and a fedora.

"Peter! I didn't expect to see you until next week." Vit helped Peter out of his coat and into one of the chairs.

"I had a feeling you'd be needing this," said Peter. He reached into the inner pocket of his jacket and pulled out a check that he handed to Vit.

Vit stared at the piece of paper. He had never expected to be in a position where he'd need an old man's money to keep Baltic Watch afloat. And for how much longer? The end was inevitable. It got him money for an intern, and time to do one last report. It would have to be a good one. Vit put the check down on his desk. "Thanks."

"What will Baltic Watch be working on next?" said Peter, looking down at his hands.

"Assuming you'd make your regular contribution, I created a position for an intern to help me do an in-depth investigation on the state of energy in the Baltics. I want to look into the new Baltic pipeline and fuel consumption projections for Europe. I want to examine the future of Russian gas, and put the nuclear power plant in Belarus into perspective. I want to investigate the newly expanded LNG terminal in Poland as well as our offshore LNG terminal in Klaipeda."

"All anyone has to do is read any of the thousands of articles already on the internet."

Vit shook his head. "I want to consolidate all of the information and paint a comprehensive picture. Even now, the Baltic countries are considering tying into the new Baltic pipeline, and people need a real analysis that points out the positive and negative aspects of all the solutions available."

"It's a waste of time. No one cares about that damn Baltic pipeline. Investigate something interesting, like the Russian military exercises going on in Kazakhstan." His face flushing, Peter shifted nervously in the chair.

Vit steepled his fingers, confused at Peter's reaction. People here *did* care about the pipeline. He'd never seen Peter get agitated so fast.

"You're going to do whatever you damn well please, aren't you?" Peter breathed heavily.

"Can I get you some water?"

"Tell me about this intern you've hired."

"Her name is Lena Markus. She's from the US."

Peter looked annoyed. "Markus is no name for a woman. Is that Markute or Markiene?"

"Americans don't use surname endings to tell the marital status of women. She's not married, so it would be Markute. But she goes by the name of Markus."

"I hate American names."

Vit frowned. "The women I know would say their marital status is none of your business."

"That may be, but I don't have to like it." Peter waved his hand. "You couldn't find anyone locally?"

"A few dozen people responded to the job posting, and most were locals. But Lena stood out because of her minor in journalism and her background in computer engineering, reinforced with job experience in databases and computer security." Vit leaned forward. "I need someone who can understand technical specifications for the pipeline's computer-controlled monitoring and pumping stations, how the flow of fuel is regulated, leak detection, and so on. Tying into the Baltic pipeline is about more than just connecting pipes. I need someone who can get a real sense of the technology. I need someone who can delve into the nuclear power plant being built in Belarus. What technology does it use and how safe is it? I need someone who can understand the operation of the offshore LNG terminal floating in the Curonian Lagoon and its expansion capabilities. It's a tall order."

"So, you found a super-woman who can do all that?"

"She has a degree from one of the top engineering schools in the US. Her writing samples were excellent. I know from talking to her that she could use a little more self-confidence, but that's easily overcome. She held down a job in the private sector for several years and wants a change. She has family here, although they're out of touch. Lena would be a fine intern. She speaks Lithuanian fluently. I was waiting for your check before making it official and actually extending the offer."

"How long is she going to be here?"

"The internship is for six months. I was able to pay her less and stretch her stay by throwing in a rent-free apartment."

"Here in the city?"

Vit nodded. "My friend has a place in Pylimo Street, near one of the coffee shops, but he had to move back to Poland for a few months—family problems. I keep an eye on the apartment occasionally, but he's happy to have someone living there. It's in Old Town, and convenient to the office."

Peter pointed his chin at Vit. "I want you to keep me informed about this energy report you're doing."

Vit gave a thin-lipped smile. "You can phone me whenever you like."

Peter sat back in the chair and wiped his brow with his handkerchief. "I'm going home tomorrow and want a good meal before I leave. The Lithuanian food in Boston is good, but you can't get everything that's available here. Take me out to lunch. Today, I feel like having *saltibarsciai*—beet soup, and some good bread."

CHAPTER 7

Vilnius, Lithuania—March

Lena Markus hadn't been this excited in years. She was about to step off the plane onto the gangway leading into the terminal at Vilnius International Airport. She had flown in from Istanbul, where she'd spent a few days seeing the sights—the Blue Mosque, the Hagia Sophia, and the Spice Market for some shopping.

Here she was at last, coming to work for a company that kept watch on the Russians. Lena often spent what little free time she had reading the *New York Times*, the *Wall Street Journal*, or watching CNN. For years, Lena had chronicled Vera Koslova's rise to power as a hobby. It was remarkable that Koslova had emerged as leader of a male dominated society that had extremely few women in political office.

But who knew what horrible things Koslova had done while in the KGB? Her sudden appointment as president of the Russian Federation had to have been the result of astute political maneuvering. Besides, there was something about Koslova's perfect appearance, perfect speeches, and perfect smile that made her unbelievable. Lena was looking forward to finding new sources of information about Koslova, hoping to find a monster behind that flawless facade.

Lena was also looking forward to finding out more about her own family. As a child, Lena heard the stories her grandmother Aldona had told of the occupation, and of Lena's great-aunt Gerde, who had been deported to Siberia in 1940. Aldona had tried to convince Gerde to come to the US upon her release, but the red tape had been staggering. Then Gerde had stopped answering her sister's letters altogether. Gerde was probably dead, but she had a daughter who might still be alive. Lena wanted to find her, but it would be hard. She didn't even have an address. Still, she had to try.

"Goodbye," said the stewardess in heavily accented English.

Lena smiled her thanks, a little dismayed that she must obviously look like an American. She wondered if a recent tooth whitening process had given her away. The few times she'd been out of the US, she'd tried to blend into the local culture. She learned as much as possible about the average person and their lifestyle. She even integrated pieces of clothing into her wardrobe like the brightly colored serape from her trip to Mexico that she still wore occasionally. However, a little amber cross always hung from the gold chain around her neck, no matter what else she had on. Lena wasn't particularly religious, although she'd been raised in the Catholic faith. The cross was important because it had belonged to her mother and before that, grandmother Aldona. It was the most precious thing Lena owned. She wore it every day.

Above all, Lena was in Lithuania because she was badly in need of a change. Fresh out of college, she'd joined a technology company specializing in computer security. Troubleshooting security problems was interesting and challenging work, and she had a knack for it. Her boss's fatherly attention and careful scrutiny of her work had made her a better computer engineer. Before long, she was well ahead of her peers. She consulted on complex projects. Her presentations to management were well-received. Then her boss retired, and her new manager was as disruptive to her career as her old boss had been helpful. The new manager challenged her every decision, and went out of his way to undercut her self-confidence. Soon, she was second-guessing herself on time-critical work, while her manager looked over her shoulder. In less than a year, she was left with a constant feeling of fatigue, a sense that life was leaving her behind, and at twenty-six years old, too many gray hairs to count. The only thing that kept her in the job was an excellent salary. She'd been able to pay off her student loans and had a tidy sum in her bank account.

The last straw came when she'd overheard the head of the division congratulate her manager for resolving a complex issue when Lena had actually done the work, spending two weeks of sleepless nights on the problem. There was no mention of her name; no mention of her involvement.

Lena resolved to find a job at a new company offering her a great salary and stock options so she could retire at forty and travel the world. Many of her friends from college were already married and burdened with kids and a mortgage. When Lena's father had died twenty years ago, her mother had aged too quickly from supporting and raising three kids alone. Lena didn't want any of that. She didn't want to be tied down to anything or anyone. She thought love should be fun. She looked forward to seasoning the world with the broken hearts of men she left behind.

But before finding a new high-paying job in the US, Lena wanted to do something fun and different. When she had noticed the opening for a short-term job at the Baltic Watch organization in Lithuania, she'd had to apply. After sending her resume to Baltic Watch, Lena had done a telephone interview. Her chat with Vit Partenkas had gone well. Like her, he was a techie. She had heard of his old company, Sagus Corporation, and they had hit it off. She had expected a job offer, but after waiting two weeks, she gave up hope. She was disappointed, but also a little relieved. She had only minored in journalism and had no experience in the field. She was worried that she wouldn't do a good job.

Then Vit's email stating the offer and modest compensation package came in. Encouraged by Vit's enthusiasm about her background and capabilities, she was more than willing to accept. She gave notice at her old job, sublet her apartment, and packed. Two weeks later here she was, embarking on the adventure of a lifetime, and feeling like an excited teenager.

Once inside the airport, Lena followed the lines through immigration. After collecting her luggage and being waved through the last checkpoint by a female officer, she went toward the exit. She looked into the collection of faces, thinking that she should change some money into euros before getting a cab to the apartment Vit had arranged for her to use.

Then she noticed a tall blond man wearing scruffy trail boots, jeans, and a corduroy blazer. His eyes were a brilliant green. He was definitely handsome, and definitely American. He walked toward her and extended his hand.

"Lena? I'm Vit Partenkas. Welcome to Lithuania."

She broke out into a broad grin. *Calm down, girl. He's your boss!*

~~

That same afternoon, Matas sat at a table near the large front windows of a coffee shop on Pylimo Street in Old Town, sipping his second cappuccino. Peter had contacted him with news that Lena Markus from the US would be working at Baltic Watch. Her job would be writing a report about energy in the Baltics that included information on the new undersea pipeline. While that in itself wasn't alarming, the fact that Vit Partenkas was going to direct the investigation was. Vit had a reputation for being thorough and relentless. He also had friends in the Lithuanian Police and its ARAS branch.

The last thing Matas needed was Vit Partenkas and a government agent from ARAS snooping around. Any suspicion of terrorism would obligate ARAS to inform the government, and then Matas would have to disband his team and go into hiding. His only chance of success was if he and his team were ghosts. That was why they met in different places, even in different countries. The Schengen Agreement allowed them to travel across the borders of member countries without a passport check. Matas had a small network of trusted friends who owed him a favor and provided locations for his meetings as well as places to stay. For this job, Matas was cashing in on a lot of favors.

Despite his desire to remain invisible, sometimes it was best to meet a threat head-on. Matas needed to learn everything he could about Lena Markus. Details such as where she lived and her daily routine could be useful. That meant following her—a skill he'd practiced for years to achieve a proficiency upon which he could rely.

He already knew what Lena looked like from photos on her social media accounts. He couldn't understand why today's young people were so eager to reveal details about themselves—what they looked like, where they had dinner, and the names of their friends. They even revealed political and social views, in stark contrast to his own practice of anonymity. During the occupation, Matas had done his best to remain unknown. Since then, it had become a lifestyle.

Few people knew anything about Matas's background. His father had been born in Lithuania under the Soviet system, and had worked as a low-level Communist administrator. The pay wasn't very good, but there were advantages. His father charged a "special fee" to expedite various transactions as the norm. It brought in more than enough money for what they needed.

After Lithuanian independence, the Soviets left the country and his father was out of work. He managed to get a job as a school administrator, but was fired because he expected a new teacher to pay a "special fee" to process her paperwork. After the backlash that followed, Matas's father couldn't find a job anywhere. Freedom wasn't good for him. It took away the pride he had from providing for his family. Idleness brought depression, which caused him to drink, and that made him even more depressed.

The evenings his father was out, Matas sat with his mother. She explained what it was like going to church before the occupation—the flowers on the altar Easter morning, the scent of the incense, mass on Christmas Eve. She said that prayers were her enchantments. They took away worry and anxiety, replacing them with calm and a feeling that in God's hands, all would be right. Her stories became the context in which Matas framed religion. He couldn't go to church, because the Soviets had converted them to storehouses and museums. But on the rare occasion when a church opened, Matas and his mother would attend service. On their knees, they repeated the words of the priest so God might hear them.

When the Soviets left in the 1990s, the churches opened again. Matas entered seminary school. His mother was proud, and his father ambivalent.

Matas's father died while Matas was away at school. During the funeral, Matas cursed the Soviets for instilling in his father a warped sense of values and spoiling him for anything but their practice of favoritism. They had ruined him as thoroughly as a bullet would, although a bullet would have put a stop to the demons of alcohol that had actually killed him.

Even though Lithuania was free, the fledging country was still organizing its government and services when his mother was diagnosed with cancer. She couldn't get the drugs she needed, and soon died. Freedom hadn't been good for her, either.

Matas finished school and became a priest. He felt his most important role was listening to the problems his parishioners were having, and giving them guidance. Older men came to the church depressed, unemployed, and fearful that the best was behind them. Matas tried to help with words from the scriptures. But how could he console these men and truthfully say *I understand* when he had no experience with which to compare it? When they stopped coming to church, Matas knew he'd lost them.

One day, a young woman in tattered clothes with skin like cream came into the church. She looked haunted and frail, like she hadn't eaten in days. When he approached her, she shrank back, apologizing for needing a place to rest. He convinced her to stay for some food. She went with him into a small kitchen behind the church. He served her a bowl of soup and a corner of bread. She ate and left. But she returned the next day, and the next, always in need of food.

After their simple meals, Matas talked of his life and aspirations. He told her about his troubled father, his devout mother, and how he had come to choose a life in service to God. Her silence spurred him to go beyond what he had ever said during his own confessions to his superiors. He grew closer to this strange woman, and looked forward to her visits. He had never felt this way about a woman and it worried him, but he couldn't help it.

One afternoon, they walked to a small patch of grass near the vegetable garden behind the church. The air was warm. Matas put his hand on her shoulder. He wanted to put his arms around her, but he didn't dare, for he was a man of the cloth.

"Tell me what's wrong," he said.

She stared up at him, looking scared. Then she let out a sob and ran away. Matas chided himself for frightening her. He should have known better. He crossed himself and prayed she would return.

Reluctantly, Matas went back inside the church to hear confessions before mass. With a heavy heart, he listened to a little boy blurt out a nasty trick he had played on his sister. He listened to a young man confess to stealing a radio. Matas assigned them penance for their sins and offered absolution. When he got ready to leave, he heard the panel move on the other side of the confessional. It was her voice. Through her tears, she explained that she had fallen in love with a Russian and was having his child. They weren't married. Her father had cast her out of his house for loving the enemy. She feared her child would be born a bastard, and heaven would be closed to her when she died.

Matas's heart grew hard. He should have told her that God was kind and would care for her and her child. But he didn't. All he could think about was her lying next to a Russian. Matas felt anger, revulsion, frustration . . . and more than a little jealousy.

When she finished, Matas couldn't speak. He couldn't say the words he had spoken thousands of times to others who had shared their sins. After waiting a moment, she left. He put his face in his hands and cried.

The next day, her body was found hanging from the rafters in a barn. A parishioner told Matas it was the woman who had come to the church.

That night, Matas stared into the fireplace, cursing the Russians for destroying her soul and God for allowing it to happen. His piety and devotion had been to a hollow master. Worse, he had been unable to reach her, either as a man or a priest. She had touched his heart in a fundamental way and he should have saved her. He stared into the flames, bereft of hope. He was an imitation priest, and a gutless man. He took off his clerical collar and tossed it into the flames, watching it burn. He left the church that night with only a small bag of clothes and a few coins in his pocket.

With no real skills and in a poor national economy, he teamed up with two men who had known his father. They traded goods on the black market. Business thrived. That led to a money-laundering scheme which eventually brought Matas to Rina and Simona, two sisters who were part of a car theft ring. From there, Matas branched out, finding things and doing things for people. Rina and Simona helped when he needed them. He never harmed anyone, and never carried a weapon. Matas believed his lies were no worse than those his father had told. Besides, what difference did it make? A man's true nature couldn't be controlled through piety and devotion to God, because God just didn't give a damn.

Matas's calm and pious demeanor served him well, and he had an unexpected talent for technology. He studied hard and worked to keep abreast of the latest electrical equipment available, in case any of his customers needed information. He became adept at using computers.

He was also very good at sniffing out trouble. That's why he was sitting in a little café on Pylimo Street, waiting for Lena Markus.

He didn't know her exact address, other than the street name and the general location, which Peter had given him. But there was a cluster of apartments near the coffee house. If his luck held out, he'd see her today. Otherwise, he'd follow her home from work tomorrow.

A red Mini Cooper pulled up in front of the building across the street. Matas recognized the man getting out of the vehicle as Vit Partenkas. A tall woman with brown hair exited from the passenger side. She was shapely and fit. When she turned to look across the street in the general direction of the coffee shop, she slipped off her sunglasses. Lena Markus was a pretty young woman with skin like cream.

Vit took out three suitcases from inside the Mini Cooper. Matas was astounded they had all fit. Vit and Lena went inside with the bags. Matas went out into the street and lit a cigarette as he watched the building. A few minutes later, a curtain moved on the window belonging to the front upstairs apartment and Lena came into view. At least now, Matas knew where she lived.

Matas took a long puff and breathed out the smoke. Lena Markus was unknowingly on the periphery of what might be the greatest political ruse of the century. He was sure Lena and Vit knew nothing of his plans, but eventually, after the pipeline was finished and the hack completed, they might piece things together. He had to make sure that didn't happen.

CHAPTER 8

Moscow—April

The Metropol Hotel made Grinsky think of Old Russia under the tsar. It was beautiful and lavish, with no expense spared to achieve perfection in architecture, food, and comfort. But with bodyguards inside his private suite and outside in his armored car, how could Grinsky enjoy life? He had no real privacy. He was never alone; his bodyguards were with him constantly. Someone was always vying for his attention. Sometimes he just wanted to escape to a park, smell the flowers, and listen to the birds without worrying whether some fanatic was going to blow his brains out or toss a grenade at his feet. It was the price one paid for a position such as his, but he wanted the prize to outweigh the burden. The only prize worth all the bother was the presidency itself.

He sat down at the table in the suite and impatiently tapped his fingers against the linen. Yuri Rozoff was late, as usual. It was fashionable to be late—Vladimir Putin was infamous for the practice, extending it to a near art form. He was often eight hours late to meetings, but people waited for him and were happy to do so. And so Grinsky waited for Rozoff, but he wasn't happy. Vera Koslova was on his mind and, as usual, the cause of his headache.

Grinsky sipped a glass of water and swore under his breath when Rozoff's bodyguards finally came in and checked the room. They also checked a second room in the suite, a bedroom, returning almost immediately to the main salon. The waiter, who had been standing by, left to bring in the food.

Then Rozoff came in, trailing the faint scent of spice from his Caron perfume—one of the most expensive scents ever made for a man. Grinsky didn't use cologne, and his wife didn't use perfume. Her natural scent, something like mint tea, had attracted him from the start. For many years, it had seemed that every time he had touched her, she got pregnant. They had had eight children, and Grinsky had lost count as to the number of grandchildren.

"So sorry. My last meeting went late. I was caught in traffic." Rozoff sat next to Grinsky at a table set for three, and poured vodka from the cut crystal decanter into his glass. In what appeared to be an afterthought, he poured some into Grinsky's tumbler as well.

"Cheers," said Rozoff.

Grinsky glowered. *What has the world come to when a Russian man makes a toast in English?*

"Are you expecting someone else?" said Rozoff, pointing at the empty seat.

Grinsky motioned the bodyguards out of the room. The big men left.

Rozoff nodded. "Even those we trust can't be trusted. What are you up to today, Grinsky?"

The door to the bedroom opened and a decrepit looking old man strode out. Rozoff put his glass down, went to the man, and put his arms around him. They stood that way for a moment. Then Rozoff helped the old man to a chair at the table.

"It's good to see you, President Fedov," said Rozoff, wiping his eyes. "A relief to know you are well."

He poured vodka into Fedov's glass. The old man gulped it.

"When Vera Koslova took the presidency from me," said Fedov, "I almost died from grief. It was over. I had no reason to live. I couldn't stand the looks of pity from my friends and family, so I went to the snow—Siberia, the soul of our country. I hid from everyone except my wife and my friend Grinsky. Every night, I dreamed of Vera Koslova's death." He held out his empty glass. Rozoff refilled it.

"When I learned Grinsky had arranged the demonstration against Koslova on her inauguration day, I knew I had a true friend." Fedov put a hand on Grinsky's shoulder. "She still doesn't know, does she?"

"I'm still here," said Grinsky.

Fedov smiled, displaying his gray teeth. "Grinsky convinced me to come here and join forces with you. I had to wait until now because it took a long time for me to recover from a bout with pneumonia. But I'm here at last. Many are still loyal to me, and will do what I say. Together, we will do what's right for *Rossiya*. I guess old bears are hard to kill after all."

"Is it a good idea for you to be seen in Moscow?" said Rozoff.

"Nobody notices old people, but the reality is the FSB is watching me all the time. That I come to Moscow to visit old friends is expected. To come here and avoid visiting you and Grinsky would be noticed more than anything else."

A bodyguard outside the room opened the door. The waiter came in, wheeling a cart covered with dishes. He made a show of serving up three plates with potatoes, asparagus, and salmon fillets, drizzling hollandaise sauce over the vegetables, and sprinkling slivers of almonds over the fish. He put a plate in front of each man, and poured the remaining hollandaise in a serving vessel. He added a basket of hearty Russian bread to the table before rolling his cart out of the room.

Rozoff took a bite of the salmon and sighed, as if his sizeable belly were aching for food.

"I hear they're testing the new Baltic pipeline," said Grinsky.

Rozoff looked up from his food. "Always right down to business, Grinsky. Yes. Everything is going smoothly. All the monitoring and controls are working, on both the Russian and German sides. The project is on schedule. We'll have gas flowing in a matter of months. This project has gone beautifully, aside from the demonstrations and political issues, but there's little we can do to control that. Not like in the old days."

"Then Vera Koslova is about to win once again," said Fedov.

Rozoff took another bite of food. "No one is going to stop that project. It's inevitable that it will be successfully completed. For the good of us all. Once China sees . . ."

Fedov pounded the table, rattling the cutlery. "Damn China to hell! Koslova is spending our money and there is no end to it. The Trans-Siberian pipeline alone will cost over three trillion rubles. She calls it the Power of Siberia—her dream. It should be called Koslova's Folly."

"It's a pipeline to China," said Rozoff. "A necessary cost that ensures our future."

"Perhaps you agree with all this spending," said Grinsky. "But I do not. I think she should be . . . handled."

"Stopping the Baltic pipeline at this stage—at any stage—would be insane. Suicide. We can't blow it up. We can't do anything. The gas must flow," said Rozoff.

Grinsky sat back and watched Rozoff chew. "There's no doubt we will all make money from her pipeline projects. Perhaps that's why you agreed when the other businessmen gave her a year to finish the new one through the Baltic. A year is an eternity, Rozoff. Why did you give her so much time? Did you speak to the other businessmen before the meeting?"

"Would I do that and not tell you?" Rozoff dabbed the corner of his mouth with a napkin. His forehead glistened. "I agree there will be money to be made once the pipelines are complete, but by then we could all be dead. Who knows? All I know is Vera Koslova doesn't keep her promises. And that will be her downfall."

"What did she promise you, Rozoff? Money? A position? Was it *my* position?"

"She's a force from hell," said Fedov. "Even God can't stop her."

"God has nothing to do with this," said Grinsky.

Rozoff took another bite of salmon. "Of course, I refused it. I would never dream of doing anything to harm you, my friend. But I wouldn't be surprised if she offered the position of prime minister to others as well. It doesn't matter to her. She gives promises of powerful positions away like candy to children."

Grinsky bristled. In her heart Koslova was nothing more than a cutthroat, vindictive bitch. He wondered how long it took Rozoff to refuse her offer of prime minister, if he'd refused it at all.

Grinsky glanced at a smiling Fedov, and his mood improved. "I hope no one expects Vera to give away such a powerful position, especially not you, Rozoff. But toying with people's ambitions is a terrible thing. She should be taught a lesson."

"You can't lock the woman up and torture her."

Fedov laughed. "Give me a cigarette, Grinsky. The doctors don't want me to smoke, but they're all idiots."

Grinsky complied and Fedov exhaled smoke through his nose. The gray cloud made him look like an angry old bull.

"The difficulty," said Fedov, "is discrediting Vera Koslova at the right time. If we depose her now, investors will think Russia is unstable, cut their losses, and leave. We can't get rid of her until after the new Baltic pipeline is operational. The first money that comes in will pay off debt. But she must be gone before the real money starts coming in."

Grinsky nodded his agreement. "Yes. There's a small window when we must strike. Once money flows like the Don in springtime, we'll never get rid of her."

"We can't do anything beforehand that she'll notice," said Rozoff. "She'll counter anything we do with a disinformation campaign. She perfected that skill in the FSB."

Fedov grimaced as he took another long puff of the cigarette. He let the smoke out slowly. "We want to build dissent among the people gradually, so she's not even aware at first. This way, people will have a negative impression that will be very hard to change, no matter what she does."

"You speak in riddles," said Rozoff. "Tell me your plan."

Fedov waved a hand. "We do several things. First, we secure our friendships with our most powerful and trusted confederates. We tell them nothing specific, but we make sure their support is firm."

"The French are considering a formal objection to the pipeline," said Grinsky. "They're claiming it's illegal for one country to own the gas as well as the means to transport it. I don't think they will ultimately do anything, but I can encourage my contact in the ministry to be vocal about the proposal and keep it in the news. That's bound to give Koslova something to stew about."

Rozoff smiled. "We should look for any opportunity that reflects poorly on Koslova and magnify it for Western news."

Fedov nodded. "Exactly. There's an element very much opposed to the Baltic pipeline. They're mostly Eastern Europeans—the Balts, the Poles, and even some Germans—everyone you'd expect. There have been a few unorganized demonstrations against the pipeline, and against Koslova. Mostly students. We need to make sure all demonstrations from now on are big and loud, to remind Koslova of her presidential inauguration when people blew themselves up because of her."

Grinsky chuckled. "That's sure to rattle her. We torture Koslova in the press, so people think the objections are directed at her alone. Make them think she's a problem that can be cut out like a cancer, leaving the rest of Russia healthy."

"We must look for anything damaging that can be used against her," said Fedov.

"But nothing that can be linked back to us," said Rozoff.

Fedov pointed a finger at Rozoff. "All of my people can be trusted. And if any of them are found out, they're just people who detest Vera Koslova, and think she's bad for the country."

Grinsky put his hand on Fedov's shoulder. "No one can know the real story about how she came to power. It would reflect badly on you, *Papochka*."

Fedov brushed away a tear. "When the pipelines are done, she'll be out, and the past won't matter anymore."

CHAPTER 9

Klaipeda, Lithuania—April

Vit steered the Mini Cooper off the ferry and onto the single road along the Curonian Split, a peninsula running through the Baltic Sea, parallel to Lithuania's mainland. There was a lagoon on one side, and the Baltic Sea on the other. At its narrowest, the Split was about four hundred meters wide; at its widest a few kilometers. It extended in the westerly direction as part of Lithuania for about fifty kilometers, until reaching the Oblast of Kaliningrad, where Russia kept her Baltic fleet and a number of nuclear warheads.

Lena leaned to the side, stretching her legs in the small car. "Are you sure we'll be back in Klaipeda in time for the demonstration against the new pipeline?"

Vit smiled. "We didn't drive all this way to miss it. But the demonstration isn't just about the pipeline. It's also about the decision of Lithuania and the other Baltic countries to tie into the pipeline. Some people object, because the countries would just be using Russian gas again. Others say it gives them an additional source of fuel, making them independent of any single supplier."

They continued down the road past patches of trees that allowed only glimpses of the sea. Few cars were out this early. Vit glanced at his companion. Aside from some small talk, Lena had been relatively quiet during the drive that had started at six a.m. He had wanted to leave early, so they'd have plenty of time to cover the demonstration and make this brief side-trip. Vit attributed her silence to jet lag and all the changes she was experiencing—new apartment, new job, and new boss. He hoped it wasn't a reaction to the difficulties they faced, because the next few months were sure to be trying, as they sought out new data sources and analyzed information for their report on the state of energy in the Baltics. He expected some people to avoid them, fearing their name in print. He expected others to waste their time with subjects unrelated to the topic. He also expected to gain a few valuable insights. Since this was likely to be the last publication from Baltic Watch, it meant that Lena would probably have to look for a new job almost right away. He assumed she needed the paycheck. Even so, she had to work hard if they were going to get the project done before the money ran out.

Vit pulled into a parking lot and got out of the car, motioning Lena to join him. She stifled a yawn.

"I could really use a cup of coffee," said Lena. "Sorry. I get better as the day goes on. I'm a night owl. Anything before ten a.m. is hard for me. Where are we going?"

"I'm about to show you."

They walked through the sand and stepped onto a narrow boardwalk heading up the side of a very large dune. There was nothing to see but sky, sand, and sparse clumps of greenery. A fifteen-minute up-hill walk took them through a range of dunes. As they approached the crest, the Baltic Sea gradually became visible, its gray-blue water looking pristine against the massive unsullied ridges of sand.

Standing beside Vit at the end of the boardwalk, Lena finally spoke. "My God, it's beautiful."

"You can't see any activity from here because we're too far away, but the Baltic pipeline is being built way out there." Vit pointed out over the sea toward the northwestern horizon.

Then he pointed due east. "Moscow is about eight hundred kilometers in that direction—five hundred miles. We were dependent on Russia for gas and oil for years. All of it came here through land-based pipelines—one for gas and another for oil. Now gas is more significant than oil, because it has a cleaner carbon profile and goes further to meeting EU clean air standards. That's one reason why Germany is so interested in the new pipeline. In one of my articles last year, I called the fuel we get from Russia black amber. You've heard of oil being called black gold. In black amber, I include oil and natural gas. Amber is precious to us like gold is elsewhere. The phrase seems to have hit a nerve."

"Black amber. I like it." Lena touched the cross hanging from her neck. "But why didn't they just build another land-based pipeline? Why go to all the trouble of building one under the sea?"

"Russia claims it's hard to keep an overland pipeline secure, even if it's buried. But the more likely reason is that Ukraine charges Russia a few billion dollars every year to transit gas across Ukrainian territory, and Russia's sick of paying the bill."

Vit pointed to the west. "In that direction, not thirty miles away, is the Kaliningrad Oblast. It's part of the Russian Federation and where Koslova keeps her Baltic fleet. Putin moved missiles there, and Koslova has been moving more missiles, troops and supplies there ever since she's been in office."

Lena spoke up. "When Khrushchev shipped Russian missiles to Cuba, it was a crisis for the Kennedy administration. When Putin moved missiles to Kaliningrad, Lithuania didn't do anything because they couldn't handle a military standoff like the US could."

Vit was impressed by her knowledge. "Living with Russian nuclear missiles just off our shore is our new normal."

"I read that Putin cursed the day Lithuania joined NATO," said Lena. "One opinion piece claimed he had a right to be angry. It would have been like Cuba actually joining the USSR. But knowing that Russian missiles are about thirty miles away has a psychological impact. Missiles can easily travel hundreds even thousands of miles. Still, having them so close is unsettling. It's probably a great comfort to the citizens of Lithuania, Latvia, Estonia, and Poland that their countries have alliances with powerful multinational organizations like the EU and NATO."

Vit nodded. "At Baltic Watch, we have to be thorough and fearless, no matter the outcome. It takes a lot to uncover a story and to see every side, despite what biases we might have. Not many people outside Lithuania know the missiles are so close. By not making it an international crisis, is Lithuania being meek or smart? In the analysis we do, we have to present issues and back up the possible solutions with data. People may not like what we conclude."

"I can tell you what I think, but knowing the solutions is an entirely different thing."

"Exactly. You have to exhaust every possible source of information. Over time, you develop a horse sense about details that if investigated further, might uncover a new dimension to your story."

Vit turned and faced southward toward the car and parking lot. "On the other side of the Split is Lithuania's floating liquefied natural gas storage and regasification unit. They call it an LNG terminal, and it's on a ship called the Independence. For decades, Russia was our only provider of fuel, and Lithuania had to pay whatever Russia demanded, because we had no other options. The Independence and the pipeline that extends from it to the port of Klaipeda gives Lithuania the ability to import LNG shipments from tankers. LNG is mostly methane and ethane gas that's been processed and cooled into liquid form, so it's safer to transport long distances. The LNG is offloaded onto the floating terminal, turned back into a gaseous state using a process called regasification, and pumped through the pipeline to the shore. There it connects with more pipelines that send it to Lithuanian homes. This capability lets us buy gas from different countries instead of relying exclusively on gas from Russia that gets here through overland pipelines. We're taking fuel shipments from both Norway and the US."

Lena smiled. "All of the Baltic countries have the ability to use gas processed offshore by Lithuania. But why should Russia care? There are so few people in these three countries that their fuel needs could hardly make a difference."

"The point is that Lithuania, Latvia, and Estonia are standing up against Russia. It establishes a precedent, and breaks Russia's regional monopoly as a fuel supplier. In fact, Lithuania kept buying gas from Russia once the offshore LNG processing facility was in place, because Russia lowered the cost. Personally, I think Lithuania didn't want to aggravate Russia even more. But it also made sense to buy from the cheapest fuel supplier. Poland is preparing to join the Baltic countries in breaking its dependence on Russia, by expanding its Swinoujscie LNG terminal so Poland can buy even more gas from different countries."

As they went back down the path, Vit continued. "Poland, Lithuania, and the other Baltic countries are a buffer between Moscow and her Baltic fleet. They're challenging Russia by aligning themselves with NATO and the EU, and breaking Russia's control over fuel."

"The question becomes what, if anything, is Vera Koslova going to do about it?"

"You've been doing your homework." Vit smiled, pleased that Lena had already grasped many of the issues.

"Keeping track of Vera Koslova has been a hobby of mine. I find powerful women who are also ruthless to be fascinating."

Vit led the way back to the car. Before getting inside, he turned to Lena. "I think your idea of interviewing some of the demonstrators today is a great idea. It'll add current viewpoints to the report we're doing."

"I can ask people if they'll let me record what they say. This device does a great job." Lena pulled out an expensive looking mobile phone from her pocket and showed it to Vit.

"It'll help that you speak the language, but people may be reluctant to talk at any length with a stranger about Russia—a holdover from the occupation when people were deported for what they said. But you can try."

"Do you think our report is going to make a difference?"

"I'm sure students will use the material as a reference in history papers for many years, but I hope it'll show our readers how far we've come. We're no longer a country forced into a government we don't want by a brutal occupation. We're modern, and have alliances to help us maintain our independence. I think Lithuanians will like reading about that, and I think it's important that they do. If we're lucky, EU leaders will see it too, and build their own energy profiles so their citizens can see what energy sources are available and the consequences of using those sources."

~~

As Vit and Lena retraced their steps back to the ferry and returned to Klaipeda, Lena could barely contain her excitement. She knew her job at Baltic Watch would be interesting when she took it, but she was going to research an important subject that had real consequences for the people involved. She may not have worked as a reporter before this, but she was determined to do her best job.

They found a place to leave the car near the site of the planned demonstration. Walking past a park with an anchor embedded in the soil, they arrived at the old square where people with signage and megaphones were already gathering. As they waited for the first speaker to step up to the podium, Lena used her phone's internet capability to bring up the picture of the organizer of today's protest.

She thought back to yesterday's elaborate process to get that picture. Vit had asked Lena to come into his office. He registered Lena's facial image with a software system on his computer, and her voice with a voice recognition biometric package. He entered a passcode, and a sultry voice from the computer said, "Hello, Lena. I'm Annie. How can I help you?"

Vit explained Annie's capabilities, and that the only version available was on the computer in Vit's office. At first, Lena didn't understand why she couldn't install Annie on her own laptop, but soon decided that even a little time with Annie was worthwhile.

It had taken Annie mere seconds to find the organizer's name: A. Sims. Lena had wanted to dig deeper, but Vit needed to work at his desk. Without email or a phone number for A. Sims, Lena couldn't make contact. But Annie had found a sketchy biography attached to a headshot. A. Sims was a woman with blonde hair hanging down to her shoulders. She had a pleasant round face, and wore glasses. According to the biography, she was a twenty-three-year-old activist from Riga with a degree in political science from the University of Latvia. Lena took another quick glance at the photograph, intending to look for her today in the crowd in addition to interviewing people.

She told Vit she'd meet him in a few hours, and set out to do her job. Lena took a deep breath. This was the first time she'd ever interviewed people. She hoped her lack of experience wouldn't show.

As the first speaker went to the podium and criticized Vera Koslova to the cheers of the crowd, Lena went up to a man in a T-shirt wearing jeans.

"Excuse me, I'm with Baltic Watch. Would you mind answering a few questions?" she said.

The man walked away.

Lena spent the next few hours stepping up to people and asking their opinion of Vera Koslova, the new Baltic pipeline, and a myriad of related subjects. Some people were polite and friendly, but they gave her no information. Many were curious about the American woman talking to them in heavily accented Lithuanian. When she finished answering their questions about how she got here and what she was doing, they nodded politely and walked away.

While the speaker boldly denounced Koslova, Lena continued to try and talk to people. Some just shook their heads. Others ignored her. She never got to the point of asking to take a picture or record a voice. Lena didn't know if people were refusing to talk to an American or disapproved of the pipelines, although a few made their perspective clear with a curse word or two. All she knew was that she was doing a bad job getting people to speak to her. Lena became frustrated. Convincing people to open up was harder than she'd expected.

The next speaker mounted the podium. He was an environmentalist who warned about the devastation a gas leak could cause to the ecology of the Baltic Sea. Oil spills were visible and could often be contained with buoys, but natural gas leaks weren't even noticeable in water. Cleanup was impossible. The only detection would be loss of line pressure detected by metering stations along the pipeline. Fish exposed to a gas leak would exhibit behavioral problems, including increased activity and scattering. Prolonged exposure would lead to chronic poisoning.

As the audience applauded, Lena edged through the growing mass of people, searching faces, comparing them with her likeness of A. Sims. She showed the photo on her mobile phone to a few folks and asked if they had seen her. A. Sims was a stranger to everyone Lena accosted, and no one had seen her at the event.

Tired, discouraged, and convinced she was a failure, Lena headed back to the statue where she had agreed to meet Vit. On the way, she noticed a small girl sucking her thumb and looking scared. Lena went to the child and squatted down so they were face-to-face. They were surrounded by a sea of legs.

"Did you lose your mommy?" said Lena.

A tear rolled down the girl's cheek.

"What's your name?" said Lena.

"Birute."

"When I was about your age, I lost my mommy, too, in a big crowd like this. But I found her because a nice lady helped me."

Birute smiled. "I'm with Tete."

"Will you let me help you find him?"

The child nodded.

"Why don't I pick you up? That way you can see everyone. When you spot your daddy, all you have to do is point and I'll take you to him. Okay, Birute?"

"Okay."

Lena picked up the child in her arms, and they went through the crowd. Before long, Birute pointed into the crowd. Her legs kicked, and her body squirmed. Lena had to put the child down for fear of dropping her. Birute took Lena's hand and guided her to a man gazing through the crowd with an obvious look of anxiety on his face.

"Tete!" called Birute.

The man pushed his way toward them. He scooped the child up in his arms and buried his face in her hair. He looked up and smiled at Lena.

"*Aciu*," he said.

"You're welcome." Lena hesitated, but decided not to let the opportunity go to waste. She had nothing to lose. "If you have a second, would you mind answering a few questions?"

The man's relief at finding Birute was palpable. He agreed to Lena's request, and even consented to have his answers recorded. A few people noticed and gathered around them. While some listened, others spoke out, and Lena was able to record everything. Upon hearing that Lena worked at Baltic Watch with Vit Partenkas, one person asked about Tilda, Vit's grandmother, a physicist and local celebrity who had died last year. At the mention of Tilda's name, even more people joined them. In thirty minutes, Lena had collected more information than she had all the rest of the day.

When they finished, Lena thanked Birute's father for the help. Birute, still in her father's arms and sucking her thumb, waved goodbye as they disappeared into the crowd.

Then she noticed Vit standing nearby, watching her.

She went over to him.

"Nice job," he said grinning. "Where'd you learn how to work a crowd?"

Lena smiled back. "I have a knack."

CHAPTER 10

The Kremlin, Moscow—April

Vera sat at her desk preparing for the next interminable meeting with her cabinet. The Minister of Foreign Affairs needed to learn how to keep his comments *brief*. His fleshy and creased face reminded her of a picture she'd seen of the mythical *Bukavac*, a monster with gnarled horns who made loud noises. A phone call came in. She recognized the number: Orlov. It had been a month since they'd last spent a pleasant evening together. She glanced at her calendar, hoping she was free tonight, but alas, was having dinner with the State Council Presidium on Housing and Urban Environments. She made a note to have her personal secretary arrange an evening meeting with Orlov. Then she realized that when the head of the FSB was in touch, it usually wasn't good news.

"My people just reported in from the demonstration in Klaipeda, Lithuania," he said.

"I'd forgotten all about it. Why did you bother to send anyone? None the protests so far have been worth our attention. Attendance has been low. The only people who go are anti-Russian radicals or tree-hugging environmentalists."

"It's what we do. There were a lot of people there. Many more than we had expected."

"The protests are gaining momentum?"

"Baltic Watch was there."

"I was hoping they'd be out of business by now."

"Vit Partenkas has someone new working for him—a Lena Markus from America. She was asking questions about the event organizer, a woman named A. Sims. Our people are looking into the background of A. Sims, but they haven't found anything yet. I'm calling you because Russia got substantial attention, and it wasn't good."

"Has there ever been a protest against the pipeline where Russia wasn't criticized?" Vera caught herself. Orlov was being deliberately obtuse. He didn't mean the protests were against Russia. He meant the protests were against *her*. "What did they say about me?"

Orlov's hesitation spoke volumes. In a moment of supreme self-control, she let the question go unanswered.

Feeling her stomach twist into a knot, she spoke. "Find out who A. Sims is and report back to me. Then I want you to investigate Lena Markus. I want to know who she is, what she's really doing in Vilnius, why she's working for Baltic Watch, what she's thinking. Hell, I want you to know how many cubes of sugar she takes in her tea."

"I'll have two of our agents stay there—Stefan and Sofia. They're older and unremarkable, but it's safer that way."

~~

After the demonstration ended, Lena convinced Vit to have a quick dinner in Klaipeda before starting the three-hour drive back to Vilnius. They chose *Stora Antis*, a restaurant situated in a nineteenth century brick-lined cellar. The dining room was decorated with old pictures, an antique cash register, and a chair that looked like it belonged in a castle. Lena ordered fried plaice, a sweet fish. Vit had the baked duck.

After the great meal and a cup of hot coffee, they headed back, arriving in Old Town just before midnight. Still energized from the day's activities, Lena asked Vit to drop her off at the office. She wanted to transcribe her notes while everything was fresh in her mind.

Lena went right to Vit's desk, happy to have some time alone with Annie. As she sipped a cup of cocoa, Lena had Annie copy the videos on her phone to a disk. Then she listened to the recorded interviews, jotting down notes and impressions. Lena was very pleased with the information. The people she had spoken with believed the Baltic pipelines were a threat to their long-term security. Russia could easily cut off the supply of gas to Europe as punishment for many reasons, including sanctions and anti-Russia press. One person said that Russia had done this before.

"Annie, has Russia ever cut off the supply of gas to a foreign country?"

"In 2013, Ukraine signed a deal with Russia for low-price gas. Then Russia hiked the price by some 80%. Ukraine refused to pay the higher price, so Russia shut off the supply. Ultimately, the issue went to the international arbitration court at the Stockholm Chamber of Commerce, but before they rendered a decision, Russia and Ukraine reached an agreement. Ukraine settled by agreeing to pay up front for its gas and paying down debt."

"Annie, will Russia ever exert political influence over all of Europe by threatening their access to gas?"

"Russia uses the income from gas sales to balance her budget. She needs the money. Shutting off or even threatening to shut off the supply would jeopardize that income, but not immediately. It takes time for countries to switch to alternative energy sources. If Russia shut off her supply of gas, it would likely affect future revenue. Controlling a supply of gas gives Russia leverage to influence European policy at the risk of future gas revenue. We won't know if Russia will use that leverage and take that economic risk until there's an international crisis."

"I'd have preferred it if you had just said no."

"I only lie when Vit asks me to."

Chuckling, Lena turned back to her notes. While she hadn't been in Lithuania for very long, Lena had gotten to know a few people who were unusually candid about their family histories during the occupation. She hadn't recorded the conversations, as they were just people interested in sharing their experiences, but she'd jotted down her impressions. The young married couple in the apartment next door had told about their grandparents fighting the Soviets during the war. The woman in the coffee shop across the street had told about her father who had refused to leave Lithuania after the Soviet breakup, because he had wanted to see free Lithuania bloom like a rose. Everyone agreed that if Russia had a means to exercise control, she would use it, especially to affect a NATO vote.

As Lena pondered over those family experiences, she remembered her own family and realized she had an opportunity. Vit wasn't around. Why not ask Annie to help with a personal matter? Eventually, Vit would probably let her use Annie for personal use, but why risk asking? What he didn't know wouldn't hurt him. This would only take a minute.

"Annie, do a search for Gerde Markus, my great-aunt."

"A Markus family lived in the village of Pabrade after WWII. Gerde Markus married Emilis Simoliunas in 1957. They had one child, a girl. Emilis died of heart failure in 1982. Gerde died in 2002."

"Is Gerde's daughter still alive?"

"She's mentioned in Gerde's obituary, but not by name. The records in Pabrade were destroyed in a fire."

"What's the last known address?"

Annie mentioned a street name in Pabrade that Lena entered into her cell phone. It wasn't much progress, but it was tangible—somewhere to take her search. Happy that she had finally found something useful about her family, she turned off the computer, shut off the lights, and headed for her apartment.

As she walked through Old Town, the charming buildings took on a mysterious personality in the quiet and the dimly lit streets. Old brick became timeless, and church spires stood out as giant beacons to the past. Lena felt pleased with the way things were shaping up. Her job was interesting and she was learning a lot. Vit was a good boss. She loved the narrow winding cobblestone streets, the beautiful buildings, and even her apartment.

Lena stopped to admire an old wooden gate that looked like it had been there for centuries. As she stepped closer and touched the wood, a chill ran up her spine. It felt like she wasn't alone. She looked around. No one was there, except for a cat running into a basement. The animal hissed and then it was quiet.

Vit had told her the area was safe, but standing here, alone in the dark, Lena wondered if he was mistaken.

~~

Matas flattened his back against the alleyway wall as Lena crossed the street. For a crazy second, he thought she'd spotted him. But a woman alone on a deserted street at night wouldn't go toward a man who was watching her. She'd run away. But Lena was American, so who knew what she'd do? The clack of her shoes against the cobblestones stopped near him. He tensed, waiting for her to scream. He could run, but she looked very fit and might be able to overtake him. He could overpower her, take her money, and be gone, make it appear to be a simple mugging. But muggings were unusual, and would involve the police. As footsteps came closer, he held his breath. He could pretend to be a vagrant. A cat hissed across the street.

After a few seconds, Lena hurried away, her footstep fading into silence.

He waited until he was sure she was long gone before returning to the sidewalk and going in the opposite direction, noting the old gate from the corner of his eye. Perhaps it was what she had stopped to look at. Americans. He pulled out a cigarette from a packet, lit it, and sucked in the smoke, trying to shake off the strain of the last few minutes.

He swore at himself for almost getting caught. He didn't have to follow her at this hour of the night, but he had nothing else to do. And sleep wasn't his friend.

Matas thought about the phone call earlier that evening from Rina and Simona on their way back from Klaipeda. Matas was staying in a three-story walkup owned by a friend who spent most of his time traveling. He was there only when he had to be in Vilnius, because he preferred the cottage he rented in Utena. The cottage was remote and virtually isolated, near where he planned to buy his farm one day.

Rina and Simona reported they were pleased with the demonstration in Klaipeda and in particular, the huge size of the crowd. But they were worried about the intern from Baltic Watch who had been asking about A. Sims, the identity Arkady had given to the protest organizer. When they mentioned Lena showing people in the crowd this fictional person's picture, Matas had felt the hair rise on the back of his neck. He wondered where Arkady had gotten the picture and if there was anything that could tie it back to him and his team.

Matas puffed on his cigarette. He believed that his plan could be in danger. Lena had found out about A. Sims very quickly. Vit Partenkas was undoubtedly involved. Success hinged on the invisibility of Matas's team. He took another puff and knew he had to take action.

He needed to know what Baltic Watch was doing. Short of bugging their offices, there was only one way to accomplish this, and that was by befriending Lena Markus.

~~

The sun had been up for hours when Lena walked into the coffee shop across the street from her apartment. Her mind was already on the meeting she was about to have with Vit. They were going to review the progress on her research report. She was anxious to do well.

Lena stepped up to the counter and ordered her usual large latte in a disposable cup. Coffee in hand, she hugged the wall to pass a couple standing in line, and a man bumped into her. Upon feeling the unexpected contact, Lena's natural reaction was to tense her body as well as her hands. She squeezed the cup. The lid popped off and the coffee spilled onto her hand and down the front of her coat. Her skin burning, she let go of the cup and it fell to the floor, splashing her pants.

"Ouch!" She turned to the culprit. "Watch it!"

"I'm so sorry. Are you all right?" The man who had caused the damage was tall, and a bit older than she.

Lena shook her hand, trying to deaden the pain. "No! I'm not all right."

"It was an accident." The man handed her a napkin.

She looked down at her coat and the big, wet stain. "Next time, watch where you're going." Lena glanced around her. People were staring. Lena's face felt hot. An employee came over with a mop and a bucket, and began cleaning up the mess.

"Let me pay to have your coat cleaned," said the man.

"I'm late for work," Lena mumbled, and hurried out the door, embarrassed at having caused a scene, wondering if she should ever go back there again.

The next morning, Lena paused with her hand on the door to the coffeeshop. Remembering yesterday's embarrassing situation, she considered going somewhere else, but she wanted her fix of caffeine. The guy who bumped into her probably wouldn't be around. She went inside. As she was about to order her usual double latte, someone came up to her. It was the man from yesterday.

"Good morning," he said.

Lena felt her face flush. "Sorry I yelled at you yesterday."

"No. It was my fault. How's your hand?"

She held it up. Her index finger was still red, but there were no blisters and it didn't hurt. "It's okay." She gazed into his dark eyes. He had a great smile.

"Let me pay for your coffee. It's the least I can do. Come join me." He gestured toward a table. "I'd like to try and convince you that not all Lithuanian men are clumsy rubes."

"It's really not . . ."

"Please. Just for a few minutes." He extended a hand. "I'm Matas."

CHAPTER 11

Pabrade, Lithuania—May

"Matas has a job for us," called Ramute, looking up from her laptop. Her son, Antanas, entered the room and sat down. The laptop's glossy exterior was a sharp contrast to the dull hand-plastered walls of the kitchen. She took off her reading glasses and lay them on the table.

"Are you sure you won't be missed at the farm supply store this afternoon?" said Ramute.

"I told them I had some family business to take care of. I'll stay late tonight to update the books. As long as the work is done by the start of business, they don't care when I do it. It's a concession they've made to the younger employees who asked for flexible time." He leaned his forearms against the edge of the table. "What does Matas want?"

"We have to pretend to be a woman's relatives."

"That should be easy enough."

Ramute went to the stove for the tea kettle caked with black around the sides from years of wear. She poured hot water into the teapot on the table. "I've been studying the woman. Her name is Lena Markus. She's from America. Her grandmother and great aunt were born here. Aldona is the grandmother. Gerde, the great aunt, was sent to Siberia. Camp Userda. She was arrested for having an American pen pal."

"That's too bad."

"It was hard, but I found a man who knew Gerde and Aldona's families when they were growing up here. He told me about the pen pal. It was unusual to exchange letters with the wife of a US politician, so people knew about it. Knowing her name, I was able to find records of the communications they sent to the Khrushchev administration advocating for Gerde's release. The pen pal's husband got Aldona out of Lithuania and she was living in the US by the time Gerde was released. Aldona settled in New Hampshire, got married, and had a child, Lena's mother."

"Guilt is a powerful motivator."

Ramute nodded. "The Simoliunas family was squatting in the Markus family house when Gerde returned to Pabrade. She married the son. They had a daughter who'd be about sixty today—more or less my age, which is good. I need to be Gerde's daughter."

"But is Gerde's daughter still alive? Do you know her name?"

Ramute shook her head. "The town records were destroyed in a fire. I looked at online ancestry programs, and examined all the records I could find from nearby towns and villages. I searched birth and death records. I found no one from the Simoliunas family, and the only Markus family members I could find are in America."

"But you're still not sure."

Ramute took a deep breath and let it out slowly. "The people who are living in Gerde's house aren't related to them and had no idea who the family was. I found the previous owners of the property, and they hadn't kept in touch with the family. All this could be to our advantage. I could be myself—Ramute. The only problem is if there were letters mentioning Gerde's daughter. They don't know about you, so you're still Antanas, and my son."

"You always say the best lies are close to the truth."

Ramute poured out the tea. "I'd feel better though, if I knew the name of the woman I'm supposed to impersonate. There's another problem. The people living in Gerde's old house need to be convinced to move out so we can rent the place."

"That means more money. I assume Matas will pay."

"He'll have to be generous so that no one talks, in case Lena Markus makes inquiries, especially with the neighbors."

Antanas buttered some bread. "People here won't talk to a stranger, let alone mention that you've been asking questions. Any more problems?"

"The sisters must have written each other. Lena Markus may have some of the letters. We need to produce one that Gerde may have received from her sister Aldona."

"We'll have to write new ones ourselves and make them look old."

"We can blame loss of most letters on Stalin's censorship, but we'll have to have at least one. Matas needs to get us more information though, like Aldona's address in the US. He'll have to tell us whether Lena has any of the old letters, even what's in them."

"That's going to be tricky. If he can't get us what we need, are we going to call it off?"

Ramute smiled. "We're a long way from giving up. I'm becoming a real researcher. Thank goodness for the internet and our network of friends here."

"If Lena suspects us, she could retrace our steps and we could be in trouble."

"Let's hope Lena Markus is so overwhelmed from finding her long-lost family that she doesn't even think of anything else."

There came a knock at the door. Antanas started.

Ramute glanced at the clock. "It's all right. I invited Dalia from town. I want her to talk about her time at the camps. You and I need to understand the Siberian experience to the degree we can. Gerde must have talked about it. That means we need to be able to talk about it. All you have to do is listen."

"I've heard all the stories. Why do we need to hear them again? Besides, once Dalia starts talking, she goes on and on." Antanas rolled his eyes.

"It needs to be fresh in our minds. Now behave. She's our guest."

Ramute answered the door, returning with an old woman walking with a cane, her back bent with age. After settling her into a chair with a hot cup of tea, Ramute buttered a piece of bread and handed it to Dalia.

"I've started to tell Antanas about our family history," said Ramute.

"The young ones don't care about history," said Dalia. "And I have no family."

"Antanas loves to hear you talk," said Ramute, casting her son a sly glance.

The old woman dropped several cubes of sugar into the tea and slowly stirred the mixture. "A detachment of soldiers came for me in

1950. I was seventeen years old. They gave me half an hour to pack bags and provisions. I didn't know how long I'd be gone. I didn't know where I was going, other than somewhere in Siberia. My mother cried the whole time I was packing. They put me on a train with others—crowded together like cattle. And off we went.

"They took my youth and my freedom. If I never see another Russian, it would be too soon. They were all cowards, scared of their own shadows. Except for that Russian woman who worked in the kitchen and fed the guards. She was all right. She gave me extra fat to eat."

Dalia pointed a finger at Antanas. "I was much skinnier than you. Fat was more valuable than gold." She slurped some tea. "I used everything I'd brought with me. When I'd worn holes through my stockings, I used them for a belt. And then as a rope to repair the cot where I slept. I had a garden in the camp where I grew vegetables. Every day I worked. Every day I prayed to be set free.

"The days were all the same. You learn how to survive, to put yourself first, even at the expense of others. I try not to think about it anymore and what I did to survive. It makes me too sad."

Ramute took Dalia's hand. It was cold. The old woman continued. "When they released me, it was the happiest day of my life. But I didn't let myself truly believe I was free until I got on a train headed home. It took eleven days to get here. Siberia is a big place. Thanks to God, I'll never see that godforsaken stinkhole again.

"I finally got to the train station near my family's house. A delivery man gave me a ride home. I had fifty rubles in my pocket, from the Soviets. Fifty rubles for all of those years in the camps."

Dalia took a breath. "Even then, as I recognized the roads and buildings after being away for so long, the idea of being home sounded too good to be true. I didn't dare say it aloud, for the house and my parents might vanish like in a dream. I pictured my father leaning against the tree waiting for me as he had when I was little.

"The driver dropped me off at the dirt road leading to the house. He wanted to drive me to the doorstep, but the road was too narrow. He offered to carry my bags and walk with me, but I said no. I wanted to give the man some money, but then I thought no. I earned every bit of it. It was mine. Then I decided not to be the woman I had been in the camps. I wanted to leave her behind. I took out some of the money and handed it to him. He didn't take it. I was relieved.

He wished me good luck, and drove off. I can still remember the exhaust fumes and the scent of gasoline from the truck."

Dalia pulled out a handkerchief from her pocket. She blew her nose and wiped her eyes. Ramute put her arms around the old woman's shoulders.

"That's enough," said Ramute. "You don't have to say anything more if you don't want to."

"I don't think about the camps much anymore," said Dalia. "I think a lot about the day I came home, though. I learned Mama and Papa were dead. They were both buried in the garden. Friends and neighbors came by as soon as they heard I was back. They were so happy to see me. They took care of me. They still do. They're my family now."

"So are we, Dalia," said Ramute. "So are we."

CHAPTER 12

Vilnius, Lithuania—May

Late Saturday afternoon, Lena stood in front of the mirror in her bedroom, holding up a floral print wrap dress and admiring how the colors complimented her light gray eyes. Matas had promised her an insider's tour of Vilnius after dinner that was bound to involve walking. High heels weren't a great choice for cobblestone streets, but they looked great with the dress. Maybe flat shoes and jeans would be better.

She smiled, happy to have been asked out by an attractive and distinguished-looking man. The years she had spent working in Virginia had been a sexual drought, unlike college, which had been fun despite the long hours studying. After she graduated, got her first job, and moved to Virginia, she'd refused to date anyone in the office, because it was bound to get complicated. And there had been no one else to date, let alone time to find someone. Those years of work were sure to be good for her career when she returned to the US, but she was glad for this break. Life was too short to spend almost every waking moment staring at a computer screen.

Matas was a bit older—she guessed forties. But he was very nice and she liked him. She even thought him sexy. He would help her get used to dating again. She certainly wanted to. Besides, she was young, pretty, and in one of the loveliest countries in all of Europe. She wanted to have a good time. She giggled, thinking what sex might be like with an experienced older man.

She went into the bathroom and brushed her hair, letting it fall to her shoulders. She didn't do much else to it, other than adding a bit of styling gel to her bangs to keep them off her face. Then she put on some makeup. Usually, she didn't wear any, but she enjoyed the novelty of putting on mascara and eye shadow—a dark plum color that emphasized her eyes.

Back in the bedroom, she put on the flowered dress and low heels. She stared at the contents of her closet, trying to decide which scarf to put on–everyone in Vilnius seemed to wear them. Before she could make up her mind, a knock came at the door. She grabbed her freshly cleaned coat and headed out.

She and Matas walked to *Lokys*, a restaurant in Old Town that he had selected. They went through a wrought-iron gate to a door under a flag with a picture of a bear. They made their way down a narrow, winding staircase to a cavern-like space with quiet corners and plenty of tables set for two. The place felt old, elegant, and very romantic.

Matas suggested she try the boar. He ordered game sausage and sauerkraut for himself, and a bottle of wine.

As they waited for the food to come, Lena pulled out her cell phone.

"Who are you calling?" said Matas.

She leaned across the table, holding the device out in front of them. "I want a picture for my friends."

Matas put his hand up in front of the phone, blocking the shot. "Please, no. I don't want my picture on the internet."

"Everyone does it."

"Indulge a man his eccentricities." Matas smiled.

Lena put her phone away, a bit dismayed at his old-fashioned attitude. *Everyone* posted photographs to the internet. She was disappointed that he wasn't hip or cool after all. She expected Matas to spend the rest of the evening telling her about himself. She was sure that an older man uncomfortable with modern ways would assume that a young woman hadn't done anything interesting in her life, and wouldn't even think to ask. She readied herself for a long evening.

The waiter arrived with the wine, and poured a little in to Matas's glass. Matas sniffed it, took a sip, and nodded. The waiter filled their glasses. Lena took a sip right away.

To her surprise, Matas asked where she was raised and where she went to school. She told him about growing up on a farm in New England. She talked about her father dying when she was very young, and the family staying to run the farm. She spoke of helping her brothers put up hay for the cows, and chopping wood for the winter. She talked about her college years in Troy, New York, at Rensselaer Polytechnic Institute, studying computer engineering and taking journalism courses. Matas asked why she'd chosen this unusual combination. She explained that writing was a passion, but she liked technology too, particularly computers. She enjoyed understanding how things worked at a fundamental level.

Lena sipped some more wine. "After I graduated, my mother passed on. We sold the property. My brothers and I went our separate ways. I don't see them often."

"You're fortunate to have family."

Lena nodded. "My mother was the glue that kept us all together. Now that she's gone, we've drifted apart. My brothers have their own families—wives and young kids. I feel like an outsider even when I'm with them."

"I doubt they feel the same way about you. Family's important, especially when children are involved." Matas swirled the wine in his glass before taking a sip. "Do you have family in Lithuania?"

"My grandmother Aldona was born here. Her sister Gerde was sent to Siberia during the war. After Gerde was released, Aldona tried to get her sister out, but Gerde wanted to stay. She had met someone and they were getting married. The sisters never saw each other again. Aldona sent packages to Lithuania, mostly clothing—warm coats, dresses, stockings. But Gerde stopped writing. Eventually, Aldona stopped sending the packages because she wasn't sure Gerde was getting them."

"You knew Aldona?"

"The women in my family tended to have children later in life. I knew her and remember her, but she died when I was a kid."

"Aldona never came here to visit her sister?"

"When the Russians were here, it was hard to visit and she was too scared. After independence, she was too old."

Matas looked down at his wine glass. "Did Gerde have any children?"

"A daughter."

"What was her name?"

Lena touched the corner of her eye. Gerde's family was strangers and the possibility of actually finding them was slim. "My mother had saved the few letters Aldona got from Lithuania in a box up in the farmhouse attic. When we were cleaning the house to sell it, I found them, but moths had destroyed them. All I remember is that Aldona and Gerde grew up in Pabrade."

Matas seemed relieved. "Too bad about the letters."

"I did a little research though, and have an address. I don't think anyone in the family still lives there—it's been so long, but I don't know for sure."

"Do you have it with you?" said Matas.

Lena pulled out her phone and showed him the information Annie had given her.

The waiter arrived with their food. Lena took a bite of boar. It was rich and succulent, like the best pork, and served beautifully with lingonberries and sweet pear.

Lena asked Matas what he did for a living. He said he was a businessman who worked on acquisitions. He transitioned the conversation back to Lena by asking about her job. He seemed impressed that her boss was Vit Partenkas from Baltic Watch. She only said a few words about the project Vit had assigned her. She was flattered that he was so interested, but she'd worked on computer security for several years. The topic was sensitive and the systems she worked on were proprietary. She rarely said anything about her work. Matas asked a few questions. She answered some, and avoided answering others. By the time they finished the wine, there were only a few other couples left in the room.

The waiter brought the bill, and Lena offered to pay half. Matas gave her a confused look so she let the matter drop.

Lena held Matas's hand as they walked slowly through Old Town. He pointed out the statue of a woman riding a bear, St. Casimir's Church, and the Alumnatas Courtyard overlooking the Presidential Palace near the University and the Baltic Watch office.

At one point, Matas stepped away to light a cigarette, and Lena surreptitiously took a picture of him standing under a street lamp. She was happy to have gotten away with it.

When they got back to her apartment, she invited him inside, but he refused. She tried interesting him in a glass of brandy. He would have none of it. He waited while she unlocked the door. They stood facing each other. He looked down at the amber cross hanging from her neck and touched it.

"Are you Catholic?" said Matas.

Lena nodded. "And you?"

He didn't answer. Instead, he kissed her on the mouth and left.

~~

Late at night, Arkady sat cross-legged on his bed in the house in Riga, crouched over his laptop computer. He lowered the screen, extinguishing the only light in the room. Arkady stared into the darkness. He was in over his head. He had talked a good story with Matas earlier that day, but felt a growing panic. He had at most six months left to do the hack, but Matas might need it much sooner. Arkady just didn't know when he'd be called upon to produce it. He understood what had to happen in general terms, but needed to figure out exactly how to hack into the pipeline. He was getting nowhere by himself.

At first, Arkady thought he could handle it. But it was turning out to be much harder than he ever expected. If he didn't produce results, he wouldn't get paid, and there's no telling what Matas would do to him. Matas hadn't said anything threatening, but he was a scary guy. Besides, Arkady couldn't fail and still call himself a hacker. He'd have to go back to his old job at the coffee shop, and that would be worse than death.

Arkady glanced at the laptop. All he needed was a little push—a few ideas to put him on track to finding a solution. He needed it now, while he still had time to work through the details.

There was one person who could help him: his old mentor, Volshebnik. But what would Arkady say? How could he approach this without telling Volshebnik all about the job? Matas had warned him not to say anything to anybody. But how would Matas ever find out?

Volshebnik was more than a mentor. He was a business partner. He was like a father. Arkady thought back to his real father who had left them when he was a child. Arkady could barely remember his face. Forced to work, Arkady's mother was gone for most of the day. All alone, the boy turned to the computer so he wouldn't feel so alone. His favorite pastime was video games, but he also spent hours trolling the internet, amazed at the troves of information available on every subject imaginable. His school work suffered. He barely passed the lower grades. But he excelled at computer programming. Spending most of his time online, he grew into a bored teenager disinterested in school and awkward with other people. Eventually, he stopped going to school altogether, spending his time watching movies online and playing computer games.

When his mother found out, she was angrier than he'd ever seen her. She forced him to get a job. Arkady managed to find something in a coffee shop in a mall in Minsk. Arkady hated it, but went to work every day just to appease his mother.

Depressed, frustrated, and having no aim in life, he thought about ending it. He had a horrible job. No friends. His father was gone. His mother thought he was a complete failure. He had no talent; his mother had told him so.

Then one day, a large, heavy man walked into the coffee shop. He had a beard that hadn't been groomed in probably years. He ordered a double espresso. He sat at a corner table, a laptop on the surface in front of him, occasionally looking up from the screen and gazing at Arkady.

A few visits and some casual conversation later, the man introduced himself. His name: Volshebnik.

"You call yourself wizard?" said Arkady, bringing him his coffee. He found the big man's arrogance oddly endearing.

"No. It's what others call me." His voice was deep and gruff.

Arkady glanced at the laptop screen displaying a rough looking man carrying a sword in a medieval castle. They exchanged a few words about their favorite computer games before Arkady went back to work.

That afternoon, Volshebnik was still at his table when Arkady's shift ended. The big man motioned him over. They talked for hours about gaming, computers, and movies. Arkady was impressed with all they had in common.

The next day after work, Volshebnik invited Arkady home to a house crammed with books and computers. Over Chinese carry-out, the two became friends.

Arkady was entranced with Volshebnik's vast knowledge of computers, networks, and programming. Arkady asked questions. Volshebnik answered with surprising patience. Soon, they were spending every evening together. When Arkady's mother asked where he was spending his time, Arkady said he'd picked up a second shift at the coffee shop.

Then, Volshebnik asked Arkady to become the contact for anyone who wanted to talk to him. Volshebnik explained that it would save him time and effort. Arkady was happy to help, and as he continued to learn, he became Volshebnik's persona to the world.

Arkady asked if he needed a tag—an online name—to protect his personal identity. Volshebnik said no—he should just be "Arkady." When Arkady asked Volshebnik his real name, the big man laughed. Arkady didn't mind. He already thought of Volshebnik as the father he never had.

Their first job together was for a Russian businessman who needed information about a competitor. Arkady handled a good deal of the work: agreeing to the job, delivering the information, and accepting the money. When it was over, Volshebnik was delighted.

"With you in my life, I'm now a ghost," said Volshebnik, slapping Arkady on the back. Arkady wasn't sure what Volshebnik meant, but was glad the wizard was pleased.

Arkady quit his job at the coffee shop. He didn't tell his mother. Instead, he bought her a new coat, and explained that he'd gotten a raise. Eventually, he told her that he'd gone into business for himself. She asked him a deluge of questions. He gave vague answers—just enough information to shut her up. He spent many nights camped out on Volshebnik's sofa, dreaming of enough money to get his own place and move out of his mother's house.

Arkady would buy a modern flat, and equip it with the most sophisticated security and computer systems he could buy. It would be his shining sanctuary. It would take a good deal of money, though. So he worked hard and saved, waiting for a big job with a big payday.

As they did more work, Arkady realized that if they were discovered by the authorities, he would be the obvious guilty party because he had handled the arrangements. Volshebnik worked strictly behind the scenes. But Arkady didn't mind. He loved Volshebnik. Besides, he believed that Volshebnik would rescue him if he ever got into trouble.

Arkady was in trouble now. He picked up his personal phone. He had promised Rina not to use it, but this was an emergency. He opened a texting window to Volshebnik.

Are you there?

The cursor blinked like a heartbeat as Arkady waited, counting the seconds.

Hello my friend. Where have you been?

CHAPTER 13

Moscow—May

Vera kicked off her pumps and stretched out her legs on the blue brocade sofa in the private sitting room connected to her Kremlin office. She took a sip from her glass. "God, I love vodka. I bring a bottle out all the time for visitors. They have some, but I just taste it. The only time I really drink is when I'm having dinner with you. Does this mean you're my enabler?"

Sitting across from Vera, Nina Ditlova laughed. In the button-down shirt and slim black skirt, she looked like a woman ready to handle anything. "You're the strongest person I know. If you don't want something to happen, it doesn't. If you want something to happen, the rest of us had better watch out. You don't need an enabler."

Vera leaned forward and the women clicked glasses over a low table laden with half-eaten plates of herring, pickles, salted mushrooms, jellied meat, and dumplings. Selected for elegance, the table was among the many antiques in the room. Other pieces were more modern and chosen for their simplicity and comfort. This room was one of Vera's favorite places. It felt like a sanctuary. She invited only special guests here, the most frequent being her advisor and childhood friend, Nina Ditlova. The two women were sisters in every way except by blood.

"We're on the brink of greatness," said Vera. "Putin had us coordinating oil production quotas with OPEC. But Russia will never belong to a cartel. Not while I'm alive. If I have my way, we'll be outproducing the Middle East in a matter of years. And no one, no one will tell me how much I can charge for my fuel—especially for gas."

"We're well on the way to supplying even more natural gas to Europe."

Vera waved her hand. "Europe is just a dress rehearsal. The real performance comes when China arrives at the theatre. They have almost twice the people—nearly one and a half billion. Can you imagine what the world will be like with Russia as one of their major providers of oil and gas?"

"Vera, do you really think that will happen? China doesn't trust us. They'd rather deal with the dictators in the resource rich countries in Central Asia and Africa than rely on Russia for fuel."

"China is already buying some gas from us. When they see how well things are going in Europe, and they realize how easily they can get additional supplies from us, they'll buy a lot more. I have no doubt."

Nina took a bite of dumpling. "Well, I'm glad the American influence is weakening. Their last president damaged the alliances they'd fostered since the war. But their loss is our gain."

"America is wealthy, but I'm sick of their hold on the global economy. It will take years for power to shift to another country, but it will. People say China will be the major power of the twenty-first century, but they're wrong. Russia will be, because of the wealth obtained from our massive oil and gas reserves. The language of commerce will be Russian. Currencies will be compared to the ruble."

"With money comes power."

Vera smiled demurely. "And we haven't even talked about India's developing energy needs. It will take a while, but their population is almost as large as China's. That, as the Americans say, is a work in progress."

She glanced at Nina. "That reminds me. We need to keep moving our money out of Russia."

"I move some out regularly. Nothing that anyone would find unusual. I use a network of accounts that would take a Svengali to unravel."

"Good. Keep it up. You and I are never going to be poor again, no matter what happens. Our lives and our future are here. But with our esteemed businessmen having put me on a schedule for completing the new Baltic pipeline, I want to make sure we have as much money as possible tucked away somewhere safe just in case."

"Are you worried?" Nina took a sip from her glass.

"Here in Russia, worrying only makes good sense."

"You know I won't let anything happen to you while I have a breath left in me." Nina put some herring on a thin slice of bread and balanced a piece of onion on top. She took a bite, her expression rapturous as she chewed and swallowed. "I hear the Baltic pipeline is almost finished?"

"I put a lot of money into getting it done quickly. It should be operational by August. The management team will make the announcement in a few weeks."

"What do you want me to do after that?"

"At our next election, Grinsky will be out, and I'll appoint you my prime minister. Together, we'll continue to perform miracles. I can already see the headlines in *Izvestia*: *Koslova and Ditlova: The Power-Women of Russia.*"

Nina put her plate down. "You promised Yuri Rozoff the prime minister's job. After the pipeline is built, I'm sure he'll try to take credit for it. After that, he'll expect to be appointed."

"It's my prerogative to appoint whomever I want, and I want Grinsky for now, but you're next."

"I'm sure he was flabbergasted when you kept him in the office of prime minister when you became president."

Vera jutted out her chin. "I want Grinsky where I can watch him. They say to keep your enemies close. It's good advice. Besides, a leader's prerogative is to change her mind. My promises are merely suggestions, not actual agreements. Rozoff would be no good in politics. He's best behind the scenes. He's a manipulator, a schemer. He should know that a visible position like prime minister would be disastrous for him. If he's foolish enough to think I would give this to him and risk the stability of my own government, then he deserves to be disappointed. Besides, when oil and gas revenues start coming in, he'll be one of the richest men in all of Russia."

"That may be, but I fear he has a long memory like most men."

"Alone, Rozoff isn't a problem. But if he aligns with Grinsky, I'll have to take action. I've warned Rozoff against it. But until something happens, if it ever does, he's just another Russian businessman. You and I both know to handle a Russian businessman. Like we handle any man: promise him everything and give him just enough to keep him interested." Vera held up her tumbler and watched the light play against the cut glass.

"What happens if he partners with Grinsky?"

"He'll become my enemy."

"Should I talk to Orlov? Have him increase electronic surveillance?"

Vera put her glass down. "Orlov's FSB is already recording everything from the people who interest us the most. I want a few of your people to continue monitoring those recordings, and report back to you. It's best that we have direct access to everything. Orlov doesn't need to know I'm involved—just a precaution."

Nina nodded. "You don't think he's involved with anything that might hurt us, do you?"

"No. I just find that keeping people uninformed prevents flies from turning into elephants. Did the report on Lena Markus come in?"

"Nothing stands out, other than she has a background in computer security, and a great aunt who was sent to Siberia during the war. The only branch of the family we could find lives in America."

"Not an uncommon story. Many families perished." Vera closed her eyes. "How many men do you think died for Mother Russia? Tens of millions. But it was the women who suffered. We raised our children with nothing but a piece of land and a cow, if we had that much. We kept things going through the worst of times. And what did we get for it? A pat on the head and another baby to raise. Now it's our turn. We'll send our daughters to the best schools. They'll become the new leaders in government and run our businesses. I can hardly wait for this new generation of women to become inspired by what we do, and continue to move Russia to new heights of achievement."

"But Vera, we have no children. We've dedicated our lives to the people. We never took the time to have a proper family. You have Michael. I don't even have a husband." Nina refilled their glasses, spilling some vodka on the coffee table and wiping it up with her napkin.

"All Russian children are ours. We are the mothers to every young person east and west of the Urals."

"To everyone!" Nina held up her glass.

Vera raised her glass. "Here's to our women poets, healers, scientists, and philosophers! May they all be great."

Both women drank. Then they threw their tumblers into the fireplace hearth, the glass shattering, the shards joining the other broken pieces already there. They both stared into the fire. Then Nina got up, went to the cabinet, and took out two more glasses.

CHAPTER 14

Pabrade, Lithuania—June

"What do people think when they see us together?" Stefan veered the Passat around a sharp curve on the 102, heading in the general direction of Pabrade. He sped up. Then he reached for the sunglasses on the dashboard, and put them on. A few flakes of dandruff fell to his shoulder.

"How do I know?" Sofia rolled her eyes. Stefan often asked pointless questions. She reached for the coffee container in the cup holder and took a sip. "They certainly don't think we're a couple of Russian agents—we're too old. Most people think the work we do is best done by young people."

"It's good to have survived long enough to be above suspicion."

"It's remarkable that we're still alive." Sofia opened the window a crack and breathed in the fresh air. "Slow down. We don't want them to spot us."

"Don't be paranoid. There are too many brown Passats on the road for ours to stand out." Stefan slowed down anyway.

Sofia took out a brush from the glove compartment and ran it through her gray hair. She pulled down the sun shade, revealing the cosmetic mirror. She leaned in close. "Too many wrinkles. I look like a witch."

Stefan smiled. "You have the figure of a forty-year-old."

"If that's supposed to make me feel better, it doesn't."

Sofia glanced in the back seat, making sure the duffel bag full of equipment was within easy reach. It was unlikely they'd need the pair of night vision goggles Stefan had bought on the black market years ago or the binoculars, but it felt good to have them close at hand. She hoped they wouldn't need the extra ammo tucked into the side pockets.

Their current assignment was surveilling a woman named Lena Markus. It didn't matter that it would be a boring job. Boring at this stage in her life was good.

She glanced at Stefan. The traces of age on his face and in his posture still surprised her. She thought of him as a young man, not that sixty-five years of age was old. They'd worked together for decades. The time had vanished as quickly as a bottle of vodka in a room full of Russians. They'd slept together many times, but only when celebrating the end of an assignment. They were considering living together, because pooling the retirement incomes received by Russian SVR agents made good sense. But they were just in the talking stage. They still had other lovers, as it was the way of people in their business. Stress and sex tended to go together like borscht and sour cream. All their superiors cared about was their ability to work together. If sharing a bed every so often helped the situation, then it was a good thing, even encouraged.

Both had had long, dangerous, and interesting careers that were ebbing now to more mundane surveillance work where their age was an advantage. Who would suspect an old couple of spying? Who'd believe it?

Stefan and Sofia were both from the Russian countryside outside St. Petersburg, and had been selected for clandestine services because of a talent for foreign languages. Both spoke Russian, English, Polish, and French. Sofia spoke Lithuanian because she was one of the few in her class able to tolerate hours of instruction from a toothless Russian teacher who had spoken it fluently. During class, she had pictured him with his clothes off, and had found it amusing. It had helped her through.

While their marksmanship skills had deteriorated with age, there was one thing Stefan and Sofia remained good at. It was keeping their mouths shut and their eyes open.

While a team of two wasn't much when the job was surveilling an active young woman, it was relatively easy. Their main problems were deciding shifts and staying awake while on duty. They made the situation workable. They were used to it. Besides, they liked to work alone, without backup teams. More people made things complicated.

Sofia squirmed out of the jacket of her pink track suit. She always wore something pink, even if it was only a bra or panties. "Where do you think they're going?"

"I would guess Pabrade, but who knows? I never expected the boyfriend to have such a nice car. Not everyone can afford an Audi. It looks new. If I knew he had a car, I'd have stuck on a tracking device."

"Right now, she's our target, not him." Sofia took another sip from the coffee container. "Who would have thought she'd get together with somebody so quickly?"

"She's an American. They're friendly people."

"Don't you think it odd that Orlov sent us here? He's not even in the organization."

"It just means this is important. If she's with the boyfriend most of the time, we can keep an eye on both of them. But if we find out he's up to something, we may have to split up. We'll have to see what happens. I don't like it when we split up."

Sofia put a hand on his knee. "It's the job."

"I don't like Orlov giving us orders. He's domestic. We're international."

"Don't worry about it. It just means that something's going on and probably high up. Keep your head down. You'll be fine."

Sofia put the cup in the holder and pulled out her phone. Her finger glided over the smooth surface. "Not much on Matas Nortas. There's a picture of him on one of Lena Markus's social media sites. But he has no social media profile. I guess it's not unusual for a man like him."

"What do you mean?"

"He has no visible means of support, but has enough money to own a luxury car."

"Don't worry. We'll find out everything about him soon enough."

~~

Lena relaxed in the passenger seat while Matas drove. It was early, and a mist rose from the fields in the distance. The sky had a pink tinge. The air was cool. The plush interior of the Audi smelled new.

They were headed for Pabrade, a little town about an hour northeast of Vilnius. Matas had said a surprise would be waiting for her there. She suspected they were going to visit her grandmother Aldona's childhood home, but wanted to play along.

"You wouldn't be taking me to meet your mother, would you?" asked Lena, smiling.

Matas chuckled. "No."

Last night, Lena had done some online research on Pabrade. It was home to about six thousand people. Images showed it to be a lovely spot, tucked in between open fields and a large wood. It was near the Vilnius-Daugpilis Railway that went from Vilnius into southwestern Latvia. It didn't seem to be noteworthy, other than possibly being home to her long-lost relatives.

Lena watched the street names, trying to match them to the address Annie had found. Her heart pumped faster when Matas turned onto the right street. She checked her phone to make sure it was what she had entered.

He parked the Audi in front of an old yellow house with a white door and green shutters. The steep roof was a red metallic material. A low wire-mesh fence separated the front yard from the road. Across the street stood a similar house, although that one was badly in need of paint.

Matas opened the homemade gate, waiting until Lena went through before following her into the yard.

"Is this where my family lived?" said Lena.

Matas smiled as he stepped up to the front door and knocked.

A young man answered. He was tall and very thin, wearing dark pants and a light button-down shirt. Lena guessed he was about her age. He smiled and gestured them inside. They went through a small foyer with boots on the floor and jackets hanging on a coat stand. The hallway in front of them led to an old-fashioned kitchen. Another door was open to a sitting room.

"Please." The young man smiled, gesturing them into the sitting room.

Lena hesitated on the threshold. Sun poured in through sheer white curtains. Items in the room were old and showed wear—a threadbare carpet, a faded pillow—but everything was spotlessly clean. The air smelled fresh, as if the room had been recently aired. Three upholstered chairs stood along one wall. In the middle of the room were straight-back chairs around a table set with plates, cups, and saucers. A tray of smoked meats and cheese sat in the center, beside a basket containing slices of dark bread.

As Lena walked into the room, a tall, older woman stepped out from the corner to greet them. Lena guessed she was in her sixties. At first, the woman's furrowed brow made her smile seem uncertain, but as she gazed into Lena's face, her forehead smoothed and her smile broadened.

Standing next to Lena, Matas spoke. "This is Ramute and her son, Antanas. I believe they're your cousins."

Lena felt her face flush. It was the right address, but it had been decades since the last letter. Why didn't they write? Have they been here all this time? She was skeptical that they were family. How could Matas be so sure?

After some halting conversation, they sat down at the table. Antanas left, returning soon with four tiny, stemmed glasses and a small decanter containing red liquid.

Ramute filled the glasses and handed them out. "I make this cordial from raspberries. I hope you like it. I only serve it on special occasions."

Lena took a sip. It was sweet and delicious. It reminded her of the dandelion wine her grandmother Aldona had made years ago. Lena and her mother had found some in Aldona's closet a few years after she died. Lena had been too young to have more than a taste. It had been wonderfully sweet too, but had a tang.

"It must have taken a lot of work to make this. Why do you bother?" said Lena.

Ramute raised her eyebrows. "My mother made a batch every year. I make it now. I don't think Antanas will keep up the tradition, but maybe you'd like the recipe."

Ramute held out the tray. Lena took a piece of meat and a chunk of cheese, laying them on her plate.

"I'm glad to be here and very happy to meet you, but are you sure we're related?" said Lena.

Ramute went to a shelf full of keepsakes on the far wall. She took down a book-size leather box and brought it to the table. Inside were small bundles of letters bound in red ribbon. She searched through the bundles, selected one, and undid the bow. Leafing through the letters, she picked one and handed it to Lena. The envelope was wrinkled and dirty—likely quite old. The return address had been ripped off and the envelope was badly mangled. The postage indicated the letter had come from the US. Lena couldn't make out the date of the postmark.

"Letters used to arrive this way. We never complained about their condition. As long as we got anything at all, any scrap of news, we were happy."

Lena took out the sheet of paper and read a chatty letter about news in town, signed by a woman named Aldona. The ink was badly faded. Some of the sentences were blacked out with marker rendering them unreadable. No doubt it had been censored. The side of the letter had been torn off.

"My grandmother's name was Aldona. She had a sister named Gerde," said Lena.

Ramute nodded as she wiped her eyes. "Gerde's my mother."

Lena read the letter again. Matas handed her his handkerchief. She didn't realize she'd been crying, too.

Ramute continued. "When Gerde came back from Siberia, Aldona was already living in the US. Gerde met my father, and when I was born, they decided to stay here in the homeland. I think even under the occupation, Lithuania was where they wanted to raise their child. After spending so much time in Siberia, I don't think Gerde ever wanted to leave Lithuania again."

Lena tucked the letter back in the envelope and handed it to Ramute, who kissed it and placed it carefully back inside the box.

"Why did Gerde stop writing to us?" said Lena. "We sent packages, but didn't know if Gerde ever got them."

"Back then, it wasn't good for people to have connections in the US. Too much mail and too many packages meant a one-way trip to Siberia, and that frightened her more than you'd believe. Gerde stopped writing to protect us. After she died, I thought about contacting you, but so much time had passed that I didn't think you'd remember us. If you did, I thought you'd be angry for the years of silence. When Matas called last week and asked if we might be related to a family named Markus in America, I was so happy I couldn't speak. He said you were here in Lithuania, so we arranged this little get-together. When I saw my mother in your face, I knew God had given me a gift."

They spent the rest of the afternoon walking around the property and narrow roads of Pabrade, talking about family. Antanas got flustered when Lena asked him what he did for a living, stammering his response. He recovered though, and spoke about the farm supply store where he worked as a bookkeeper. Lena took it to be nerves. Maybe he wasn't accustomed to visitors claiming to be family.

When it was time to go, Matas waited in the doorway as Lena and Ramute hugged. Lena felt like she was hugging all the family that had been lost to her until today. When they parted, Lena's cheeks were wet.

Ramute wiped away the moisture with her fingers. "It's tears like this that I don't mind seeing."

In the car heading back to Vilnius, Lena tried to compose herself. Without Matas, she might never have found Ramute and Antanas. He'd given her one of the greatest gifts of her life.

"I'll never forget what you did," she said, putting her hand on his knee and gazing out at the road.

~~

Matas placed his hand over Lena's as he steered the car onto the motorway. He knew the afternoon with Ramute and Antanas would cement his relationship with her. The visit mattered to Lena. She wouldn't forget that he had found Ramute and Antanas, and had brought them all together. It was just a matter of time before Lena confided in him about everything, including what she was learning from her research at Baltic Watch. Her tears were a very good sign that things were going his way. He was relieved at how easy it had been to fool her.

Halfway home, Matas noticed the Passat that had been behind them on the way out to Pabrade—at least, he thought it might the same car. He got that tight feeling in his stomach that told him something bad was about to happen.

He pretended not to notice, and said nothing about it to Lena. He took her to her apartment. She invited him inside again. He refused, for he had work to do, although it would have been easy to stay.

After Lena was safely inside, he drove through the streets, constantly looking in his rearview mirror for the brown Passat. He didn't see it, but it could mean the driver had skills. Matas wound his way to the E272 and headed north. He got off at a shopping mall, parked the car near a travel agency, and waited. Still no Passat. He took a roundabout way back to Old Town and the garage he rented for his car.

After parking, Matas walked parallel to Pylimo Street and down an alleyway across from Lena's apartment. Glancing at the street, he noticed the brown Passat parked at the curb. Two people were inside—a man and a woman. They weren't young.

They had chosen to stay with Lena as opposed to following him. That meant they were probably interested in her and not him. While that was a relief, it meant that Lena or her work was important to someone who had the resources to have her followed.

Matas had to get even closer to Lena, to find out what was really going on. He pictured Lena's creamy skin, recalling the woman he had failed to help long ago when he was a priest. He hoped Lena's story would have a happier ending.

CHAPTER 15

Joniskis, Lithuania—June

Rina eased the car through a wooden gate into a small yard as the headlights shone on an old house with a thatched roof. Surrounded by a tall fence, the car and even the house windows weren't visible to anyone passing on the street. No doubt the reason why Matas had chosen the place.

Simona was in the passenger seat and Arkady was napping in the back. The drive from Latvia hadn't taken a long time, but it was well after midnight.

Rina cut the engine and got out of the car. She used the light on her mobile phone to help find the house key under the second gnome to the right of the front door. She went inside and walked through the eat-in kitchen, sitting room, and the two bedrooms, checking that all the windows were locked and ensuring that no one was there. Rina knew the place was supposed to be empty; Matas had told her it would be. But she liked being cautious. In her line of work, it just made sense. At the door, she signaled Simona and Arkady it was safe to come in. Rina went back outside and opened the trunk so her companions could get the bags.

Then Rina locked the gate and the car, went inside, and went to bed.

As usual, Rina was the first up the next morning. She dressed and splashed some water on her face. She made a pot of coffee—it was ready by the time Simona came in. Arkady joined them a few minutes later, carrying his laptop. Rina handed Arkady coffee in a cup bearing the words *I'd rather be in Latvia*. She didn't bother to say good morning. He never spoke before having coffee. But today, he looked surprisingly alert. Rina guessed that he'd been up for a while already. The circles under his eyes had grown darker over the last few weeks, and he'd spoken out in anger about the smallest things—the soup wasn't hot enough, she and Simona weren't being quiet enough, his bed wasn't comfortable enough. Signs of stress.

Arkady settled in at the table, his glasses resting on the end of his nose. He sipped coffee, his gaze on the screen of his laptop. The interior lights were on, the closed blackout curtains preventing the sunlight from coming in. Rina cracked eggs into a bowl and stirred them before pouring them into a pan warming on the stove. She moved to the side and Simona opened the oven, placing a tray of bread inside. The scent of toast made the room homey. The women put the eggs and slices of warm bread on plates and carried them to the table. Arkady picked up a plate, held it close to his face, and shoveled the food into his mouth with a fork. Rina and Simona sat down, glanced at each other, and buttered slices of toast.

Rina glanced at Arkady. "Matas phoned me yesterday. He said the pipeline dedication ceremony is being planned for the first of August. He wants you to do the hack on the twenty-sixth, at midnight."

Arkady slowly put his plate down.

Rina continued. "I want you to explain what you're doing again. If Matas asks me anything, I need to be able to tell him. Simona, too. He said he needed to know everything."

Arkady looked nervous. "Are you sure he said the twenty-sixth of August?"

"Midnight. What's the matter with you?" Rina ate a bit of egg.

"If Matas wants to know anything, he can talk to me directly. Besides, isn't it better if you two don't know what I'm doing?"

Rina gave him a dirty look. She was getting sick of his attitude.

"What? He doesn't trust me and wants you to check my plan?" said Arkady.

"Matas doesn't tell me who he trusts and who he doesn't trust." Rina took a bite of toast.

"All right," said Arkady. "I'll go over it one more time, and that's it. I can't keep wasting my breath on you two, or this'll never get done."

"If you want us to bring you any more food, you'll do what Rina says," said Simona.

Arkady pushed his glasses up to the bridge of his nose. "I've been working my ass off these past months, getting past preliminaries and collecting background information. I looked at the list of companies and services Matas gave me a few months ago. I focused on all the companies supplying the computers, software packages, and communications equipment for the pipeline control room in Zug, Switzerland. I went to online professional networks and job boards to find people working for those companies."

Rina flinched. "What are you planning to do with that information—find out where they live and force them tell you about the control station?"

"We don't do that sort of thing." Simona looked up from her plate of eggs.

Arkady exhaled, as if the explanation was exhausting him. "I went to social media sites, looking for common interests among the people I found at each company. I found one company where a number of people posted photos of themselves having dinner at different Thai restaurants. I sent them an email about a Thai restaurant that included a link to a new menu, but the link was infected with my virus. When people opened their email and went to the bogus website, the virus automatically downloaded to their computer. My virus tracked keystrokes on the computer where it was loaded, and sent it back to me along with all the networking information I need—IP address, network connections, usage ports, the applications they're running. All sorts of stuff, including how they connect to the control room computers. Another company had people who liked to ski, so I sent them email about an early bird ski pass discount with a link containing my virus. I did this for all the companies working on the pipeline that had something to do with the control room. I got a lot of data back, and am in the process of narrowing it down. Once I do, I'll have enough information in theory, to hack into the control room computers. At that point, I'll be able to change the parameters that control the flow of gas."

"I don't get half of what you said," said Simona, munching on a slice of toast.

Arkady ignored her. "A lot depends on how well secured the control room is. It might have an isolated network, and somebody might be monitoring network traffic. If they detect communications they don't expect, they could enforce extra security, like making everyone change their passwords."

"How long would it take to recover from something like that?" said Rina.

"If my virus is still running on their computers, it won't take all that long to recover from password changes. But if they rebuild the machines, then I would have to start over, and that might take a long time. A lot hinges on one of these affiliate companies having a connection into the control room that isn't as secure as it should be, or is temporary. I think our chances are good close to deployment time when they finally turn on the gas. People who supply software and hardware used in the control rooms will need to be certain that everything's working, so they'll be monitoring like crazy, and potentially showing their bosses nice real-time graphs and other things. If there's a problem, people will have to diagnose it, and I doubt that they'll all fly to Switzerland just for that."

"I don't know how I'm going to remember all this, but you sound as though you know what you're doing," said Simona.

"You can tell Matas it's all based generally on the cyberattack on the Ukrainian power grid in 2015. I use the same principles, although my virus is much more sophisticated, and the way I download it to computers is well, brilliant. It's a well-targeted attack. Just like the one in Ukraine."

"That's nice," said Rina. "But Matas probably won't care about that. He'll want the details and if you can't explain what you've done, you'll be in trouble."

"He'll want more than what I just told you?"

"Who knows?" Rina shrugged.

"Do you think he's going to come here?" Arkady adjusted his glasses again.

"No. Matas will stay away. He'll probably phone me and ask to talk to you." Rina pulled out her phone, looked at the screen, and put it back in her pocket.

Arkady leaned forward. "And when's that going to be?"

Rina glared at him.

"You never tell me anything. Fuck off!" said Arkady, turning to his laptop. "I'm not standing around waiting for Matas to phone. You can't interrupt me all the time. I need to concentrate. You people give me the creeps."

"Well, you're stuck with us, so get used to it. Besides, Matas wants you to deepen the A. Sims background. Baltic Watch has been making inquiries about her."

"Easy. I can give her a credit card and more online material." Arkady thought of the photo for A. Sims he had taken from an obscure database in Finland. After he'd captured the photo, the computer it was on had crashed and Arkady had gone on to do other work. To be safe, he should hack into it again and remove the photo. But right now, he had more important things to worry about.

"How long are we going to be here?" he said.

Rina looked at him suspiciously. "You're in a fine mood today. We just got here. Why do you want to leave?" The stress was obviously affecting him, which was to be expected. If he didn't calm down, she'd need to say something to Matas.

"How long?" Arkady looked angry.

"A few days. Then we move again. We stick together like glue until this is done."

"Where are we going next?"

"You'll see when we get there."

"Leave me alone then. I have work to do."

~~

Late that night in his bedroom, Arkady took out his personal phone. The cottage was quiet—Rina and Simona were probably asleep. He cursed that they were with him almost all the time. Either Matas still didn't trust him, or the job was far more sensitive and important than he had imagined. Either way, August twenty-sixth was two months away. And he was nowhere near ready.

The next conversation with Matas was coming up soon, and Arkady needed details he didn't have. Volshebnik had told him exactly how to write the virus. After Arkady had installed it on the targeted computers, it had worked beautifully. Using the most advanced cyberattack techniques available to exploit flaws, the virus had provided Arkady with a large collection of data. But now, he had to sift through all of the information looking for precisely what he needed, assuming he knew what he needed. Volshebnik had to help him again, but what if he refused? All would be lost—the project doomed to fail. If Matas found out Arkady was in touch with his old mentor. . . Well, he couldn't find out. Rina and Simona couldn't find out. Arkady felt like his head was in a vice.

Matas wasn't a computer geek, but he was smart. Their conversations had proved that Matas asked good questions and knew the terminology. If something didn't sound right, Matas would sniff it out. He'd get suspicious. Arkady couldn't fool him. He had to be prepared.

Arkady picked up his phone and began to type. *Are you there?* Arkady pressed the 'send' key.

Still here. What do you need now my little friend?

Arkady was so relieved, he wanted to cry.

CHAPTER 16

Vilnius, Lithuania—July

On Sunday, Lena joined Matas on a trip to Trakai to visit the restored island castle. She spent a lovely day with him looking at all the treasures, and shopping in the open air market. She bought a few pieces of amber jewelry. They ordered pizza in a little restaurant down the street.

As they ate, Matas asked her about the project at Baltic Watch, which only endeared him to her even more. Ever since that day at Pabrade, she felt comfortable being open and candid about her work. After all, there wasn't anything secret about her job at Baltic Watch. She told him about the lost little girl at the demonstration in Klaipeda, her research on the LNG terminals in Lithuania and elsewhere in Europe, and even mentioned the mysterious A. Sims.

Then she asked when they were going to visit Ramute and Antanas again. Matas mentioned that Antanas was busy with inventory at the farm supply store and was working day and night. It would have to wait a few weeks. Lena was surprised Matas had been in touch with them, but said that would be fine. They agreed to visit Ramute sometime in the future.

After they drove back to Vilnius, Matas walked her to her door. He stepped in close. It was good to feel his strength and warmth.

She tilted her head back, and pulled the lapel of his coat down so that his lips were mere inches from hers. He kissed her. It felt like she was floating. She opened the door and took his hand to pull him inside.

"Why don't you stay for a while?" said Lena. Her heart was racing. It had been a long time since she'd been with a man.

He cupped her face in his hands and kissed her again. Then he touched the cross at her neck, stroked her hair, and left.

Lena closed the door and leaned against it, a little disappointed that she was alone, but pleased with the kiss. She was already daydreaming about Matas. She dwelled on his touch. It was good to feel close to someone. It had been a long time. Already, she looked forward to seeing him again on Tuesday for dinner, before flying to Germany for what was likely to be the last demonstration before the new Baltic pipeline opening ceremony. Tuesday seemed far away.

The next morning, Lena stopped at the coffee shop across the street. Waiting for her latte, she recalled Matas bumping into her and the coffee spilling all over her coat. It was a story she might tell grandchildren one day. Then Lena caught herself. Falling in love with an older man and having a family with him wasn't part of her plan to retire early and travel the world. She took her drink, went out into the street, and shook off the weekend's pleasant memories as she walked to work.

At the office, Lena settled into her chair. Her desk was a mess of pens, yellow sticky notes, papers, and pipeline maps, a sharp contrast to the stark looking office.

Her report on energy in the Baltics was shaping up. She had recently added consumption projections over the next ten years for Europe. The only thing missing was the analysis of Vera Koslova's intentions, which is what Lena really wanted to work on. Unfortunately, Vit didn't agree.

She had talked to him about it last Friday, stating outright that she planned to do an analysis piece on Vera Koslova.

"No," he'd said. "I didn't hire you to bash Vera Koslova."

Lena felt her face get hot. "I believe I can write a very fair-minded piece about her."

"When we have reason to do an analysis piece on Koslova, I'll talk to you. Your focus is energy in the Baltics, and that's it. This may be the last report people see from Baltic Watch in a long time, and it has to be good and completely accurate. You should be spending your time double checking your facts."

Vit had gone on to tell her not to editorialize at all. She rolled her eyes at the recollection. Her boss was just wrong. She was certain he would need an analysis of Vera Koslova eventually, and she'd have one ready.

Lena drank some of her latte while gazing at her laptop screen and the picture of A. Sims that displayed in the background whenever she powered up the machine. As with Vera Koslova, A. Sims had gone from being a challenge to an obsession. Whenever Lena had a moment, she asked Annie a new question to help identify the damn Sims woman. Nothing had come up. The most obvious conclusion was that A. Sims didn't exist.

But Lena refused to believe it. She grabbed her cup, the maps, and her laptop containing all the notes she'd been amassing, and headed into Vit's office. He was at the university spending the morning with an old friend, and she had the place to herself. She touched the chassis connecting the computer to the desk, wondering whether Vit trusted her, but let it go. After all, he let her use Annie most of the time, and Annie was a great resource.

Lena asked Annie to check all variations of A. Sims—male, female, on all social media platforms. She did this regularly, in the hope of finding new information. The data came back quickly. There was the usual biography and headshot that Annie had found months ago, but this time, there was something new. It was a grainy photograph of a women's rugby team with a caption listing A. Sims as a member. The image resembled her, but it was hard to tell.

There was another piece of information—a credit card. A. Sims was young. Maybe this was her first one. Vit had mentioned that Annie was specifically blocked from investigating finances, but somehow Annie had found the card.

Lena furrowed her brow. She was getting nowhere. Then in a moment of inspiration, she asked Annie to compare the *picture* of A. Sims with all the photographic images stored in public databases on the internet. Annie found the exact image in an obscure database of seamstresses in Finland. Why was a political science major working as a seamstress?

It seemed unlikely that Finland was involved in the demonstrations, although activists from that part of the world might be concerned about the pipeline's potential impact to the environment should a gas leak develop in the Baltic Sea. A seamstress might have political passions, but it was a stretch to believe one could organize and run a demonstration in Lithuania.

Lena rubbed her eyes. Who was this woman? If A. Sims was real, why hadn't she come forward? Why hadn't she attended the demonstrations? Why hadn't she spoken a few words to the crowds? Locally, she'd be a hero. Almost everybody in Lithuania and the other Baltic countries were against the pipeline anyway, so why hide? Perhaps she feared reprisals from the Russians. Maybe she was reluctant to talk openly just like everyone else.

Maybe A. Sims was a fake identity. Maybe someone had created A. Sims to mask their own role in organizing the demonstrations. But who would do that—and why would they want to? Russians wouldn't organize a demonstration against a pipeline that clearly was in the best national interest of their country. Who was behind this? Baltic activists? European environmentalists? And what about the credit card? Lena struggled to understand.

Vit came in carrying a business size envelope. He greeted her and sat in one of the guest chairs. Lena began collecting her things to bring back to her own office. Vit told her to stay as he was only going to be there for a minute. He picked up a map from the desk. It showed a spiderweb of lines across Eurasia.

"Russia has over a million miles of pipeline and she's building more," said Lena.

"Good to know. Ready for the trip to Germany?"

"I was planning to leave on Wednesday."

"I got you an interview with one of the managers who'll be at the pipeline landing site in Lubmin tomorrow afternoon. His name is Harold Weber. He won't have much time, but you'll get to see what the receiving station looks like."

With a twang of regret, Lena realized she wouldn't see Matas until the end of the week at the earliest. "Oh. All right."

Vit gave her a half-smile. "Matas will manage somehow while you're away."

"I'm glad you two were able to meet, even though it was just for a drink. We'll all have to have dinner together one night."

"He seems like a nice guy." Vit handed her the envelope. "Here's your ticket and itinerary. With your extra time in Germany, you can look for this A. Sims character, if she shows up at all. Annie's still not finding out anything more about her?"

"Nothing substantial; just a blurry photograph and a credit card. I'm beginning to think I'll never find her. Will I be going back for the inauguration ceremony next month?"

"Not sure it would be worth the trip. Koslova announced she won't be there, only Prime Minister Grinsky. With his security detail and the security details of all the other dignitaries there, you won't even get close. You'll get a lot more out of covering this week's demonstration in Greifswald. Ever been to Germany?"

"Yes, right after high school. Just Frankfurt and Berlin, though."

After a few more minutes of small talk, Vit left the office to go home.

Lena glanced at her ticket. She dialed Matas's number and got a not in service message. She dialed it again. Same response. This number had worked the few times she'd used it. What was going on?

Lena glanced at the computer and asked Annie to look up Matas's phone number. In a minute, Lena was punching a new number into her mobile phone. Matas answered on the first ring.

He sounded surprised. "This is a brand-new phone. How did you find the number?"

Lena laughed. "I have my ways."

In the second of silence that followed, it felt like something was very wrong, that she had crossed a line and shouldn't have called him.

Lena broke the silence. "I'm flying to Germany first thing in the morning, and won't be able to have dinner with you tomorrow night. Vit wants me to leave early to see if I can find out more about the leader of the demonstrations."

Matas's pause lasted a beat too long. Was he upset that she had to break their date?

"What did you find?" he said.

"I'll tell you next time I see you."

Another pause. Then, "When will you be back?"

Lena told him late in the week. Matas wished her a safe trip, and suggested they have dinner together when she returned.

After hanging up, Lena looked down at her mobile phone. Maybe Matas didn't like spur-of-the moment phone calls. Or perhaps they were both just tired.

"Annie, how did you find this number?" said Lena.

"Matas Nortas has no number on contract with a service provider, but he has a mobile phone. I used his last known number to see who he called. I used those numbers to find their calling number. Three couldn't be traced, meaning they're burner phones. I gave you the first number of the three."

"Why would Matas need a burner phone?"

"There are several possible reasons. Burner phones can be used for calls and texts that you don't want going to your primary phone. People use them for dating applications, campaign contributions, and when selling items through online services. People who aren't signed up with a carrier can use them for emergency calls. They're good backup devices for phone calls and texts when traveling, or if there's a problem with your primary phone."

Lena really didn't know a lot about Matas. Still, he had been very kind to her. They'd kissed several times. He'd reunited her with lost family, for God's sake. She should trust him. She *did* trust him. But she wanted to find out more. She wanted to get to know him better. Why shouldn't she? He couldn't possibly have anything to hide.

Why not take advantage of Annie's considerable skills?

"Annie, would you please do a background investigation of Matas Nortas?"

"Certainly, Lena."

"When you finish, send me an email with the information." She paused. "By the way, I took a picture of him several weeks ago. His face is at an angle and he's not looking directly at me, but you might be able to use it for facial recognition against any online photos. And look in local archives. Many have come online since the occupation ended. You might find something there."

Lena logged off Vit's computer and shut down her laptop. She took her things back to her office, and packed everything into the worn canvas shoulder bag she always carried. It was big enough for her wallet, notepad, and even her laptop. Then she grabbed her sweater, and headed out the door.

~~

Sitting on a bench across the street from the Baltic Watch office, Matas looked at his phone, stared into space, and then carefully put the phone in his jacket pocket. His trembling fingers pulled out a packet of cigarettes. Lighting one, he inhaled, exhaled, and inhaled again. *How the hell did she get this number?* He stared at the partial view of Lena's office through the tree leaves as he searched for answers and came up with nothing.

He could have spent the night with her after the trip to Trakai Castle. Hell, he could have spent the night with her after Pabrade and the visit to Ramute. Lena would have let him—he was sure of it. But he hadn't. He'd ignored the opportunities. Or was it that Lena reminded him of another woman from long ago?

If he'd slept with her, she might have explained how she found the number of his brand-new burner phone. *Was she trying to find out more about him?*

He wasn't sure if the new information Lena had related to A. Sims would lead her to Arkady. If that damned hacker left some breadcrumb behind, they were doomed. The project couldn't go on. If Baltic Watch knew that a hacker from Belarus was behind the demonstrations, they would keep digging until they actually found him. Arkady would tell them everything and that would be the end of them all. Matas raised his eyebrows. Worse, what if the *Russians* found out about what they were doing and got to Arkady?

And who in the hell is following Lena? Never had anyone been this close to the lies Matas had fostered. He assumed the couple in the Passat were following Lena, but he wasn't completely sure. *What did they want? Who had sent them here?* To protect them both, he had to worry about them both.

Matas puffed his cigarette. He wasn't accustomed to worrying about someone outside his team, let alone a strange woman. He pictured the swell of her breasts. Only an old *fool* would let himself get emotionally involved.

At least he had the image of the couple in the Passat. That had been a bit of luck. He'd asked a kid en route to school if he wanted to earn a couple of euros. The kid got a clear photo on Matas's phone of the man asleep behind the steering wheel, and the woman looking at her manicure. He had sent the photo immediately to Rina and Simona.

Matas pulled out the packet of cigarettes again before noticing he already had one burning between his fingers. The uncertainty about Lena's safety was real, but he couldn't fly to Germany without raising her suspicions. Still, Rina and Simona would be there. He had warned them to look out for the Passat and the couple. If *anyone* was following Lena, Rina and Simona would notice.

The door to Baltic Watch building swung open and Lena came out. She was wearing a blue sweater and jeans, looking young and fresh as ever. She carried her shoulder bag, as usual.

When she had passed from sight, Matas got up from the bench and glanced over his shoulder. No cars were allowed in this area. If that couple was still following Lena, it had to be on foot. He didn't notice anyone in particular, but there were people who could make themselves practically invisible. He had to assume they were out there, somewhere. Matas moved into a crowd of students passing and walked with them for a distance. He pulled out a cap from his pocket and put it on just as he left them at an open gate to a courtyard shared by a number of apartments. He threw his phone into a dumpster, and went down a side street to Pylimo, where he waited for fifteen minutes, more than enough time for her to walk home. Then he went up to the door of Lena's apartment building and rang the buzzer. As he waited, he looked down the street and spotted the Passat.

He heard a window open above him. He looked up. It was Lena, checking to see who was there before opening the door. *Smart girl.*

In a moment, he was inside her apartment.

"What are you doing here?" said Lena.

Matas tried to kiss her.

Lena squirmed away. "Are you angry that I phoned you?"

"Just surprised. I didn't have time to give you the new number. How did you find it?"

"Why? What happened to your old phone?"

Matas thought fast. "I was visiting a friend at his machine shop. I put the phone down. The next thing I knew it had fallen into a vat of acid. The whole thing was destroyed."

"I thought you were angry about something," said Lena.

"I was. At myself for being so stupid."

Matas took off his jacket and draped it over a chair. Then he pulled her to him and kissed her. She smelled like a rose. He murmured into her ear. "I couldn't stand the idea of not seeing you all week."

"I'm only going to be away for a few days." Lena looked up at him and then kissed him back.

I have her.

Matas gazed at her flawless skin and her softness. Around her neck, the amber cross glowed. He closed his eyes and kissed her again.

CHAPTER 17

Vilnius, Lithuania—July

It was the first time Matas had made love to a woman in years, and it was an American. His motive was deplorable–tricking Lena into talking about the demonstration organizer before leaving for Germany. At least it was no worse than fooling her into believing Ramute and Antanas were her relatives. He tried not to think about it, but it was impossible not to.

Lena turned toward him. She nibbled his ears and stroked his chest. Matas tried not to respond, tried not to take advantage of her again, but he couldn't help himself. He forgot about everything, and just lived.

And yet, after breaking their embrace, he didn't ask about A. Sims. Instead, Matas told her about his wish for little homestead in Utena on the edge of a forest, with room enough for a garden and maybe some fruit trees. Lena talked about the farm where she had grown up and her mother. He felt a connection between them. He couldn't help it.

Then Lena talked about Vit Partenkas and Baltic Watch without even being prompted. Matas only had to listen to learn that she knew nothing about Arkady. His relief was marred knowing he had taken advantage of her for nothing. *But why did he care?*

He stayed awake most of the night with Lena curled into his side, her head resting on his shoulder. Her mouth was open. She was gently snoring. He recalled her fingers trailing down his chest and wondered if this incredible young woman might have feelings for him. He couldn't allow it. He wouldn't drag her into his dark world of invisible people who naively believed their lives would begin when they got out. No one ever got out. Not entirely. Not even him. He was a criminal, for Christ sake!

But then he pictured Lena with him on the little place he wanted to buy in Utena, and wondered if he had feelings for her. *I'm a damned fool.*

She deserved more than a broken man who was old enough to be her father.

His job was to protect himself and his team, not to indulge himself with feelings for this spoiled American. He couldn't afford it.

Lena stirred. Even asleep, she was lovely. She propped herself up on an elbow and kissed him. She got out of bed, fumbling for her robe. She left the room, and came back in a few minutes with two cups of coffee. They talked a little in bed as they drank. She got up and packed, then took a quick shower. He watched her dress.

"I'll take you to the airport," said Matas.

"No. Stay and get some rest. I can take a taxi."

"I want to." Matas pulled on his pants. The Passat was probably still parked outside on the street. He at least wanted to see her safely to the airport. "I'll go and get the car. It'll only take a few minutes."

She put her arms around his neck and kissed him again. "Okay."

~~

At least it's not another damned church, Matas thought as he sat on a bench overlooking the massive outdoor statue at the Ninth Fort, a large prison that had been turned into a museum in Kaunas. It was dedicated to the fifty thousand Jews killed there during WWII. Peter had honored his request not to meet in a church, but it felt like the old man was toying with him. Here, thousands of people paid their respects to the dead every year. Matas glanced up at the early morning clouds, hoping rain would hold off for a while, but the gloomy day comforted him more than sunshine ever did. He wondered what Lena was doing at this hour in Germany—maybe still sleeping.

He didn't think the brown Passat had followed him here. He'd taken a roundabout route. Still, he wasn't sure. He'd grown accustomed to living in a world of shadows, where only a select few people knew anything about him. It comforted him to know he was a ghost. No one judged him for his failure as a priest. No one chided him for having a father who was a Communist. No one cringed at the illegal means he used to make money. No one knew him, except for his team. Even most of the people who hired him had never seen him. He usually made arrangements through middlemen who preserved his anonymity for a cut of the profits.

But Peter insisted on face-to-face meetings. Due to the fact that Peter was paying him exceedingly well, Matas was willing to go along. He hoped it wasn't a mistake.

This last-minute meeting with Peter just weeks before the Baltic pipeline would be declared operational seemed a waste, unless there was news, or if Peter wanted something more. Matas wasn't in the habit of changing agreements halfway through a job, and he wasn't about to start now.

A black Mercedes pulled into the lower parking lot. The car went very slowly and had trouble turning into a slot. *Probably Peter.* It backed up and readjusted position before finally stopping. *Definitely Peter.* It seemed to take an eternity for him to get out, walk a few steps, go back for something, and finally make his way along the upsloping path to the bench where Matas waited.

Peter was breathing heavily when he sat down. They didn't acknowledge each other—just two strangers on a bench in a park that happened to honor the dead.

Matas took out a cigarette, offering one to Peter. Peter took it and leaned toward the flame from the lighter Matas held. The old man greedily puffed.

"My doctor would have a fit if he knew I was smoking a cigarette. But you only live once," said Peter.

"What do you want?" said Matas.

"I want to know if you're ready. And I want to know how you're going to do it."

"We found a way."

"Tell me."

"You'll read about it in the newspapers."

"I'm paying a lot of money for this, and I want to know that you're taking care of things. That you're doing it right. We have a lot to lose if they find you."

"You mean if they find *us*."

Peter chuckled, then coughed. He took out a handkerchief from his pocket and covered his mouth. After he finally stopped coughing, he wiped his eyes, finished the cigarette, and stubbed it out under his foot. "Even if they arrest me, I'll be in the US by then. With lawyers involved, by the time they extradite me to Lithuania, I'll either be dead, or too old to care."

"How convenient for you."

"But that won't be the case if you or your team is caught. If the Russians realize that Lithuanians were behind the pipeline shutdown, they'll come after us. As far as Koslova is concerned, we're just a doormat between Ukraine and the Baltic Sea. People here are worried about an invasion. Russia won't come here unless there's a reason. This gives them one helluva reason."

"There'll be sanctions placed against them if they make a move." Matas tried to sound bored, but he was worried about the Russians, too.

"Don't you get it? We have to convince the world that Russia stopped the flow of gas. Then people will look back at history, and what the Russians are capable of doing. Only then will they adjust their plans, and stop buying fuel from the devil."

"We're taking all possible precautions. And it doesn't help that you want to have these chats. The less we're seen together, the better."

"Who's here?" Peter gestured at the statue in the large open field. Aside from an older man and an older woman in a pink jumpsuit sitting all the way over by the statue, there was no one.

Seeing them, it occurred to Matas that the couple had been there for a while. "That's what we thought during the occupation, only to find listening devices planted all over the country. The Soviets recorded everything. Nothing was private. No one can be trusted. Not even you."

Peter blew his nose. "After this is over, you're going to have to take care of Arkady, the Belarusian. No one can ever know what we did. He's not one of us. He can't be trusted."

You're not one of us either, thought Matas. "He's being paid well to keep his mouth shut."

"I don't trust him!"

"You're paying me to do a job, and that's what I'm doing. I'm not being paid to take care of people, as you put it. Arkady is on my team. He won't be a problem." Matas hoped he was right.

Peter's face turned red. "It's my money. I give the orders!"

Matas scowled. "If you take it upon yourself to harm *anyone* on my team, I will find you. If you consider withholding your payment to me for whatever reason, I will find you. Wherever you are. And it won't be pleasant. For you, that is."

The old man banged his cane on the pavement. "Damn impudence!" He stood, and walked back down the path. The lady in the pink jumpsuit looked over at them.

Matas took out another cigarette and lit it as Peter drove away. Rina and Simona had vouched for Arkady, so he *shouldn't* be a problem.

Lena, however, might be. That she was spending an extra day in Germany looking for A. Sims worried him. But there was no A. Sims to find, no loose thread to unravel—at least that's what Arkady had led him to believe. But Lena was smart and had resources. How else could she have found his phone number? That alone bothered him. It wasn't that he didn't trust Arkady. Matas didn't know if Arkady was smarter than Lena, Vit Partenkas, and all their resources at Baltic Watch.

If Arkady left something behind that linked him to A. Sims, Lena might actually find Arkady. He would talk. Eventually, everyone talked.

Matas could try misdirecting Lena, although he was loath to do it, especially with Vit Partenkas involved. Vit would probably see through any deception. It probably wasn't necessary anyway. Lena was already talking about the investigation, keeping Matas up to date, and even telling him what she was thinking. She wasn't holding anything back. She trusted him.

If she suspected him of anything illegal, he'd see it in her face. Lena, like all innocents, wore her emotions on her face.

Matas tossed away the cigarette and rubbed his eyes. It would be so much easier if he could sleep. Even if just for one night.

Perhaps he was overthinking it. If Arkady could control the pipeline, people would naturally conclude it was the Russians. A few breadcrumbs pointing to Russian interference as punishment for the demonstrations was all they needed to convince the world. Rina and Simona had already prepared material for social media that would blame Russia for the hack. They'd post it after Arkady had done his job.

But the Russians would look into everything with unrelenting determination. If they found Arkady, Matas would be the next target. They'd get to Lena, too. Bottom line, it wasn't Baltic Watch and Arkady that Matas had to worry about; it was the Russians.

The brutal truth was that they couldn't all survive this. Matas didn't know if he had the nerve to do what might be needed, even in the direst circumstances.

He pictured Lena's broad open face and sparkling eyes. He might not be able to save her. He thought of another woman from long ago whom he had failed to save—her loss had driven Matas to a life in the shadows. Lena could pull him into the light if he let her. But he didn't belong there. Not anymore.

CHAPTER 18

Lubmin, Germany—July

Lena felt her heart beat in time to the constant vibrating hum from the pumping equipment as she waited on the pathway just inside the gate to the Landfall Station. This was where the massive undersea pipes emerged from the Baltic Sea and made their way onto land to connect into the European gas grid. The six-hectare area was a marvel of gray valves and enormous pipes with stairways built around and over them. Along the pathways, workers in hardhats monitored valves, adjusted settings, and strolled in groups to the large warehouse and train tracks.

Other areas abutted this section, all dedicated to the sacred substance that could vanish into the air and water, or explode with merciless violence. The Landfall Station was built to control the beast.

The pipes and buildings were surrounded by an iron perimeter fence. In the distance, the Baltic Sea was an icy gray. A few scraggly trees were visible along the beach. Looming on the horizon, were stacks of a nearby power plant.

A man approached Lena. He was wiry, had a thin mustache, and a twitch in his left eye. He introduced himself as Harold Weber.

"I don't have much time," said Harold, checking his watch. "Besides being a manager and an engineer, I'm the public liaison to the control room in Zug, Switzerland. Everyone seems to want some of my time these days."

He handed Lena a bright yellow hard hat and safety vest, helping her put them on.

Harold continued. "Here in Lubmin, the pipeline connects into the EU grid, allowing the gas to flow into European countries. Zug is where we actually control and monitor the gas for Germany and the rest of continental Europe."

As they walked the gravel pathway next to the pipeline, Harold pointed to the gas and flame detectors. "The sensors detect any problems and can immediately shut the pipeline down, just like that." He snapped his fingers.

They passed an odd-looking solid cylinder, about seven meters long. Harold explained it was the pipeline inspection gauge, or the PIG. "It's a high-tech internal pipeline inspection tool and very expensive. We have it outside today because a film crew will be here later doing a documentary. Normally it's stored inside. The PIG travels through the pipeline with the flow of gas, and measures material integrity of the pipe—wall thickness, internal geometry, corrosion, curvature, all in one unit. Usually, we run the PIG through the pipeline once to establish a baseline. Any later measurements by the PIG are compared with the baseline to see what has changed."

"I'm sure you don't expect any issues, but how often do you expect to run the PIG through the pipeline?" said Lena.

"We're fully prepared to handle anything that comes up, and we do everything possible to avoid problems. For example, the PIG allows us to proactively check the health of the pipeline. European regulatory requirements determine how often we use the PIG, probably every few years. We put it in the pipeline in Russia and extract it here in Germany. It takes several days to travel the pipeline. Then we check all the data collected. If the PIG sensors detect anything abnormal, we know where and probably what happened. The pipeline's life expectancy is about fifty years, and with this level of maintenance, we shouldn't have any problems."

"Does that mean you'll replace it in fifty years?"

Harold laughed. "We'll see."

He pointed out the massive valves connecting different pipelines, explaining that they had to handle the different pressures. "The Slavanskaya Compressor Station near Narva Bay in Russia builds up the pressure of the gas, so it can travel all the way through the pipeline without additional compression. In Germany, the compression is adjusted again before it's transported through the European grid."

"You monitor everything from here?"

"There's monitoring here, but our primary monitoring is in the control room in Zug, Switzerland. There's another control room in Kingisepp, Russia. In both locations, through a series of cable and satellite connections, we can monitor and manage the pipeline remotely. The system worked very well for the first pipeline ten years ago, and we expect it to continue to work well when we open the new Baltic pipeline, especially with all the software and hardware updates we've made.

"In Zug, we have display screens showing statistics, real-time monitoring, and the entire pipeline geography. We can remotely control the valves at the landfall sites. We have the ability to show the chain of command in pipeline operations so we know who to inform should it be necessary. We even have access to the backup control room. It's high tech all the way. Here in Lubmin and in our sister site in Russia, we have instrument equipment rooms with workstations that also can control the valves."

"Isn't the inauguration officially opening the pipeline next month? Is gas already flowing?"

"To make sure everything is working, we test with water early-on, and then we monitor real-time conditions with gas in the pipeline. How else can we tell if everything's all right?"

Twenty minutes later, Lena took off her hard hat and vest, handing them to Harold before bidding him goodbye. As she drove back to her hotel in Greifswald, she reflected on the enormity of the pipeline project. It involved thousands of people, advanced technology, international cooperation, billions of dollars, and years of preparatory work all for energy to heat homes and run power plants for fifty years. If Russia acted purely on business interests, their profits could improve the lives of one hundred and fifty million Russian citizens and secure the supply of energy for all of Europe for decades. But would Russia behave? Would Russian citizens benefit from the pipeline profits? Would Europe ever be willing to go to war to ensure their access to Russian gas?

Lena had the unsettling feeling that the report she was working on for Vit was only the beginning. Her questions needed to be answered, and the most difficult ones involved Russia.

~~

Rina pulled the car up to the curb and parked. Simona was with her. It was about ten in the morning. They were a good distance away from Greifswald Center, so they could leave when they wanted without being caught in traffic. The town was about twenty kilometers from the Landfall Station in Lubmin and the closest a crowd could get to the secured facility that was being prepared for the collection of dignitaries who would visit for next month's inauguration.

Rina wore an ankle length flowered dress. Underneath, strapped around her midsection, was a pregnancy pillow. She waddled when she walked, although sometimes she forgot to. She carried an embroidered handbag containing a phone, two floppy hats, some money, and a tablet computer.

Simona had on cargo pants and a long-sleeved T-shirt. She carried a new mobile phone, bought for the quality of its video recordings.

Both women wore wigs and special sunglasses designed to hinder any facial recognition software from identifying them, even on a video. Since their tattoos were distinguishing features, Rina had covered the burning tree on her left shoulder under a thick layer of makeup. Simona's shirt covered her shoulder tattoo. Both women used heavy makeup to cover the ring tattoos on their fingers. They had considered wearing gloves, but decided against it. They didn't want to stand out in any way. Even wearing light gloves in the middle of summer might be noticed.

They strode together along the meticulously clean streets toward the demonstration that was due to start at noon.

"Arkady is driving me crazy," said Simona. "He complains too much."

Rina frowned. "So what? We're getting paid. Just do your job."

"I think many people are going to be here today. There was significant chatter on social media about the demonstration. Some of it was downright hateful, especially toward Vera Koslova."

"She deserves it, and as long as the press covers the event, we'll be okay. Just in case, we'll have our own little show." Rina stopped, and pressed a hand into the small of her back. She'd seen many pregnant women do this.

Simona held up the mobile phone. "I'm all set."

They continued walking to the large open area of the Greifswald square. It was completely surrounded by buildings, mostly stone, many painted in pastel colors. The steep rooflines looked distinctly German. Tables and chairs in front of cafes made the place look inviting. A block away, stood the dark round tower of St. Nikolai

Cathedral. The demonstration area had been cordoned off by German police. Officers in riot gear stood around the perimeter.

The women sat in an outdoor cafe along the square for a light breakfast, watching people arrive. A few rode in on bicycles. Some came in vans and cars. Excitement grew as groups poured in, probably from buses parked outside the square. People brought their own signs—most written in German, but there was a smattering of the three Baltic languages, and some Polish, English, and Russian. A few people held onto their signs, while others set them in piles for later use.

About an hour and a half later, Rina and Simona went to the area where the demonstration would be held. Before being allowed entrance, they went through a portable metal detector. Rina had to turn on the tablet to prove it was just a computer.

About noon, the crowd began chants that grew gradually louder. *We don't want the pipeline. We don't trust Koslova. Down with Vicious Vera.* They became boisterous. When a news helicopter hovered over the square, the crowd got even louder, shaking their fists and waving their signs.

Rina poked Simona in the side and took two hats out from her purse. Both women put them on. The broad brims covered their faces. As the news helicopter hovered above the crowd, Rina screamed and fell to the ground.

"Help," cried Simona.

"Oh my God!" shouted a voice.

"Is she all right?" shouted another.

"He pushed me down! Over there." Rina kept her head down as she pointed at a group of nearby demonstrators.

"He hit her!" cried Simona, also pointing into the crowd.

"Why would anyone do that?" said a voice.

"And she's pregnant, too," said another voice.

A small crowd gathered around the demonstrator Rina had identified. The man looked astonished. Someone even poked him in the chest. Angry retorts and some shoving were quickly quieted by the police. Folks helped Rina to her feet, asking if she was all right. She nodded. Simona put her arm around Rina, and the two women walked away—no harm and no foul. They went to their car and left.

They drove to the outskirts of town, stopped on a deserted sideroad, and changed clothes inside the car. It wasn't difficult. All they had to do was remove the outer layer. Under the dress, Rina had on chinos and a T-shirt with spaghetti straps. Simona unbuttoned her shirt with the T-shirt underneath. They put the pregnancy pillow, wigs, and Rina's dress into a plastic bag to drop later in a trash container outside a petrol station. Simona's clothes were so nondescript that it wasn't necessary to throw them out, although she rolled up the cuffs of her pants to mid-calf. They wiped the makeup off their fingers using towelettes from a package of baby wipes.

They stopped at a café that offered internet service in a small town not far away. The women took espressos to a table, and turned on the tablet computer. Simona logged in as A. Sims. She took the video card out of her recorder and put it into a slot on the tablet. Using a video editor, they cut out everything in the recording except for the loudest, angriest expressions criticizing Vera Koslova, Rina's pregnant body lying on the ground with her face obscured, and the fortuitous footage of the back view of a man looming over her. When they were done, they uploaded the edited video to several prominent and public internet sites under the title, *Pipeline Demonstration in Germany Turns Violent: Pregnant Woman Targeted.*

When they were done, the two women got back into the car and started the twelve-hour drive back to Lithuania. Rina expected to be at the safe house with Arkady in time for an early breakfast.

~~

Arkady was exhausted. He'd been up all night and all day, using every second of time alone to work through the details of his hack. Thank God Matas had stayed away. Finally, he had something that had a damned good chance of working, thanks to Volshebnik.

Volshebnik had saved him. His mentor's advice had been logical—find the accounts he needed to get into the control room by looking at the names of people and computers. *Make assumptions. Try things.* Arkady had, but without success. Then in a moment of inspiration, Arkady had tried factory control settings for various accounts, and found one that hadn't been changed. He discovered how the account had connected into the control room and followed the same process—he'd gotten in and out like a feather drifting to the ground.

He hoped he wouldn't need Volshebnik's help anymore. Arkady hadn't mentioned the pipeline or control room, only referring to it in a general way as a SCADA system, supervisory control and data acquisition. There were many in use all over the world. Volshebnik could only guess what Arkady was working on.

Arkady wanted to believe he was safe. *Volshebnik would never talk about this; he'll keep it a secret.* But if the authorities somehow found out that Arkady was behind the hack, they might find Volshebnik, too. Arkady would never implicate his mentor. He retraced his actions, wondering if he had left behind any shred of evidence that might lead to them both.

~~

The only light in Vera's Kremlin office came from a lamp on the desk and her laptop. The rest of the room was dark, hiding the luxurious furnishings and the portrait of Catherine the Great hanging on the wall in the shadows behind the desk.

Vera clicked the mouse, playing a video that had been posted only hours ago. Already, it had almost a million views. Glimpses of the old square in Greifswald—she'd never been there, then a closeup of a sign waved by a man with a goatee: *Stop the pipeline*. She put a hand over her stomach. Another scene of a very pregnant woman on the ground, curled in a fetal position, obviously frightened, and the back of a man looming over her. "He hit her," cried a voice. Another man waved a sign that read *Vera's gas for your freedom*. Another voice: "Why did you hurt her?" In the background, someone screamed. The crowd chanted *Stop Vicious Vera*.

Vera clicked again, replaying it from the start. She didn't know how many times she had watched it already, but she couldn't help herself. She searched for some sign that the anger wasn't directed at her, but she knew the truth. Wishful thinking had no place in her world.

Her enemies would be salivating over this. Grinsky, Krum and the rest of the damned oligarchs, maybe even Rozoff. Too many to feel safe.

She remembered the demonstration on the day of her inauguration as president of the Russian Federation. It should have been the happiest day of her life, but a large gathering protesting her rise to power had turned violent. Suicide bombers in the crowd had blown themselves to bits. They killed everyone standing near them. A child was crushed in the panic. Her FSB agents had never identified the perpetrators. At one point, she'd thought Grinsky had been behind it, but there wasn't a hint of his involvement, and she wasn't sure anymore. The person responsible was still out there.

The demonstration in Greifswald had no explosives and no one died, but the protest clearly targeted her. Vicious Vera. Voices on the video. She turned off the laptop. It would consume her if she let it. She had never let anything consume her. Still, it felt like she had been stabbed in the stomach. She couldn't move. Vicious Vera.

She picked up the phone and dialed a number she knew by heart.

A man answered, his voice expectant, as if he had been waiting for her call. "Orlov."

"The demonstration in Greifswald. Did you see the video?" She felt the energy drain from her body.

A pause. "Yes."

"Find out who was behind it. And this time, I need you to be successful." Vera hung up the phone, turned off the light on her desk, and stared into the darkness.

CHAPTER 19

Vilnius, Lithuania—July

On the plane to Vilnius, Lena typed furiously on her laptop, drafting a scathing report about Vera Koslova. Fueled by what she had learned at the demonstrations, her years studying the woman, and the insights she'd obtained from researching energy in the Baltics, Lena felt she knew Koslova. Besides, Lena's time was running out. Before long, she'd be back in the US at some technology company making lots of money, and her opportunity to have exposed Koslova as a ruthless tyrant would be gone.

In the report, Lena concluded that Koslova's goals were threefold. First, she wanted to sell lots of gas and expand the bank accounts of Russian oligarchs and politicians. Secondly, she wanted the ability, if necessary, to influence the votes of European NATO members—essentially exchanging gas for votes. It would take a crisis, and it would cost Russia future fuel revenues, but that doesn't mean she wouldn't do it. Finally, Koslova wanted to do whatever was necessary to become a major gas supplier to China. If Vit posted it, the Koslova analysis might even bring some paying subscribers back to Baltic Watch.

Lena wished she had more data to back up her hypothesis, but when she showed it to Vit, she was sure he'd be pleased. All she had to do was edit it, and then convince him to read it. But he'd been distracted lately, probably worrying about the financial difficulties plaguing Baltic Watch. She also had to make sure he saw her report on energy in the Baltics first, because that's what she was being paid to write.

When the pilot announced they were about to land, Lena turned off her laptop and put it in her shoulder bag under the seat in front of her. She smiled, thinking of Matas and their night together. She'd been with other men, but he was different. He was gentle, even though very passionate. When she moved back home, she was going to miss him. She didn't want to think about that yet.

Her trip came to mind—overall, it had been a good one. Her talk with Harold Weber had gone well. He'd even given her a rudimentary diagram of the systems used in the control room at Zug, boasting that it was the best technology available. The information was on the internet and publicly available, but it was a nice diagram that pulled things together. There'd been a disturbance involving a pregnant woman at the demonstration. By the time she reached the scene, the police had taken back control and the woman was gone. Lena gathered some information about the incident before returning to her quest to find A. Sims. No one knew or had seen this elusive woman. Lena was now convinced beyond any doubt, that A. Sims didn't exist. It was likely a fake name to hide the identity of the protest organizers.

After an uneventful taxi ride, Lena was back in the office. She reached for her mobile phone to call Matas and tell him she was in Vilnius, but remembered the background search she'd asked Annie to run. Lena had noticed the message earlier—she hadn't had time to check it during the trip. She thought it might be fun to read the report before calling him, and surprise him with a fact or two about his life. Then she thought better of it. Remembering his reaction when she had found his new phone number, she knew that Matas didn't like surprises. Still, excited to learn something more about him, she opened the email.

She couldn't believe what she was reading. Annie's message claimed that Matas had been a Catholic priest, and his father had been an administrator in the Communist party. It wasn't that she objected to priests, or even Communists. It hurt that the man she was sleeping with had consciously chosen to omit telling her anything about these major events in his life.

What else hadn't he told her?

Lena read Annie's email again, hoping for even more, but there was nothing. She glanced at her watch. It was late and when she usually did her best work. She had notes to review, and information to summarize for her report. She tried putting her feelings aside and focusing on her work, but it was impossible. She was tired and annoyed with Matas and his damn secrets. All of a sudden, Vilnius wasn't so charming. Neither was Matas.

Lena put her laptop in her shoulder bag, grabbed her wheeled overnight bag, and went downstairs, slamming shut the outside door. She stepped onto the cobblestones and headed home. She heard footsteps coming from behind her.

"Lena."

She stopped at the sound of Matas's voice, but didn't turn to face him. He moved around to face her. As he lowered his head to kiss her, she turned away.

"What is it?" he said.

"You were waiting for me?"

Matas adjusted the cuff to his shirt. "I wanted to surprise you."

"You were a priest?"

"How did you . . ." He stared at her with wide eyes.

"I'll take that as a yes."

Matas squeezed her arms. "How?"

Lena squirmed out of his grasp and pushed him away. "Annie found an old photo of you."

"Who's Annie?"

"None of your goddamn business. She matched your face to an old online photograph of the first newly ordained priests in Lithuania after the Soviet breakup. And there you were."

His lips faded to a thin line. "You took a picture of me? I asked you not to."

Lena turned and walked away, but he caught up with her. He looked nervous, agitated, even a little scared.

"Please don't be angry. I never talk about it," he said. "I'm sorry."

"What difference does it make? You don't owe me anything."

"Let me explain."

Lena folded her arms and stared at him.

"Not here." Matas took her elbow in one hand and her luggage in the other. It made a thumping sound as he rolled over the uneven stones to the coffee shop where they'd first met. He bought her a latte and a cup of coffee for himself. They sat at the table they always used—in the front by the window.

"I was ashamed," said Matas.

"There's nothing wrong with being a priest."

"People needed me and I couldn't help them. A man of God who couldn't do more than mumble a few prayers and send them on their way is useless. They needed someone to understand their burdens, and I couldn't. I was just a stupid kid. I had to leave the priesthood because they expected me to save them. And I couldn't."

"That's why you left? Why is that such a secret?"

Matas stared into his coffee. "There was a woman."

Lena sat back in her chair and waited.

"It's not what you think. I never touched her. I wanted to. She was pregnant, homeless, and needed help. Instead of really helping her—finding her a place to live and reconnecting her with family, I kept thinking how good it would feel to hold her in my arms. She committed suicide."

Lena was stunned.

"I couldn't see past my own desires. She's dead because of me. That's why I left the church. It's not something I talk about."

They went up to her apartment. Sitting on the sofa with a stiff drink in his hand, Matas had the look of someone with regrets. Lena sat next to him, waiting for him to say something more.

Matas spoke haltingly about his mother's religious devotion, admitting it was she who had pushed him toward the church. He had gone willingly. Maybe it was a way to distance himself from his father, a corrupt administrator for the Communist party. He talked about the men his father's age who came to him for guidance. He couldn't help them, either.

Still cradling the untouched drink in his hands, Matas sat back and closed his eyes. He was so still, Lena thought he had fallen asleep. She'd read that could happen when a person released a burden they'd been carrying for a long time. She got up and gently lifted the glass from Matas's hands. She put it down on the table.

Lena could wake him and send him home, shutting him out forever. It would be the smart thing to do. But it felt like she was just starting to know this man, and she was curious. He wasn't rich, although he didn't seem poor. He had taken her to wonderful restaurants. He had a great car. She had never seen where he lived. She didn't know exactly how he made his living. She didn't know his friends. She knew nothing about him, except that he had been driven from his faith by circumstances over which he had no control. It would be easy enough to tell him it was over and send him away, but he had reconnected her with family.

Lena wanted to believe Matas was like the other Lithuanians she'd met who were reluctant to talk, although Lena was hardly a stranger.

She felt an attraction to him that she couldn't deny. She'd heard about women who had lost their fathers at an early age and had dated older men. Was she looking for a father figure? No. She had been looking for fun when Matas came along. And then something happened. He made her feel wanted. He knew how important it was for her to find her family, and he had found Ramute. She cared about him, and maybe even loved him.

His eyes opened. "I'm glad I told you about the little farm I want with a garden and fruit trees. It's not much of a dream, but it's mine."

"I don't want you to lie to me anymore. And no more secrets."

Matas let out a long breath. "You still like farms?"

Lena nodded.

~~

The day before the pipeline inauguration ceremony, Lena typed on her laptop with the flourish of a concert pianist. Then she clicked the 'save' button. Her report on energy in the Baltics was done. *I hope he likes it.*

As she waited for two copies to print, she realized she was humming. Things were better with Matas. He'd opened up to her and they were connecting. She'd even given him the keys to her apartment. If her report did well, maybe enough money would come in for Vit to extend her internship.

Then she thought of her report on Koslova. She'd spent many nights revising and editing the material she'd put together during the flight from Germany. It was ready, and if she was going to hand it to Vit, now was the time. She printed a copy, put both reports into a file folder, and carried them to Vit's office. She knocked on his open door. He looked up. She entered, and carefully placed the report on energy in front of him on the desk.

He smiled. "All the changes are in?"

"If you want me to make any more modifications, just let me know." Lena sat down across from him, the file folder containing the report on Koslova on her lap.

"I'll give it a quick run-through, and probably just post it."

"To our adoring public, who subscribes to our service and pays the bills."

"No. This one will be free. People need to see this. It's important they understand where their fuel is coming from, and what their options are for the future. Besides, we don't have many subscribers left."

Lena sighed. "That bad?"

"I was hoping for better response from our ad campaign. I ran one finally, because we need the money so badly. Unfortunately, there hasn't been a sensational story here since the Darius Artis case and the nuclear threat to Ukraine. People have let their subscriptions lapse. The new pipeline is an issue, but it's been very well covered in the international press. We hadn't contributed much new material on the subject until you came along. You got people on the street to open up. One cornerstone of Baltic Watch has been incorporating local opinion. People will like reading about that."

Lena leaned forward. "The report has no real political analysis on Russia or Koslova. It would definitely add dimension."

"What's Vera Koslova going to do? Invade Lithuania? Hold the gas hostage to avoid EU sanctions? The problem is we won't know what she has in mind until there's a crisis and she takes action." Vit continued leafing through the report.

Lena put her hand over the file containing the Koslova analysis resting on her lap. She wondered if there would be a better time to give it to him. "How long do you think Baltic Watch will stay open?"

Vit hesitated. "Your internship lasts for another month. I'd like you to help me close up shop. You won't be doing any writing, though. We'll be archiving files, contacting old customers, that sort of thing. Then you'll be as free as a bird. I'll write you a great reference."

"Thanks, Vit. I'm going to miss it here." Lena glanced around the office. "But I think I'm going to travel a bit through Europe before going back to the US."

"I suspect you'll be leaving behind a man with a broken heart?"

"Matas?" Lena blushed. "Maybe."

She looked down at her lap, picked up the file, and handed it to him—her analysis of Vera Koslova's political motivations and ambitions.

He looked at her. "What's this?"

"A going away present. I made some observations about Koslova that I think your subscribers would be very interested in reading."

"You were supposed to be working on energy in the Baltics."

"I did. And I also did this."

His brow furrowed, Vit quickly leafed through the report. "How much of this is based on actual fact?"

Lena's stomach sank as she waited for Vit to finish. It took only seconds.

"You wasted your time. I can't post this. What we write here is based on fact and only fact, not our personal opinion."

Lena bit her tongue. "But you haven't read it yet."

"And I'm not going to. This wasn't your job. Our last posting will be on the state of energy, not some hate piece about Koslova." He raised a finger. "And I'd better not find this on the internet."

"I wouldn't do that unless you approved." Lena tried to sound defiant, but she wanted to crawl into a hole. She told him good night, and left the office.

CHAPTER 20

Lubmin, Germany—August 1

Grinsky straightened his tie—the blue one his wife had said brought out the brown in his eyes. Behind him stood a tremendous portable dome where the inauguration ceremony for the new Baltic pipeline would take place. His security team shifted nervously as he took a last look around the Landfall Station. He had to admit it was impressive, especially the spiderweb of pipes that reflected the immensity of the project.

Much to his dismay, the project had gone well. France had declined to pursue an objection on the basis that it was against EU policy for one country, namely Russia, to own both the pipeline and the gas. Ultimately, France agreed that pipeline oversight would come from Berlin.

Then the problem with Denmark was resolved. Sweden, Germany, Finland, and Russia had approved the pipeline construction in their territorial waters long ago. Denmark was the only country to hold off approving the one hundred and seventy-seven kilometer segment of the pipeline slated for her economic zone waters. This area was designated by the Law of the Sea as exclusively hers for marine exploration and energy production. Cutting through it was the most efficient path to Lubmin. Grinsky had hoped that Denmark's reluctance would delay the project for longer than the year Vera had been given by the oligarchs to finish the work. Then the Baltic Pipeline AG used their sophisticated underwater surveying vehicles to mark a path routing the pipeline around Denmark's economic zone waters so that approval wasn't necessary. Accountant Krum had objected to the new route, claiming it made the pipeline even more expensive, but Nina Ditlova had convinced the others to go ahead with the new plan. Then at the last minute, Denmark approved—extra money wouldn't be needed; the project wouldn't be delayed any longer. Vera might have had a role there, too. He expected nothing less.

Vera Koslova had emerged victorious, even after the demonstration in Greifswald where she had been vilified, thanks in part to the people he had sent there. He wondered if she had even seen the videos where the crowd had chanted *Stop Vicious Vera*.

He had done all he could. Despite a few sessions with Rozoff and several discussions with Fedov, they had no real plan to further discredit Koslova, and no sure means to strip her of power. Grinsky's people had scoured Lena Markus's social media postings and had found nothing other than a boyfriend. Oddly enough, his people weren't finding much information about the boyfriend Matas Nortas or the organizer of the demonstrations, A. Sims. He didn't really know if A. Sims was Lithuanian, Latvian, Finnish, or from the damn moon.

He had no choice but to wait for an opportunity. Sometimes opportunity never came, and the possibility of failure rattled him.

Even here in beautiful Lubmin, there was failure. It was a small seaside resort that had been critical to Germany's energy profile for almost fifty years. Then in 1976, a fire at Lubmin's nuclear reactor had destroyed all but one water pump. The surviving pump managed to draw off enough hot pressurized water from the core to prevent a meltdown, but just barely. It could have been another Chernobyl. The East German officials had kept the near-disaster a secret until 1990. After the Berlin Wall was brought down, Germany began dismantling the nuclear facility, and they were still far from finished.

These days, Lubmin housed the Landfall Station for the pipelines. The first Baltic pipeline, also built by Russia, was operational in 2011. At one thousand two hundred and twenty-three kilometers, it was the longest subsea pipeline ever built. The new Baltic pipeline, whose inauguration was the object of today's visit, followed in the same general path as the original. The new pipeline doubled the capacity and improved all aspects of the technology from installing pipe to controlling gas flow. Building it was a massive job that included coordinating efforts of dozens of companies. Crews had installed a staggering three kilometers of pipeline per day. It was a true accomplishment, for which Vera Koslova would surely be remembered. The thought galled him.

Grinsky heaved a sigh and glanced up at the sun. At least it was a beautiful day.

He entered the dome through the side door. Most of the dignitaries were already inside, including the board members of the Baltic Pipeline AG, a corporation admired all over the world as an extremely efficient international shareholder consortium. Its most prominent members were Germany and Great Britain, but also included representatives from Denmark, Austria, France, and Russia. Katharina Becker, CEO of the company, was a personal friend of Vera Koslova's.

Hundreds of people were inside the portable domed structure. Every seat was filled. He looked up at the ceiling, awash with one hundred and eighty degree images taken during the Baltic pipeline construction. There was a video clip of the ships laying pipeline, and hyperbaric tie-in equipment splicing together undersea sections. There was a video of the pipeline emerging from the sea like a great monster, and videos of welders. All were playing simultaneously on the circular ceiling in a tribute to the massive project. It was breathtaking.

A ripple of applause greeted Grinsky as he made his way to his seat. He waved in response.

The first speaker was the German chancellor, a brilliant woman who expressed in clear terms Germany and the EU's need for fuel, and the business arrangement with Russia. Her request inviting everyone involved in the pipeline to stand brought the entire assemblage to their feet, amid stunning applause.

Katharina Becker was next. The plump and friendly-looking German spoke of the challenges faced in overseeing the entire project. She spoke briefly about the healthy business relationship Germany was enjoying with Russia, calling their alliance political history.

Joe Day, head of Britain-Energy and a board member of the Baltic Pipeline AG, talked about the financial success they could all share, now that Europe's energy needs had been satisfied for the foreseeable future. He gestured with hands so thin they were practically translucent. Grinsky wondered how the man could be so skinny and still live.

Grinsky scowled at the next guest's introduction, the primary speaker of the day. Vera Koslova was joining via live satellite link from her villa in Sochi. Grinsky had expected to say a few words himself on behalf of the Russian Federation, but Vera had decided to participate after all. *That bitch robbed me of another opportunity to speak for all of Russia.*

The lights dimmed just a little. Pictures of Koslova shone on the 180-degree dome: Vera at her desk in the Kremlin, Vera waving from the bleachers at the May Day parade, Vera shaking hands with the German chancellor at a diplomatic meeting. She filled the room. Larger than life. The audience gasped.

Then Vera Koslova and her husband Michael filled the massive screen behind the speaker's podium. In a red business suit, the color mimicking the flowers in the beautifully manicured garden behind her, Vera Koslova smiled and waved as Michael receded into the background.

Vera's voice filled the stadium. She eloquently spoke of a common continent with Europe and Russia, and her hopes for a free-trade zone. She expressed her gratitude at being able to help Europe overcome its shortfall in energy supplies by providing access to Russia's massive gas reserves. She expressed hope for political closeness over time. She remarked that the Baltic undersea pipeline made the world safer, by avoiding overland pipelines which were a constant target for terrorist attack. *She actually sounds sincere.*

Vera waved goodbye to shouts of approval and thunderous applause.

The head of EnergyLine, major supplier of pipeline for the project, and other speakers followed. Grinsky didn't pay any particular attention to them.

In the final event of the ceremony, the senior representatives from the major countries involved in the project gathered around a massive valve atop a section of pipeline, over which the entire dome had been constructed. Grinsky's hands, along with the others, turned the valve, officially allowing Russian gas to enter German territory via the new pipeline. But that, too, was just to impress, because the gas had been flowing for weeks.

~~

That night, with a bodyguard to either side, Katharina Becker strode into the lobby of the Regent, one of the most elegantly appointed hotels in Berlin. She wore a long black dress that almost made her look slim. The diamonds around her neck sparkled. The pipeline was done. The dedication was over. She was ready to celebrate.

The trio stepped aside to let a bomb-sniffing guard dog and his handler exit the lobby, no doubt having finished a last-minute sweep of the structure. Katharina's bodyguards had checked the hotel earlier that day. Two were still there; two others had returned to Katharina's residence to escort her to the event. Hotel security unobtrusively guarded every door. Bodyguards and security details melted into the steady flow of men and women arriving for the private party.

Katharina passed the baby grand piano and entered the Langhaus Salon, whose walls glowed in the soft light cast by crystal chandeliers. The tables were set with white china and cut crystal glassware. Waiters circulated through the crowd with trays of champagne, vodka, and bite sized hors d'oeuvres with a distinctly local flair: fingertip sized pieces of warm crusted German brie, tiny ham and sauerkraut rollups, bite-sized pieces of rye bread with a rosette of salami garnished with cornichon.

She smiled and waved upon recognizing Nina Ditlova. The two women exchanged a kiss on the cheek.

"Thank goodness Denmark approved the pipeline through their economic zone waters," said Nina.

"Pressure I imposed on behalf of the German government and the many late-night phone calls you made were enough to convince the Danes the pipeline is just good business." Katharina winked. "How's our mutual friend?"

"She never admitted to worrying about the project, but I know she's relieved it's finally over." Nina smoothed the skirt of her silver suit and then took two tumblers of vodka from a passing waiter. She handed one to Katharina. They clicked glasses.

Katharina leaned closer. "If Vera hadn't insisted that you join the project team, we'd still be laying pipe."

Nina smiled. "Thank you for saying so. I think the same thing about you."

"I hate it that Rozoff tries to take all the credit."

"Vera knows what's going on."

"I've missed her. Would you tell her? I understand the pressure to keep our friendship quiet, but it takes a toll."

"You shouldn't worry. A little passing time means nothing to Vera."

"Let's go skiing this winter like we used to. Just the three of us. I bought a place in Fichtelgeberge a few years ago. No one will find us there."

"It's hard to get away. Besides, Vera and I haven't been on the slopes in years."

"I hear it's like riding a bike."

As the women laughed, Joe Day and Yuri Rozoff joined them.

Rozoff kissed Katharina on the cheek and nodded to Nina. "Here we all are. The management team that made the pipeline a reality."

"They said it would take twice the time," said Joe Day.

"Denmark had me worried, but they succumbed to my charm. It saved us considerable money," said Rozoff.

Katharina glanced at Nina who coughed.

"Charm?" said Joe Day. "I don't think the Danes could be charmed into changing their minds about anything. I think they realized the pipeline had to go forward. We finished faster than I ever expected." The tendons in his neck stood out.

"We did it," said Katharina. "Now that we have a sufficient and guaranteed supply of gas, Germany is celebrating. With the gas we're sending into the European grid, many more countries are celebrating, too. We thank our Russian associates for a tremendously successful project, and for setting a very competitive gas price."

"You're welcome," said Rozoff.

Nina glared at Yuri. "I think we're charging a fair amount considering market value. I know President Koslova is delighted with the results."

Katharina raised her glass. "To Russia, our greatest business partner yet."

CHAPTER 21

Moscow—August 26

From her bed at the Cape Idokopas presidential residence outside Moscow, Vera tossed and turned. Michael wasn't here—he was in Sochi for the rest of the summer. She'd flown back to Moscow right after her appearance at the pipeline inauguration ceremony a few weeks ago. Unlike her husband, she wasn't on permanent vacation. She had work to do.

She'd chosen the backdrop of Sochi for the pipeline inauguration broadcast because she wanted people to believe she lived like a queen. While she slept in dachas, ate the best food, attended the finest dance performances and concerts, she spent most of the time working. She was at the Kremlin early each morning, and stayed late almost every night. A few times a week, she forgot her troubles on the tennis courts. In the winter she played inside; in the summer she played in the sun. Often, she came away with fresh perspective.

Now that the pipeline project was done, she should be relieved. Gas was flowing. The Germans were delighted. The Brits were happy that the European grid was delivering fuel to the Bacton gas terminal and onto the UK. In her collection of congratulatory messages, there'd been a sense of relief that Europe's energy future was finally secure. Businesses could prosper. There was nothing standing in the way of making this the most prosperous decade in a century.

To Vera, it was merely one step along the way to providing Russian gas to China, and becoming the richest nation on Earth. When *that* was done, perhaps she'd be able to sleep.

She had met the one year deadline set by the oligarchs with time to spare. When they met again in January, they would have nothing but praise for her. Money would be coming in by then, for a while, until she diverted the profits into finishing the Power of Siberia pipeline that would bring Russian gas to China. Then the oligarchs would no doubt complain again. They'd give her a period of time in which to finish the project. Again. When it was done, they'd be happy. *Russian businessmen have so little vision.*

But instead of relaxing and enjoying her success, Vera fretted on a bed covered in the finest silk sheets in one of the grandest residences in Moscow. The work was done. Her enemies had been silenced. Russia was on the verge of greatness.

So why couldn't she sleep? Did she fear success? Absolutely not. Were her enemies out there waiting for her to fail? Certainly, but that would never change. Did she have more work to do and more problems to solve than ever? Always.

When she was a little girl, Babushka had told stories of the Domovoy, the house spirits. Legend said that a bit of bread and a pinch of salt left at night by the kitchen hearth appeased the spirits and kept them from causing mischief and creating illness in the household. Babushka had believed in the Domovoy, as had Vera's mother. They had carried out the tradition faithfully, and in their own ways had led very successful lives. Babushka had raised an intelligent and beautiful daughter, Vera's mother, and had left a modest family legacy in the samovar Vera kept in her Kremlin office. Vera's mother had run away from a selfish husband to help Nina's mother settle in a place far away from her physically abusive spouse. They'd helped many people achieve literacy in the cold of Siberia.

Vera had never left food out for the Domovoy, and they hadn't prevented her from leading a country.

The ring from her bedside phone startled her. She glanced at the clock on her nightstand. *Twelve seventeen a.m.* She took a deep breath, her stomach already tense. No one ever phoned at this hour with good news. She answered. "Out with it."

Nina Ditlova said, "The gas in the pipeline stopped flowing."

Vera was stunned. She had expected someone to try and blow up one of the ships supplying the pipeline crews, but never thought they'd have an operational issue so soon. "What broke? Didn't they test it?"

"They're not sure what happened. They're checking for a systemic failure. But our people think it might be cyberespionage."

"Terrorists." The mere word shook her. "Do we know who did it?"

"No idea."

"Was it the Balts?"

"We don't . . ."

Vera felt her heart race, the political consequences of what had happened already coming to her. "My enemies would do anything to discredit me."

"Who do you . . ."

"Was it Grinsky?"

"Vera, we're not even sure what really happened."

"The West would love to blame me for this. They'll vilify me in the press. They'll say I did it to exercise control."

"Our best people are already . . ."

"We have to find out who did this. People will say I ordered the gas be held back as punishment for the negative press at Lubmin."

"No, it's too early to . . ."

"I bet Grinsky is laughing right now."

Vicious Vera. She could almost feel the wolves nipping at her heels.

~~

Grinsky stirred from a sound sleep at the ring of his phone. He turned on the light and answered.

"What!" he said.

His wife rolled over, shifting her back to him.

"It's Yuri," Rozoff said, laughing.

"Are you drunk?"

"I have the best news possible. I couldn't wait to tell you."

Grinsky sighed as he glanced at the clock. *This insufferable idiot had better have something good to say.*

"No gas." Rozoff said, and laughed even more.

"Fool! What are you talking about?"

As Rozoff told him what had happened, Grinsky sat up in bed, his smile growing.

"And they don't want to turn it on yet, because they're worried about a problem with the controls. They're running a full suite of tests," said Rozoff.

"Excellent!"

"There'll be so much negative press, it's sure to include claims that Koslova rushed the job. That's something we can blame on her and fix once she's gone. It's the end of her. I feel it in my bones."

"Does Fedov know?"

"He was my first call. He laughed so hard, I thought he was going to choke."

"Could it have been a cyberattack?"

"Possibly. We'll know soon."

Grinsky considered this theory. If it was a computer crime, he wondered what it would take to find the perpetrators. He even imagined thanking them and protecting them so no one else would find them. He wanted Vera to shoulder the blame.

This could topple Vera from her throne. Then he could run the country. Feeling completely happy, Grinsky leaned against the headboard and smiled.

~~

Peter was the only person left at the South Boston Lithuanian Club other than the bartender. The large windowless room was quiet, the tables and chairs behind him devoid of patrons. The linoleum floor had already been mopped, and the tables cleaned. No noise came from the kitchen, open only on weekends, as the cook and her helper had left hours ago.

He savored his beer, Utenos, a brand made in Lithuania and the only thing he drank, although he liked vodka for special occasions. He rarely drank it though, because most was imported from Russia. He'd rather die than drink Russian vodka. This bar was one of the few places that sold good Lithuanian brands like Vodka Unique, but tonight Peter wasn't celebrating.

He'd given up hope that the pipeline would fail. All the money, travel, and anticipation had led to nothing. Matas had failed him. Peter should never have given him complete control. Peter had done his best to leave a legacy, and failed. He would go to his maker a broken man. There was nothing left to do but die.

Wrapping his hands around the beer bottle, Peter thought about Uncle Peter, his namesake, who had no doubt suffered through his last hours with the Soviets. That was a hard way to go. Peter remembered his father, active and productive until the day he dropped dead of a heart attack while walking the dog. That was a good way to go. Clean. No burden to anyone. No health worries.

He hoped his own death would come quickly. The worst fate Peter could imagine was to lie in bed slowly withering away while remembering his failures, and thinking how he could have done things differently.

"It's late. You should go home and get some rest," said the bartender, untying the apron around his waist.

Peter nodded and lifted the bottle to his lips. His gaze went to the TV mounted on the wall above the bar. They'd had it on for the Red Sox game, and had turned the sound down when it ended. The station was issuing a special report. The caption on the screen mentioned the new Baltic pipeline. Peter called to the bartender. "Turn the sound up on the TV."

A female reporter was speaking. "While investigation into the cause of the outage has just begun, experts won't rule out the possibility of a cyberattack. The question the world is asking is, *Who would have done this?* It could be any number of terrorist organizations. It could be Ukraine retaliating for the power grid outage in 2015 and the NotPetya attack in 2018. The outage could have been perpetrated by Russia in response to the violent anti-Koslova demonstration in Germany last month. Experts have already begun to convene in Zug, Switzerland to analyze the outage. We hope to have more information soon." Footage from the Greifswald demonstration played behind her.

Thank you, God. Peter gestured to the bartender. "Get out the Vodka Unique. And two glasses. We're going to celebrate."

"What are you so happy about all of a sudden?" said the bartender, opening the refrigeration case and pulling out an opaque black bottle. He filled two tumblers part way with the clear liquid and handed one to Peter.

"I'm happy to be alive, my friend."

~~

At the house on Kalnciema iela just outside the heart of Riga, Rina, Simona, and Arkady huddled around the tablet listening to an internet newsfeed about the pipeline shutdown. Arkady was so relieved he wanted to shout for joy.

"Job's done," Rina said.

"I'm glad that's over," said Arkady. He'd done it. He'd had help, but as long as Rina, Simona, and Matas didn't know, it would be all right. This had been the most difficult job he'd ever had. He ached to tell Volshebnik all the details—how hard it had been, how impactful the job was, how he had hidden in hovels throughout the Baltic countries. The old man would be proud of him. But of course, Arkady couldn't say a word.

"Remember," said Rina, "you're not to take on any work for another month. At least. We don't want anyone noticing you back online the day after the outage. It's too much of a coincidence."

"What do you expect me to say if anyone asks about me?"

"Just what we discussed. You had a lot of jobs lined up and burned out from too much work. Then you took a rest."

"Fine. But when I get back online, my friends might ask if I had anything to do with the pipeline. They're sure to be talking about it for weeks. It's bound to be a big discussion. I'll have to leave a comment or two."

"No bragging," said Simona. "And no telling anyone what you did or how you did it. As far as you're concerned, this never happened."

Rina spoke. "If we hear anything about this on the internet, Matas will come looking for you, and it won't be good."

Arkady nodded solemnly. His internet friends were sure to think Volshebnik had something to do with the shutdown. The old man would deny it, but would they believe him? Would they then suspect Arkady?

"What are you two going to do now?" said Arkady.

The women exchanged a glance.

"We'll be out of commission for a while, too" said Rina. "Don't even try to reach us, because you won't be able to."

"You're not going to tell me anything, are you?"

Rina shook her head. "Can we drop you somewhere?"

"No thanks. I'm going to walk into town later today for the bus to Tallinn."

"Why Estonia?" said Simona.

"Eventually, I'm going to Belarus and home. But I want to catch the ferry to Helsinki first. I want to do some shopping."

"Electronics?"

Arkady shrugged. "Of course. What's Matas going to do now that this is over?"

"Who's Matas?" said Rina, smiling.

"I get it. This never happened. Tell him goodbye for me."

Rina took Arkady's computer and dropped it into her bag, along with the tablet and the mobile phones they had used for the project.

"I hate to see all that equipment go to waste," said Arkady.

"Everything has to be destroyed. Remember. This never happened," said Rina.

Simona gave him a kiss on the cheek. "Let's go. I want to be out of here before sunup."

"See you next time," said Arkady as the women went out the back door.

He sank into a chair, looking forward to the next days of worry-free rest. A buzz sounded from his personal phone, indicating an incoming text message. It was from Volshebnik.

How much did you get for the job?

What job? answered Arkady. His hands shook.

Lol. It's all over the news.

It wasn't me. Arkady felt like he was choking. He struggled to breathe.

If you say so.

~~

Matas slowly lifted his arm out from under Lena's head. This was the night he had been waiting for, the night he'd know if Arkady had done his job. Lena turned to her side and snuggled under the blankets. He waited a moment to make sure she was asleep before getting out of bed.

He pulled on his pants and went into her living room, quietly closing the door. He switched on a lamp and picked up the remote control. He pressed the power button. The TV came on. He lowered the volume and sat on the coffee table, clicking through the channels, looking for news, but it wasn't necessary to go through many. Several stations were already reporting the breaking story that the gas had stopped flowing through the new Baltic pipeline.

The news reports claimed the cause might have been a physical malfunction, but some were already speculating that it was a cyberattack. One report raised the possibility that Russia was behind it. Either the diatribe Rina and Simona had posted from A. Sims blaming Russia had taken hold, or the world was reaching the conclusion he wanted all on its own.

His relief at finally being done with this job was immense—greater than he'd expected. No more meetings with Peter. No more skulking about after Lena. He could finally buy his farm and leave the turmoil behind. Still, there were certain worries. What about that couple following Lena? Would Arkady keep his mouth shut? What about the inevitable Russian investigation? What if they found out the truth?

He fought off the distress. *The worst is over.* He thought of the fruit trees and what he'd plant in the garden. He could go there now, and step into his future as a rich man, who had finally done something good for his country. He felt a sense of pride for having told Russia in a very public way to watch out—the world was wary of her.

Then he thought of Lena, and all the lies he had told her. If he had any sense, he'd leave tonight. But Lena might look for him. Maybe he should wake her up, pick a fight, and storm out. He could claim it was over, that she was too young and immature for him. She'd cry. He didn't want to see her cry.

Breaking it off would hurt her, no matter how he did it or when. He didn't want to break her heart, but he had to do it. It would be the best thing for her. She was young and resilient. She'd find someone closer to her own age. Leaving was the sensible thing to do. If he stayed, he'd certainly ruin her life and he might end up in prison or out in the woods with a bullet in his head.

Why should he care what that couple in the Passat wanted, or why they were following her? Lena could take care of herself. She'd be going home to the US before too long, and she'd be safe there. In the meantime, Vit Partenkas could worry about her. He glanced at the bedroom door, wondering what life would be like without her.

CHAPTER 22

Moscow—August 26

Orlov felt sick. It was the middle of the night, and he was sitting in a chair across from Vera's desk at the Kremlin. Nina Ditlova was next to him. Vera drummed her fingers on the polished wooden surface, looking as angry as a bear.

"Was Grinsky behind this?" said Vera.

"We don't know." Orlov coughed, hoping it hid his unsteady voice.

"What exactly did your people find out about this Lena Markus?" said Vera. "Could she have done it?"

Orlov shifted his weight in the chair. "SVR has been watching Lena Markus for a few months, and we've had eyes on her boyfriend, Matas Nortas."

"Tell me."

"She's been investigating the new pipeline, among other things. She attended the last few demonstrations—her only international travel had been to Germany. Baltic Watch just issued her energy report that our agents say is merely a snapshot of the current state of affairs. Other than working and seeing her boyfriend almost every night, there's little to report."

"What about the boyfriend?"

"We had Stefan and Sofia keep tabs on him as well, although their focus was the girl." Orlov cleared his throat and tried to speak more slowly. He hoped it wasn't obvious. "Matas Nortas, the boyfriend, has means, but it's unclear how he makes his living. He met several times with a Lithuanian businessman living in America, Peter Landus.

They were together a month ago in Kaunas. Our agents saw them. Peter Landus's family was involved in anti-Soviet activity after the war."

"Who organized those demonstrations?" Vera pursed her lips. "Why is Matas Nortas meeting with a subversive from America? Does Vit Partenkas have a role in all this? I want answers! Get Bok in there."

"He's on an important mission right now. He's . . ." Orlov swallowed hard.

"Your people found nothing. I want someone in there who will get the job done."

Orlov bristled.

Vera continued. "I don't care what he's doing. I want Bok!"

"Last I heard, he's in northern Europe. I assume he could be in Vilnius in a matter of hours." Orlov hoped he was right.

"Have Bok start with the people at Baltic Watch, especially that woman and her boyfriend."

"But our people have already . . ." Vera's scowl told him it had been the wrong thing to say.

She broke in. "Find out if they're behind this, or know who is. Those people would do anything to discredit me."

"The more people we send to Lithuania, the more dangerous it is for them."

"You have your orders. Get going!"

Orlov opened his mouth to speak, but thought better of it. Good agents were hard to find. Sometimes, it was even harder to keep them alive. But for now, all he could do was give Vera what she wanted. He stood and left the room, closing the door quietly behind him.

~~

Vera stared at the door after Orlov walked out, trying to clear her head. She had to do something, but what? She turned to Nina. "I want you to launch a disinformation campaign."

"Certainly. Did you want to blame this on the Croatian Tartars or the Balts? Perhaps the CIA? There's always the Ukrainians."

"Yes, the Ukrainians. I want an announcement claiming the Ukrainians did this in retaliation for the power grid outage in 2015, and the cyberattack in 2018 on their NotPetya financial system. Do this from multiple sources, as usual."

Nina sighed. "They're going to think it was us Russians, no matter what we do."

"Do it anyway. Then get our best cybercrime people in the GRU involved. The Main Center for Special Technology. If it was a cyberattack, I want to know who did it, and how. And fast."

"A team of our cyberexperts is already on the way to Narva Bay."

Vera tented her fingers. "Honestly, Nina. Why would I stop the gas from flowing? Why would I jeopardize that large and important a source of revenue for Russia? We need the money from gas sales to pay our bills. How would retribution for the demonstration in Lubmin be at all beneficial to us? Yet, if I deny any involvement, my enemies will accuse me of lying. This will be the one time I can tell the absolute truth, and I guarantee you, no one will believe me. But I can't say anything."

"Bok will get to the bottom of this. You know how he is."

"A sadistic killer? I'm willing to overlook a few faults, as long as he gets the job done."

~~

Lena turned into the warmth she expected next to her, but Matas wasn't there. Sleep interrupted, she got out of bed, put on a robe, and found him sitting on the coffee table in her living room, watching TV.

"Can't sleep?" she said.

Matas gazed up at her, his eyes wide. She sat next to him, and they watched the news about the pipeline outage.

Lena was mesmerized. She couldn't take her eyes off the TV. As bits of news came in, the commentators tried to piece together what really happened. When she realized what time it was, Lena went into the bedroom. She came back fully dressed and carrying her shoulder bag. She stopped at the dining room table and put the laptop inside the bag.

"You're going to the office at this hour?" said Matas. "I'll give you a ride."

"No need," said Lena giving Matas a quick kiss. "I'll be there in ten minutes."

"I have to tell you something. It's about us."

"Later. I've got to go." She headed for the door.

He got up and grabbed her arm. "It can't wait."

Matas looked tormented.

"What is it?" said Lena.

For a moment, he didn't speak. Then his shoulders slumped and he stepped away from her. "Just be careful."

Lena looked at him quizzically. Then she glanced at her watch. "We can talk when I get home."

She gave him a quick peck on the cheek and left the apartment, feeling a sense of unease. Outside the building, she glanced up at her window. Matas was looking down at her. She blew him a kiss. He waved back.

No one was out on the street. As she hurried along, she pulled out her phone and punched in Vit's number. He answered, sounding groggy. She told him the news, and they agreed to meet at the office as soon as possible. She slid the phone into her pocket, and then looked over her shoulder. Pylimo Street was deserted, but it didn't feel like she was alone. She hurried toward the office.

~~

Vit arrived at the office fifteen minutes after Lena's call, as he lived only a short walk away. Dressed in jeans and a T-shirt, with the shadow of stubble on his face, he switched on the computer and brought up a display to a cable news channel. He felt his expression harden as he listened to a report on the pipeline situation. *This was damn serious.*

Lena came in from the kitchenette carrying two cups of coffee. She handed him one.

They huddled around his desk, alternately viewing information Annie displayed on the Ukrainian power grid cyberattack from several years ago, and the cable news. A reporter mentioned alleged Russian retaliation causing power grid problems in Crimea.

For a crazy moment, Vit considered making Annie more powerful and asking her to break into the control room to show them how it could be done. But with all the control room engineers inevitably watching for any unusual activity, Annie breaking in would fuel the flames and lead the investigation back to him. His changes to her capabilities would be discovered. It would be better if Annie could help the engineers figure it out for themselves. But how?

"A pipeline was attacked tonight," said Vit. "I'd like to rule out the possibility of a cyberattack, but we need more information. It would be great if we could see log files and talk with someone in Switzerland."

"How about the pipeline manager?" Lena picked up her mobile phone and punched in a number. She put the phone on speaker. Harold Weber answered, sounding out of breath. Lena identified herself.

"I barely have a minute," said Harold. "CNN International just arrived."

"In Germany?" said Lena.

"I'm in Switzerland."

"This is Vit Partenkas of Baltic Watch. Have you confirmed that it was a cyberattack?"

"Unfortunately, it appears so, but we haven't yet confirmed it."

"Can you get me access to the log files?" said Lena.

"We have our best engineers working on the problem. All I can say is that the attack was coordinated, multifaceted, smart, and extremely well-timed."

"Harold, can you release the files to us?" said Vit.

"Absolutely not. Not until this matter is thoroughly investigated. We can't risk a security leak."

"Was it the Russians?" said Lena.

"I have to go, Ms. Markus. Goodbye."

The line went silent. Lena and Vit looked at each other.

"What now?" she said.

Vit got up and stood by the window. "This is a long shot, but I have an idea. If we think about the control room at Zug—its computers, networks—everything you found in your research, we can work with Annie to come up with a plausible scenario of what might have happened. Then Harold will have to bring us in because he'll be too scared not to."

"Why would Harold care what we have to say? He thinks we're just a couple of reporters," said Lena.

"The name Baltic Watch still carries some weight. And if we show him how it could have been done . . ."

Lena shook her head. "The best cybersecurity people in the world are in Zug right now analyzing this. They have computer files, access to the physical systems, all of the specifications and manuals. I have nothing. Even if he agreed to talk to me, what do you think I could possibly contribute?"

"They're analyzing the data." Vit rubbed his chin. "Why don't you and Annie write a program that simulates or behaves just like the control room? You'd be able to run it and see how the simulation reacts to different scenarios. They could even experiment with it in Zug to figure out what the hackers might have done."

Lena slouched her shoulders, already looking defeated. "It would take weeks, possibly months, for me to research control room operations in detail before even thinking about writing a simulation."

"We have one thing they don't. Annie."

Lena didn't look convinced.

Vit needed Lena on board with his idea. Fast. There might be a way.

"This is the kind of crisis that would call for an analysis piece on Vera Koslova." Vit watched her, hoping his positive reaction to her previous work would give Lena the confidence she needed to think through the simulation idea.

"I can send you my analysis and links to the references I used if you want them."

"Thanks. Sorry for being so hard on you. I've been wracking my brain trying to figure out how to keep the company afloat, and I guess I took it out on you." As he spoke, Vit realized his apology was long overdue.

Lena smiled weakly. "Don't worry about it."

Vit continued. "While you're working with Annie, I'll do an analysis for our subscribers explaining what happened based on the news feeds, and mention the countries with enough motive and talent to do something like this. I'll ask you to read it once I have a draft."

"I considered Russia's enemies in my piece on Vera Koslova."

"I know."

"You read it?" Lena looked surprised.

"I may have told you not to do it, but I'm not going to ignore a good piece of analytical work."

Lena smiled. Then her expression turned serious. "When I was in Lubmin, Harold gave me a rough high-level diagram of the systems used in the control room. Many of the specifications for those systems are in the public domain—I checked when I was doing my report. If Annie creates a program that simulates the basic function of the control room, we can give it to Harold. He can add information like the precise network configuration including firewalls and other parameters. Putting it all together should identify weak spots."

Vit nodded. *She was on board.*

Lena continued. "Once the simulation is done, I can run it against hypothetical configurations just to show what it can do." She gave Vit a worried look. "It's going to take time, though."

"I can rev up Annie's engines."

Lena look at him quizzically. "What do you mean? How are you going to do that?"

"Don't ask. Just leave me alone with her for an hour," said Vit turning to his keyboard. "It'll only be temporary. And for God's sake, don't tell anyone."

CHAPTER 23

Vilnius, Lithuania—August 26

From a car parked directly across the street from Lena Markus's apartment, Bok watched her building. After receiving Orlov's phone call, he'd been able to get here in a few hours from Poland. That the head of the FSB had requested an SVR agent for a job meant that Vera Koslova was behind it. Bok didn't care for Lithuania, but he'd do anything for Vera.

Nothing moved along the street, though there wasn't much activity at this hour of the night. He was tired, but years of surveilling people from parked cars made it almost impossible for him to sleep while in any vehicle. So, like a big cat alert and waiting for his prey, Bok sat in a nondescript rental in the middle of Vilnius, waiting for Lena Markus to appear.

Bok liked to work alone, but after reaching Vilnius, he had contacted Stefan and Sofia. They had given him the particulars he needed: the addresses of Vit's apartment and Lena's, the address of Baltic Watch. Bok got Vit and Lena's normal work schedule, and a few more details.

Bok typically refrained from any kind of group communications, as he hated hearing voices in his head other than his own. All he had was his mobile phone, and he could contact Stefan and Sofia if needed, so he told them to stay back. He wanted to tell them to return to Russia, but Vera Koslova needed a job done. For her, the only important thing was the result, so he used all resources available, and hoped he could tolerate Stefan and Sofia for the duration of the job.

For weapons, Bok had a knife—a Benchmade folder with a three-inch blade in his pocket, and a Glock in his glove compartment. He used the Glock when he had to, but he enjoyed the intimacy of a knife. In a black canvas tote, he had a lock pick set, a Wi-Fi jammer, and other tools of his trade.

To his surprise, at three a.m. lights appeared from inside Lena's apartment. Soon after, the door to the building opened and Lena came out into the street, carrying a bag over her shoulder. She looked up at her apartment and blew a kiss to someone; the boyfriend. Then she hurried along. She went north on Pylimo Street and turned right. Knowing the area from many visits here, the possibility of following her by car was nearly impossible. Many of the streets were blocked to anything but pedestrian traffic.

As she was already out of sight, Bok got out of the car with his bag of tools and jogged after her. When he spotted her, he slowed down and practiced the craft he knew well. He observed without being observed, as any master in the art of foot surveillance would.

But Lena Markus didn't appear to be evading anyone. She was just going fast, and that in itself was a problem. A man dressed in black running after a woman in the middle of the night wasn't the picture Bok wanted to project, even to the few people out this late. Following at a distance, he determined she was likely headed for the Baltic Watch office. He cut through a park, intrigued with the possibility of having a chat with this attractive woman. He loved chatting with strange women. The building that housed the offices was sure to be vacant. Lena was sure to be alone. He'd have his chance. Bok couldn't wait to get to know her.

He got to Baltic Watch in time to see her go inside. A moment later, upstairs lights clicked on. As he came closer, a group of students appeared, obviously drunk. One bent at the waist and vomited onto a small patch of grass. The others laughed. They wove down the street and disappeared from sight.

Bok took a last look around and headed for the door, already reaching inside his pocket for the kit containing his tension wrench and pick. Before getting close, he did the first thing he always did: check for cameras. This building had them along the front entrance. Before Bok could check the back, a disheveled looking man appeared.

Bok had no choice but to retreat and blend into the dark side of a nearby structure.

When the man entered the building, Bok got a glimpse of his face. Vit Partenkas was one of the few who had survived a chat.

Bok's suspicions were confirmed when a light went on next to the first set that had been clicked on by Lena Markus. No doubt, they'd be busy investigating the pipeline outage for some time. But Bok didn't care what they were doing. He only cared about getting his job done, which included searching the apartments of the two Baltic Watch employees.

He called Stefan and Sofia, ordering one of them to keep an eye on the Baltic Watch office, and the other to continue watching Lena's apartment. Then, because it was so close, Bok went to Vit Partenkas's apartment. The U-shaped building was separated from the street by a wooden gate and a courtyard. Bok didn't see any security cameras, but took the precaution of putting on a cap and keeping his face down anyway.

Vit's apartment was a ground-floor unit with broad windows looking out into the courtyard. Bok looked for more cameras and saw none. But a computer expert like Partenkas was likely to have at least one installed somewhere for surveillance purposes.

Bok went around the side of the building to the cable juncture. Reasoning that a computer expert would connect any surveillance equipment to the internet for real-time viewing, Bok looked for the wire providing internet access to the building. If he cut or disconnected it, there'd be no internet. But the cable connection was near the roofline and out of reach. He found an unlocked window at ground level on the north side of the building, and let himself into a dark basement. Forced to risk a light, he used his flashlight to find the interior cable connection. Before disconnecting it, he activated his powerful wi-fi jammer, in case interruption in the cable connection triggered a text message to Vit's phone. Retracing his steps, Bok went to Vit's door, picked the lock, and let himself in.

There was no door alarm, but there was a camera. The wi-fi jammer should have blocked the camera's internet connection, but as a precaution, Bok took his time to cover it with a cloth from his bag. He did the best he could to keep his face blocked. Sometimes the mere shape of a jaw was enough for an expert to identify a person, but very few people knew what Bok looked like. Vit Partenkas had seen him, but the room they'd been in had been dark.

Bok took out his portable Geiger counter—another precaution that had saved him twice before. He didn't like to take chances. He checked the reading. There was nothing to worry about. He put the device back in his pocket.

Confident he was invisible to any surveillance, Bok began his search. He went quickly, although taking the time to put everything he touched back in its place, as there was no point in advertising he'd been there. He scoffed at a short stack of DVDs in the living room. *No one uses DVDs anymore.* Nonetheless, he put them in his pocket, along with some USB storage devices from the desk. There might be something useful on them. One never knew. To hide the fact that he'd taken the disks, he replaced the exact number he had taken with fresh ones from a nearby stack, still partially covered in plastic.

He continued to search, going methodically through each room. He found nothing more that was interesting, except for a watch, signet ring, and some cash in the bedroom. He considered taking the money, but decided against it.

Having finished, he retrieved the cloth covering the camera, and left the same way he'd come, stopping to get the wi-fi jammer. He kept his face down in case any nearby cameras had a partial view of the courtyard. He hurried along, because dawn was breaking and an early riser might come out. Nothing happened.

Returning to Pylimo Street, Bok double-checked the security cameras in the area. Several coffee shops had them, but the apartment building didn't. Such inconsistencies were his friend.

Then he contacted Sofia. She'd been watching Lena's apartment building. She confirmed that Matas Nortas was still inside. To deliver disks and USB sticks to her, he put them in a small paper bag and placed it beside the rear wheel of his car. As he sat behind the steering wheel, Sofia strode by in a pink T-shirt and jeans. She bent down to tie her shoelace. Bok didn't even bother to check that she'd taken the bag.

The sun came up and people came out into the street. His phone vibrated. He answered.

Sofia said, "There's nothing on those disks or on the sticks. Only old Baltic Watch reports and data files. You can find most of this crap on the internet," she said.

"Are you sure?"

"If I said so, I'm sure."

"Why are you angry with me?"

"Because last time you saw me, you almost killed me, even though it was just business."

"If I had really wanted to kill you, you'd be dead."

"Don't expect me to send you flowers, Bok."

Bok sneered, hoping the job would be over soon. "I'll watch the apartment for now, but when the boyfriend leaves, I'm going inside. Keep watch for the girl. If she comes back, call me. Tell Stefan." He hung up.

An hour later, Matas came out of the building. He paused at the outside door, looking down at his keychain. Curious. Bok was struck by the man's somber appearance. Matas looked up and down the street as if he suspected he was being watched. Bok snickered, knowing he would have been hard to spot by a professional, let alone somebody's boyfriend. Matas headed south.

Bok waited a few minutes in case Matas came back for something. Then with the canvas tote bag over his shoulder and the knife in his pocket, he crossed the street to Lena Markus's building. He buzzed every apartment until someone unlocked the door. Then he went inside.

He was looking forward to searching Lena's apartment, and helping himself to some food. Women often had good things to eat in the fridge. Bok would enjoy some time on her comfortable sofa as he waited for her to come home. Then they would get to know each other.

Bok went up the stairs to number 2C. He knocked, calling out "Maintenance." Even though he knew no one was inside, it paid to be cautious if only for the sake of a nosy neighbor.

CHAPTER 24

Vilnius, Lithuania—August 26

All day, Matas walked aimlessly through Old Town, smoking one cigarette after another. He was doing the right thing—taking care of himself. And he was saving Lena from even more heartache. Her last kiss before she ran out would be the last she'd ever give him. He hadn't the heart to pick a fight before she left. She was gone before he could even think of the words, let alone say them. Leaving her keys on the coffee table should give her a clear message. Even if she tried to find him, he knew how to hide.

He remembered her touch and her laugh, thinking how much he would miss her. With a pang of regret, he remembered how he had taken advantage of her. How he had lied to her. But he had no choice. The job was more important than his feelings, even more important than her feelings. Now she could probably ask him to do anything and he would. Not that it mattered, for they'd never see each other again.

He'd almost left her a note. It would have been an act of kindness to leave a written confession. He hadn't been to confession in decades. Better a written one than a spoken one, because he could choose his words carefully and say just enough. But what would he say? That he didn't want to ruin her life? That she deserved better? That he was a criminal, responsible for carrying out the most dangerous transgression against the Russians in fifty years? A hundred years?

The job was done, and he had succeeded. Money would have already been wired to his account. All he had to do was to forget he'd ever met Lena, and get out of Vilnius. That was the smart thing to do. He turned around and headed for the garage where he kept his car.

Soon, he was on the A2 motorway and headed for his beloved Utena. Usually he enjoyed the end of a job. It gave him a sense of pleasure to have nothing else to do, at least not right away. It just didn't feel like this job was over.

He got all the way to Utena before getting off the motorway and heading south toward Pabrade. He told himself he just wanted to thank Ramute for her help, knowing it wasn't that at all. He wanted Ramute to say he wasn't a lousy son-of-a-bitch for what he had done to Lena.

Ever since he'd helped Ramute's husband out of his depression after the occupation, they'd been like family. Matas had found Ramute's husband a job driving truck for a local farm supply company. He thought nothing of it, but Ramute said it had saved them. The job had given Ramute's husband purpose and pride from once again supporting his wife and son.

After the husband passed on, Matas asked Ramute to pretend to be his older sister to help gain the trust of a potential client. It had worked. Ever since then, Ramute and Antanas worked for Matas whenever he needed family members for a job.

But there was a risk to contacting anyone who'd been involved in a job so soon afterward. This one had been political and very dangerous. He shouldn't contact anyone, especially Ramute, for a year or even more.

It was dark when Matas arrived at the yellow house. He opened the rickety homemade gate, and knocked on the front door without even thinking about what he was doing.

Ramute answered. She looked behind him quickly before pulling him inside. She locked the door. She wore an apron and her hair was messy. "What's wrong?"

Matas gave her a kiss on the cheek before going into the sitting room and plopping into a chair like a man who has been a long time coming home. Ramute joined him a moment later, with her decanter of raspberry cordial and tiny glasses. She poured some out.

"*Į sveikatą*," said Ramute.

They clicked glasses and sipped.

"Where's Antanas?" said Matas.

"He went home to our house. I'm the only one staying here now. Thank you for the money."

"How long will you be here?"

"We rented the place for three months, just in case we needed it. The old couple who lived here didn't want to leave, but they needed the money."

"They won't talk?"

Ramute shook her head. "No. They're like us."

"Good."

Ramute looked worried. "There is a problem?"

"I know what I should do. I should go to Utena and buy that little place I found out in the woods. But Lena . . ."

"I see. What did you expect would happen, after spending time with such a beautiful young woman? You should have prepared yourself for this."

"I wish I'd never met her."

"Well, it's too late for that. What are you going to do now?"

"I told her you were her family. I lied to her about the one thing that was important to her."

"You had your reasons." Ramute refilled the glasses. "Are you going to see her again?"

"Knowing how hurt she'll be when she finds out what I did makes me sick." Matas stood and went to the shelf of keepsakes.

"How will she ever find out? Certainly not from me or Antanas."

Matas nodded. "The letter you showed her was ingenious. Lena completely believes you're her cousin."

"I do my research, but I've never seen you pine for a woman. When a job is done, you move on. Not today. She has touched you. You're thinking it may be the last time any woman affects you this way. Maybe you want Lena to be with you. If that's true, you have to go find her and tell her how you feel."

"What good would it do? She's the one person who could put everything together and land me in prison, or worse."

"If she loves you, she'll be silent, and we'll all be safe. If you're not sure, you have to let her go." Ramute went to him. "You helped my husband when Antanas was just a baby. You gave my son a father he could love. Do you know how important that was to me? What you did makes us family. I would do anything for my family."

"Everything Lena and I have together is based on lies. If she ever learns the truth, she'll hate me. A person doesn't forgive the things I've done. I've hurt her enough already."

"You never accepted that you helped some people, because you dwelled on the people you couldn't reach. If you want Lena to become part of our family, I will embrace her with my heart. Decide what's right for you, Matas. She doesn't have to know who I am if you don't want her to know."

"You'd be willing to carry out this lie for the rest of your life?"

"I would do it for you. Do you love her?"

"I suppose I do."

Ramute put an arm around him. "Then your path is clear."

~~

The evening ferry to Helsinki was full, but Arkady managed to get a seat in the upstairs lounge on a broad sofa next to a window. Nearby, parents sat watching two kids play on the floor. Arkady ignored them.

His phone beeped, indicating a text had come in. Volshebnik.

I see a tidy sum was wired to your offshore account recently, said the message.

Arkady responded. *I told you I was working. I got paid.*

Let's say you give it to me.

Why should I?

Didn't I do most of the work? And remember, my little friend, my silence is expensive.

Arkady felt faint. Volshebnik must have known about the pipeline from the start. *Volshebnik knows everything.*

If he didn't pay Volshebnik, the old man might talk. That might implicate them both, but Volshebnik was good enough to create breadcrumbs that would lead an investigation right to Arkady, and only to Arkady. But if he paid, Volshebnik might ask for more money later.

In truth, Arkady had no choice. He had to pay. He only hoped that would be the end of it.

He used his mobile phone to transfer the money. He had worked so hard and had endured so much. He was going to use the money to get a place for himself. He tried to tell himself he couldn't miss what he never really had.

Arkady had to get back to work. He had no choice. He had promised Rina and Simona to stay offline for a month, but he couldn't afford to any longer. He had to kill his identity—to kill Arkady. Then he could come back as someone else—with a new name. But it meant starting over.

It meant he couldn't go back home, because Volshebnik might find him there. He had to close his bank account and stop his credit cards, so Volshebnik couldn't trace his finances. It meant his friends wouldn't be able to reach him. His old business contacts would be useless. He had to take every precaution and be careful, because Volshebnik was a crafty bastard. The only good news was that Matas wouldn't be able to find him either.

Arkady wondered where he was going to live.

When the ferry docked in Helsinki, Arkady waited until almost everyone was off. As he stepped off the boat, he let his phone slip out of his hand into the water. He didn't even stop to watch it sink into the Baltic Sea.

CHAPTER 25

Vilnius, Lithuania—August 27

Lena was tired and hungry by the time she got up from behind Vit's desk. Vit was sitting in one of the guest chairs, nodding off. She stretched out the kink in her back from sitting so long. It was already dark outside. They'd been working for twenty-two hours straight. It was already one a.m. and she was both exhausted and exhilarated.

"Annie, let me know when the simulation has finished running," said Lena.

Skeptical that Annie would get substantial results, Lena wanted to get out of the room for a moment. Sure, Annie was capable and Vit had done something to improve her abilities. But creating a simulation with the complexity of the control room should take weeks, not a single day. She went into the kitchenette and opened the refrigerator. All she found was yogurt. She took out two containers, picked up spoons, and went back to Vit's office.

Lena touched his shoulder. "Have a bite to eat. You must be hungry."

Vit sat up and took the container of yogurt. "Thanks."

"Did you post your initial analysis of the pipeline outage on the Baltic Watch website?"

"I did. Thanks for helping me with it. You know, one day you could have your own byline. I'm glad you gave me your notes along with the report. They saved me a lot of time getting the analysis together. The thing is, there are so many groups who hate Vera Koslova, I only included the top contenders. Anyway, I made the analysis public so everyone can see it, not just our subscribers. Tomorrow, when you finish the work with Annie, you can help me do an update on the pipeline status. People will expect it."

Lena nodded, excited about the upcoming work, as there were political ramifications, probably extreme ones, if they proved that Russia had caused the outage.

Annie spoke. "The simulation finished running, Lena. I'm displaying the results."

Lena exhaled, relieved at the collection of graphs, histograms, and charts. As she examined the results further, she was amazed at the level of detail resulting from Annie's unbelievably quick work. Lena was glad to be proved wrong. Vit moved his chair behind the desk, joining her.

They had made assumptions about several things, including the network. The simulation allowed more access than likely, but it was a start. They could refine this, and the other assumptions, by merely entering new values into the simulation. Ideally, Harold Weber could tell her the exact parameters, and she could run the simulation to show the vulnerabilities that Annie had already predicted. One possible vulnerability was using default accounts for normal control room tasks. Some software used well-known accounts for install and set-up. The account name and password should be changed as a precaution, but sometimes people forgot. Lena needed to talk to Harold and get as many details as possible.

Half a dozen windows on the screen showed graphic depictions of the security weaknesses identified by running the simulation. Others displayed graphs of network speed, access time, and pipeline parameters that could be modified from the control room. Lena sat back in the chair and rubbed her eyes. "You're a genius, Annie. At least the basic program is finished. All we need now are the details. We can get some information from online specifications for the various products in the control room and make educated guesses. It's still a lot of work, though. But with that information, you can run the simulation again for better results."

"Anyone can run the simulation by copying it to their own computer, Lena."

"Great job," said Vit, glancing at his watch. "It's been a long day. Let's call it quits. Go home and get a few hours of sleep. Let's say we meet back here at eight a.m. and pick things up again. If all goes well, we'll phone Harold Weber sometime tomorrow."

~~

Vit walked to his apartment, pleased with Lena's ability to change gears from reporter to computer programmer without complaint. It showed she was a real soldier. He was going to miss her. Maybe if he sold his artwork, he could pull together enough money for her to stay a few more months. Detailed political analysis would be needed with this pipeline shutdown, and he knew she'd love to work on it. He couldn't believe Koslova had been so stupid as to order the pipeline attack, and maybe she hadn't. So far, his assumptions were heavy and his evidence light.

Cutting across the courtyard, he put his key in the lock and opened the door to his apartment. He flicked on the light, which automatically turned on the TV-like screen to his home computer hidden in the desk. Instead of displaying the usual four windows, one from the camera in each room, there was a dark screen displaying a pop-up message 'Service interrupted.'

In all his time here, he'd never seen this. The cable service in Vilnius was excellent. It rarely went down. Vit took out the wireless mouse from the desk drawer, and activated the video replay of his cameras. Nothing.

Concerned, he went to his desk and turned on what looked like another TV screen. He used a wireless mouse to run a video that had been automatically created and stored to disk just this evening from the well hidden camera in his bedroom. When he had moved in, he'd installed a wire from that camera directly to his computer. This allowed him some basic security while the cable company processed his request for service. He'd taken great care to snake the wires through the walls, making them completely invisible. Then when he had access to cable, Vit had kept the old system running, resisting the temptation to upgrade. He reasoned that a thief expecting a sophisticated surveillance system wouldn't look for this old-school, hard-wired approach.

The video showed a man in dark clothing and a cap searching the bedroom. Stunned, Vit watched the video again. The man didn't appear to be a thief, but there was something about him that was familiar. He thought of the Russian who had held him at gun point in the *sodyba*, but this couldn't be him. Still, the possibility drove Vit to the door where he engaged the deadbolt.

Vit watched the video again. The thief examined the signet ring and watch, and put them back on the bureau, then found the money clip in the drawer and hesitated, but put it back. Vit went into the bedroom and checked that his valuables were still there. They were.

Back in the living room, Vit scratched his head. Someone had broken in, probably disabled the internet, and searched the place—looking for what? As far as he could tell, nothing was out of place. His books were where they belonged in the floor to ceiling bookcase, but since he normally kept them in random piles on the shelves, it was hard to tell if anything was gone. The artwork on the walls was untouched. The folk art wood sculpture by Ricardas Vainas was still sitting on an end table—a thief surely would have taken it, for it was worth a good deal of money and easy to carry.

When he examined the contents of the bookshelves more carefully, he noticed that the stack of used DVDs on the middle shelf had been tampered with. He picked one up and saw it didn't have a label. He always labeled his DVDs. Some contained old surveillance video, and others had old reports and research data. There was nothing of interest to anyone but himself, in case he wanted to write a book one day about his time at Baltic Watch. Looking more closely, all the DVDs were unlabeled. Vit rubbed his chin. Someone had broken into his apartment and taken worthless DVDs, but had left the expensive artwork. It made no sense.

Upon closer examination, his USB sticks were missing, too. Why the hell would anyone want them? His company was a few weeks from closing. Now his apartment had been broken into and searched. The only items taken were computer storage devices.

Vit reached for his phone and called the one person he could rely on when things went haywire: Zuza Bartus. When she answered, his heart fluttered. He said someone had broken into his apartment. When she said she'd be right over, he thought how good it would be to see her again.

CHAPTER 26

Vilnius, Lithuania—August 27

As she walked home, Lena realized she hadn't talked to Matas all day. He'd wanted to tell her something this morning before she hurried out, but the day had been so busy, she simply forgot to phone him. She dialed his number to tell him she was on her way—no answer. She recalled the story of his old phone disintegrating in a vat of acid. It was an odd way to lose a phone, buy why would he lie to her about that? Why wasn't he answering his phone now?

The windows were dark. She wondered if Matas had gone to bed already, or if he'd stepped out for a while. She inserted her key into the outside door and went up the stairs.

When she'd arrived in Lithuania, she hoped to find someone who'd show her the sights and share a few laughs. Things with Matas had gone far beyond a few casual dates. The better she knew him, the more she liked him. Going into the priesthood even for a short time showed conviction and character. By finding her lost cousins Ramute and Antanas and taking her to meet them, Matas had shown extraordinary kindness. Then he couldn't bear the thought of her going to Germany for a few days, and had surprised her with a visit. They'd spent the night together.

She took a deep breath at the top of the stairs. Falling in love wasn't part of her plan. She was still annoyed that he was a master at keeping secrets, and liked to practice on her. They needed to talk, and they would, but hopefully not tonight. There'd be plenty of time once the pipeline crisis was over. She was tired and wanted to put the excitement of the day behind her. She could do with a hot bath and some food.

As she put the key into her lock and turned it, she pictured Matas in bed. She might forgo the bath and food, and just curl into his warmth.

She smiled, turned the key, and went into her apartment.

~~

Sitting on Lena's sofa in the dark living room, Bok smiled at the scratching noise coming from the door lock. *At last, she is home.* The anticipation from waiting all day had led him to this near orgasmic moment. He went behind the door, so there'd be no chance of her seeing him. He loved surprising people—especially women. He pulled out the Benchmade knife and extended the blade.

The room light clicked on. Bok blinked to adjust his eyes. Her back to him, Lena closed the door. Already, he could smell her scent. What a lovely creature. *And so young!*

He seized her around the neck and shoulders. His hand tightly pressed her mouth. She immediately began to struggle. He liked feisty women, but this wasn't the time to enjoy a tussle. He pressed harder and held the knife up in front of her face so she could see it.

"Be still," he said.

She stopped moving. Her back stiffened. Her warmth felt good against his chest. He whispered in her ear, "Don't scream."

He slipped a blindfold over her eyes and moved her toward a chair.

"Sit," he said. He tied her hands to the arm rests with nylon cable ties—portable, light, easy to use, and extremely strong—a testament to how advanced civilization had become. It only took a few seconds. He hadn't heard her voice yet, and yearned to. He gently ran the blade tip down her cheek.

"What do you want?" said Lena. Her voice was shaking. He loved that.

"I want you to tell me your secrets."

"There's money in my purse. Take it. You can have it all." She cocked her head as if listening for sounds from the hallway outside the apartment.

Bok chuckled. "No one's going to save you. We have all night to get to know one another. By the way, you shouldn't leave spare keys out. I found them on your coffee table." He rattled a keychain with two keys on it next to her ear, smiling as Lena's head jerked toward the sound.

Bok continued. "Were you leaving them for your boyfriend? Or did he forget to take them when he left this morning? I tried them. They work perfectly. I think I'll keep them."

He stroked a lock of her hair and she shrank away. He nuzzled his nose against her ear. "I want you to tell me what you know about the pipeline."

~~

Relieved that Zuza had gotten to his apartment quickly, Vit let her in. He couldn't help but hug her. Her hair smelled of lavender. Their time apart faded.

"It's good to see you," he said lowering his arms.

"Somebody broke in? How can you tell? The place is a mess as usual," said Zuza, stepping away from him.

Vit played the security video that showed a man searching his bedroom.

"You record what happens in your bedroom? All those times we were in there together you were taping it?" Zuza put her hands on her hips and glared at him. It looked like she was going to spit nails.

"It's just for security reasons."

"Have you watched them?" Her lips were a thin line.

"I don't keep anything." It was true, but he had watched before deleting them. Vit felt his face get hot. A corner of Zuza's lips hinted upward, but it was so brief, he might have imagined it.

Vit played the video a second time. "There's something about that guy that seems familiar. Remember when we were chasing Darius Artis? Annie identified the man who tried to drive me off the road near Visaginas. The same guy broke into our sodyba in Utena. Alexy Bok. It couldn't be him, could it?"

Vit felt Zuza's gaze. He tried not to look scared.

She spoke slowly, even thoughtfully. "His face is hidden so well and his clothes so dark that it's impossible to do a positive ID. But he'd be a fool to come back into the country."

Vit relaxed a little. He showed her the stack of unlabeled DVDs. She mumbled something about the geek using older technology.

"He left my jewelry, money, and art behind," said Vit. "But he took all my computer storage devices. Isn't that strange?"

"What have you been working on?"

Vit told her about the report Lena had written on energy in the Baltics, and the analysis on Vera Koslova he'd posted on the Baltic Watch blog just hours before.

Zuza reached for her phone and punched in a number. She spoke into it, giving Vit's address.

Vit assumed she was calling her office for assistance.

"The police will be here soon. This is a problem for them, not for me and ARAS." Zuza walked around the room. Then she went into the bedroom. In a few minutes, she came back. "Why do I think there's something you're not telling me?"

"Don't you think I learned my lesson with Darius Artis?" Vit wanted to add *before we broke up*, but thought against it.

"It looks like a simple break-in," said Zuza, "but it's strange they didn't take the money. There's always the possibility that this is connected to something at Baltic Watch. You have an intern working for you, right? You should call her and make sure she's all right."

"Her name's Lena Markus." Vit smiled. That Zuza knew he'd hired someone meant she'd been reading the public Baltic Watch social media site where he posted updates about the company. He wondered if Zuza's subscription to the ezine had lapsed. He rang Lena's number. No answer. His stomach sank. He rang it again. Same result.

"What do we do now?" said Vit.

"We wait for the police to arrive and file a report. In the meanwhile, keep trying to reach Lena."

"You're going to stay for a while, aren't you?"

Zuza nodded. "I think the team at ARAS might be able to do without me for a few hours. You know they still owe me for solving the Darius Artis case." She smiled as she punched more numbers into her mobile phone and turned toward the window, speaking softly.

Vit was entranced. She was as lovely and tough as he remembered.

When she hung up the phone, Zuza said, "I can always count on you to make things interesting. However, it would be nice to hear from you when you don't need something."

That hurt. Maybe he had been an ass for cutting her out of his life so surgically, trying to hurt her for having hurt him.

A knock at the door. Zuza opened it and two uniformed police officers—a man and a woman, entered the apartment.

Vit and Zuza talked with the officers, who jotted down information in small notebooks. As much as Vit wanted to believe this was a random break-in, he didn't. The pipeline outage had just occurred. The demonstrations Lena had covered had been about the pipeline. She'd asked dozens of people about A. Sims, the only name related to the demonstrations. Even her boyfriend Matas had come into the picture just after she'd started asking people about this mystery woman.

Vit regretted not asking Annie to do a background check on Matas. Given his age, Matas seemed a harmless companion, but Vit only knew what Lena had told him. She was very attractive and could have anyone she wanted. Why Matas? Why now?

He thought about the DVDs and USB sticks. Someone was after information, although Vit couldn't imagine what specifically it could be. The burglar had searched his apartment. If Zuza thought Lena's apartment might be searched, too, maybe the Baltic Watch office was next. Then Vit felt like he'd been gut punched. Maybe Annie was the target.

Vit scribbled down Lena's address and pressed into Zuza's hand. He bolted for the door. "Go see if Lena's all right. Please. Hurry!"

"That's where we're headed as soon as we're done here."

He raced out of the apartment, shouting, "Gotta go to the office!"

"What in hell for?" Zuza called after him.

Vit didn't bother to answer. He just ran. His phone rang; Zuza. He ignored it. *She's going to be pissed at me.* He was winded by the time he got to Baltic Watch. He looked up at the dark windows. The place seemed quiet and deserted. He let himself in with his key and turned on every light as he searched every room. Certain he was alone, he made sure the doors were locked and went back to his office. He turned the computer on. "Hi Annie."

"What can I do for you, Vit?"

Good question. He didn't know if he had minutes, hours, or days. All he knew was that someone might be after Annie. He'd left her vulnerable to any thief, because he was a very stupid man. Given an hour he could save her, undo all the fiddling he had done to make her more useful although far less secure. But he might not have an hour. Should he risk trying to save her? If she fell into the wrong hands, her enhanced capabilities could be disastrous. If anyone figured out how powerful Annie was, they could do incredible damage: break into private accounts, hack into the most secure government web sites, hack into banks. The list went on.

But time was ticking, and Annie was waiting for instructions.

"Do a full backup of all of Lena's data and your simulation program to my USB stick." He inserted the device into the computer. He glanced at the clock. That would take a few minutes.

As Annie worked, his mobile phone rang again. This time, he answered.

"When I call you, answer the damn phone! Why did you run off?" Zuza asked.

"I had to take care of something extremely important."

"Look genius, did it ever occur to you that your office is about to be ransacked and the guy might be there waiting for you?"

"No one's here. Just give me a few minutes. I'll come back. I have to do this. Go and check on Lena!"

"I'm already on the way. Meet me at her apartment. And be quick about it." Zuza hung up the phone.

Annie spoke. "The simulation and data were copied to your portable storage device, Vit."

He took the USB stick out of the computer and put it in his pocket. Then he reached out and touched the computer screen, thinking how odd it was, his need to caress a piece of plastic, but it was the only thing he could do. "It's been a great run, Annie."

"Thank you, Vit."

This is on me. Mrs. Brown warned me, but like a jackass, I ignored her. Now I have to pay the price. How am I going to live without Annie?

"Self-destruct, Annie."

"There's no recovery from that command, Vit."

"I know. Do it."

"Good bye, Vit."

He stared at the screen counting the seconds until Annie was gone. He felt as bad as when Zuza had left him.

Annie's last act would be to shut down the computer. She was always thorough. He waited. The screen went dark and she was gone.

~~

Lena's neck throbbed where Bok had pressed his hands. She tried to remember what she'd heard about defending herself against a rapist, how making it personal could work in the victim's favor. Make him see her as a person, not an object.

Oh God, what should I say? "My name's Lena."

Bok laughed.

"Who are you?" said Lena. *Think!*

"No darling, I don't have a name."

He spoke Lithuanian fluently, but with a Russian accent. She was sure of it. "Why do you want to hurt me?"

He ran a finger along the contour of her ear. She wanted to crawl out of her skin. She twisted her body against the restraints, scraping the chair against the floorboards. He quickly put a stop to that, putting his hands around her neck and squeezing.

She thought she would die! She couldn't breathe. When he released her, she sucked in air. Tears streamed out from under the blindfold and ran down her face. *Just survive, Lena. Just survive.*

"You really need to learn to cooperate." He stroked her cheek. "It will go so much better for you."

Her phone rang. Matas! If she didn't answer, he'd come to the apartment looking for her. *Please God.*

It stopped ringing. "There, that's better," said Bok.

It rang again. Hope leaped into her throat. Again.

"Your boyfriend is a persistent fellow, isn't he?" said the man.

Then a different phone buzzed. After a moment, he said, "How close?"

She couldn't hear the voice on the other end of his phone.

"Damn!" he said.

Seconds later, he quickly taped her mouth shut. He stroked her cheek. The darkness behind the blindfold grew darker after a click she assumed was the light switch. The front door closed quietly.

Lena felt a moment of intense relief. But was he really gone? Maybe it was a trick. *If only I could get this damned blindfold off.* But he had the keys and could come back at any time.

She'd better change the locks. But first she had to get loose. *Where are you, Matas?*

Then she remembered the keys Matas had left on the table. *Maybe he wasn't coming back.*

Eventually, Vit would miss her and come looking for her—have the landlord unlock the door for him. But not until sometime tomorrow. It might even be the next day. *What if the Russian came back before then?*

Lena strained against the plastic restraints until her arms ached. All she could do was wait and pray that someone would find her. She willed Matas to come back. If only she'd stayed with him that morning and listened to what he had to say. He'd said it was important, but she didn't have the time. She wanted to scream. She wanted to go home to Virginia. She wanted someone to save her!

She tried counting the seconds, and fell into a cloud of fear and desperation.

Then came muffled steps—someone walking down the hallway. She strained to hear. Was it the Russian coming back already? Her stomach tensed. She thought she was going to be sick.

A knock the door. "Lena!"

Her heart leaped into her throat. Matas's voice. Thank God! But she couldn't answer with tape covering her mouth. She made noises in her throat. *Stupid! No one can hear me.* If she didn't answer, he might go away, leaving her tied to the chair. *He didn't know about the Russian.*

She *must* get his attention. She pounded her feet on the floor. *Not loud enough!* She squirmed in the chair, scratching the chair legs against the floor.

Another knock at the door. *He can't hear me!* She coiled her leg muscles, and hurled herself toward the door. The chair rocked to the side. She swayed her shoulders. The chair tottered dangerously to one side, balancing precariously. Then it came crashing down. She felt a sharp pain on the side of her head and saw stars.

CHAPTER 27

Moscow—August 28

Before daybreak, Vera entered the breakfast room at her Moscow residence where she'd gone for a few hours of restless sleep the night before. She sat at her usual spot at the table covered in impeccable white linen. The maid squelched a yawn as she set down the usual plate of scrambled eggs and hearty Russian bread. Michael came into the room. He ate breakfast with her every morning they were together, no matter how early it was.

The usual stack of newspapers lay next to Vera's plate. She picked up the *New York Times*. She was fluent in English as well as German. As she read, she felt her face twist into a scowl. She ripped out the front page, rolled it into a ball, and threw it across the room. It hit the red velvet wallpaper and fell to the breakfast buffet, landing on top of a chafing dish filled with sausages.

"The buzzards are already circling the carcass," said Vera.

Her husband Michael glanced up and tilted his head, looking confused.

Usually, foreign press was the last thing Vera looked at in the morning. First, she read the press clippings prepared by her office staff and delivered to her wherever she was. Then she scanned the tabloids to learn what real Russians were thinking. After that, she looked at the Russian quality press—her favorite columnist was Sergei Kolesnikov. Only then did she look at the foreign press.

But today was different. She wanted to see what the international press was saying about her first, and it was bad. Very bad.

A maid picked up the wadded paper from the buffet table and carried it out of the room.

"The people love you, my little rabbit." Michael put a piece of soft sausage on a slice of bread, making an open-faced sandwich. He looked very relaxed in his burgundy silk robe. Even that irritated Vera this morning.

"You have absolutely nothing to worry about," he said.

She looked at him with disdain and picked up the next newspaper from the stack on the table. It happened to be *The Times* from London. Its headline: *Baltic Pipeline Disaster*. She skimmed the article and went to the editorial section, where absolutely nothing good was said about her, or Russia. One article discussed the emergency sessions of the EU that were being held in Germany later today.

She threw the paper on the floor. "Why don't they believe what our people are telling them? We have the best cybersecurity people in the world. If we say it was the Ukrainians, they should believe it was the Ukrainians, no matter what anyone else says. But no. They claim it has to be the Russians, because the Ukrainians are incapable of pulling off something like this."

"Did they really say that?" said Michael.

"They don't know what they're talking about. The Ukrainians are very skilled hackers. Some of our best work has been done by Ukrainians, and Belarusians for that matter. Those idiots in the West know nothing."

Die Welt was next on the pile, with an article advocating a prompt shift to a majority of non-Russian energy sources, including LNG from the US. "Where are the Germans going to get the money to pay for this non-Russian energy? We give them the best price possible. Where are they going to process the liquified gas? Where are they going to store it? Or are they going to build a damn pipeline under the Atlantic Ocean? It will take years for them to shift to other energy sources. Years! I'm bringing all the gas they could possibly need right to their doorstep. Idiots! Next thing you know, they'll be talking about building nuclear power plants."

She read some more. "They say the attack was multidimensional and extremely sophisticated. They have no idea what actually happened. And yet, they blame me."

Vera crumpled the paper. "Why would I order the outage? It does nothing but harm Russia. They're not thinking clearly, but they're quick to condemn."

Michael carefully placed the sandwich on his plate. "Western press just prints lies. If they ever saw the truth, they wouldn't print it, because they'd think it was a lie. I'm waiting for someone to say it was the CIA."

Vera stared at him blankly. "They already have. Yesterday, Baltic Watch posted an analysis of all countries and organizations capable of doing this who have a reason to hurt Russia. The CIA was on the list, but they said it wasn't likely, given the current political climate in the US. But the CIA blew up one of our pipelines in Siberia in 2004. Who's to say they didn't have something to do with this? I wouldn't be surprised if they helped the Ukrainians."

Michael looked at her with a sad expression on his face. She threw *Die Welt* to the floor and shoved the remaining newspapers off the table with her arm. They landed with a thud. Another maid ran over, picked them up, and clutched them to her chest as she left the room.

Vera picked up the remote control next to her plate of cold eggs and untouched bread. She pointed it at the Aivazovsky seascape hanging from the wall and clicked. The painting rose toward the ceiling revealing a large plasma TV, the picture already coming into focus. A reporter from one of the Russian news channels was explaining that terrorists had mounted a cyberattack on the pipeline. Early evidence indicated that Ukrainian pro-Western national democrats could be behind it. Normal operation would not resume until a full triage had been performed, and the security of the entire system checked.

"At least our Russian news is getting it right. The Western press is screaming at me, saying I ordered the outage in retaliation for the pipeline protests. Ridiculous. Russia is dependent on hydrocarbon revenues to balance our budget. That they even consider I would retaliate pains me. It makes no sense! I'm logical and disciplined, obviously intelligent. Do they think me so fragile that I can't take a little criticism? Why would I care about the demonstrators, or what they say? I have more important things to worry about than what some headline-hogging pro-West liberals say."

"You are right, my love. Who cares what the rest of the world thinks? Besides, Europe has enough gas for a while, through normal channels. Things will settle down soon enough."

"Don't be so sure. Europe has almost no storage capacity. They'll scream about us and try to figure out some way to control our hand. Sanctions will come next. That's what the EU will be discussing today in Germany no doubt, especially if the Americans are there. They shouldn't be, but they stick their nose into everything. I hate sanctions almost as much as I hate the Americans."

"This will pass. Be happy, Vera."

She sat with her arms crossed, almost feeling steam rise from her head. "Shut up."

Michael tilted his head, an expression of surprise on his face. "What did I say?"

Vera got up and left the room.

~~

Lena opened her eyes. Her throat hurt. Her head felt fuzzy. She realized she was in her apartment, lying on the sofa. Her thoughts flashed back to the Russian, his hands choking her, the blindfold, the desperation. She touched her thighs. She was still wearing the jeans. At least she hadn't been raped. Yet. Her hands were free. She remembered Matas at the door, calling to her. She remembered falling. Voices. The Russian may have come back. She jerked her head to the side, trying to see better. A stab of pain hit the back of her eyes. A man sat on the coffee table beside her.

"Matas!" Her relief lasted only a second—he might be in danger, too. "Where is he?" Lena whispered.

"He's gone. Relax. You're safe," said Matas.

Lena slowly sat up to a dull pounding in her head. "Why did you leave the keys behind? He took them."

"It won't matter. You can get a new lock when you have the door repaired."

Although the door was closed, the wood around the lock was badly splintered.

"How did you get into the building?" Lena massaged the side of her head.

"It took a few minutes, but someone let me in."

Vit came toward the couch. He looked concerned even though he was smiling. "Thank goodness you have a good hard Lithuanian head."

"The guy wanted to know about the pipeline," said Lena.

"Someone broke into my apartment. I came over to check on you. You weren't answering your phone," said Vit, his tone serious.

"I thought it was Matas." Lena rubbed the sore spot on the side of her head. "How long was I out?"

"Minutes," said Matas. "They got here soon after I did."

A woman came over. Vit introduced Zuza.

"We should get you to a hospital and have you checked out," said Zuza.

"No. We have too much work to do. I'll be fine," said Lena, hoping her words were true. She leaned back and the pain eased a bit. Matas sat next to her and put his arm around her shoulders.

"That's your choice," said Zuza, "but these officers will want to take your statement about what happened."

Two uniformed police officers, a man and a woman, introduced themselves and took notes as Lena told them her story and Matas held her hand.

It seemed a long time passed before the officers left. Sitting on the sofa next to Matas, Lena felt drained. His arm was draped around her shoulders. She wondered why a man as thoughtful and deliberate as Matas would leave his keys behind. She didn't think he ever forgot his keys. If he'd left them behind deliberately, then why did he come back?

Vit handed her a cup of tea. Lena took it and cradled it in her hands, enjoying the warmth. Zuza sat on the love seat across from them.

"We got so close to figuring this out, Vit," said Lena.

Vit stroked the nape of his neck. He looked awful.

"It's not your fault," said Lena.

"I got you into this. You were working for me, on a subject I told you to investigate. Next thing I know, some psycho busts into your apartment and asks you about the pipeline."

Lena shuddered. Matas drew her closer to him.

"Are you sure he was asking about the pipeline?" said Vit.

Lena nodded. "I got that message pretty clear."

"And you have no idea who that man was?" said Zuza.

"He was Russian," said Lena.

Zuza looked confused. "You said he spoke Lithuanian. How do you know he was Russian?"

"I know a Russian accent when I hear one."

Vit and Zuza exchanged a glance.

"What?" said Lena.

Vit bit his lip. "When we were chasing Darius Artis, Zuza and I had a brush with a Russian who spoke Lithuanian like a native. Not many Russians know the language."

"Lena," said Zuza, "even if you only got a brief glimpse, I'll need you to describe his face to a sketch artist."

Lena pressed her hand against her throat. This was harder to talk about than she'd expected. "He was behind me when I first came in, and then he put the blindfold on me. All I know is that he's strong. He kept whispering in my ear." She shivered. "I thought he was going to rape me."

"Any distinguishing marks or tattoos?" said Zuza.

"He was wearing a nice watch."

"Russians like watches," said Matas.

"Did you see what make it was?" said Zuza.

Lena shook her head. "Large and silver. That's all."

Zuza pointed her chin at Matas. "What do you do for a living?"

"Businessman," said Matas.

"Where's my computer? Did he take it?" Lena twisted around, looking for her shoulder bag.

"It's here," said Matas. "Your bag looks so worn that the Russian probably thought nothing valuable was inside."

"Thank goodness." Lena released a breath. "I have some files that Annie needs for the last bit of work on the simulation."

"About that," said Vit, running a hand through his hair. "I had to destroy her."

"What? Why? I can't finish the simulation work without her," said Lena. Her heart raced—she couldn't take much more bad news.

Vit slumped his shoulders. "I had no choice but to wipe her clean. Someone searched my apartment. I assumed it had to do with Baltic Watch. I couldn't risk Annie falling into the wrong hands. Now that I know you were held captive in your apartment at knife point, I'm glad I did it."

Vit sat down beside her. "I'm sorry I got you into this Lena, and I'll get you out somehow. But first, we need to figure out a plausible cyberattack scenario and give it to Harold Weber. You said the simulation was essentially done. You've got to finish it without Annie."

"I don't even have the program or the data we used. Nothing. I'll have to recreate everything and I'm not sure I can." Lena rubbed her temples.

Vit held up the USB stick. "It's all here."

"You expect me to take over where Annie left off?" After the night she had, Lena could barely remember her name, let alone work on one of the most complex programs of her career.

"You worked on computer security for years before coming here. You can do this, Lena," said Vit.

Lena shook her head. She felt like a fraud. Annie had done the work, not her.

"Why don't you start by telling us what you and Annie did?" said Zuza, watching them with an expression of complete focus.

Lena spoke haltingly at first, but felt more confident as she explained the basics of the simulation and its ability to take different parameters as input. She talked about Annie's initial assessment of the satellite and cable connections into the control room, and added her own observation. "Many companies provided hardware and software for the control room. While the pipeline was being built, I'm sure people got in remotely to check that everything was operating properly. They might still be able to get in remotely. If even one person short-circuited security, a hacker could find that vulnerability and exploit it."

When Lena finished, she felt better. Talking about the simulation had kept the Russian's voice at bay. She picked up her shoulder bag from the floor where it landed when the Russian had grabbed her. She took out the laptop, put it on the dining room table, and started it up. She took the USB stick from Vit and inserted it. All the results from the last simulation run came up on the screen. Relieved, Lena checked that the simulation program was there, too. It was. Maybe she could make some progress without Annie. At least she could try.

As Vit, Zuza, and Matas crowded around her, Lena explained what the results meant. Vit asked a few questions. It felt like he was guiding her along.

"We need to talk to Harold Weber," said Lena. "He can confirm our assumptions, and if necessary, change our input parameters. We need concrete data to make our results plausible. When we have the data, we can run the simulation again."

"And it will show us if there are any problems," said Vit.

Lena nodded. "Annie said there were. But Harold won't talk to us until we have results, and we won't have results until after we talk to Harold."

"What information do you need?" said Matas.

Lena patted Matas's hand. "It's all right, you don't have to worry about this. You've already done enough by coming back when you did. I might be dead if it weren't for you."

Zuza turned to Matas. "Are you saying you know something about the pipeline?"

Matas stared into space. "I read a lot."

"I'm going to get to work," said Lena.

Matas pulled out the chair next to her and leaned toward her. "Aren't you tired?"

"Sure, but I've got to do this." She glanced at Vit and Zuza. "Vit, would you get me some more tea?"

Vit shrugged. He and Zuza went into the kitchen.

"I know some things. Tell me what you need," said Matas.

Lena stared at him. All the pieces fit together somehow—the pipeline, the hack, the Russian, the break-in, Matas. She, too, was a piece in the puzzle. "If you were behind this, they could put you in jail." She glanced nervously toward the kitchen.

"In telling you anything at all, I put my life in your hands."

"This isn't a game, Matas. Were you involved?"

He put his hand on hers. "I know what's at stake. Let me do this and prove to you I'm not a bad man."

~~

Vit smiled when Zuza patted the cushion on the loveseat and motioned him to sit down next to her. Their shoulders touching, he was grateful for the closeness. They had a perfect view of Matas and Lena hunched over the computer on the dining room table.

"Do you think the Russian who attacked Lena could be Alexy Bok?" said Vit.

"I already alerted ARAS that he might be in the country. I know Bok brings back bad memories—for me, too. When he jumped out of the window at the sodyba, I shot at him. I could have sworn I hit him. Then he came out of nowhere and almost ran me over with his car. If Bok is in the country, they'll pick him up."

"They didn't get him last time, did they?" Vit didn't think of himself as squeamish in any way, but Bok was his nightmare.

Zuza pointed her chin at Matas. "Who's that guy?"

"I told you. Lena's boyfriend."

"Is he a computer expert?"

Vit shook his head. "Not that I know."

"They seem to be pretty tight. He's talking and she's typing. Does he have anything to do with this? How else could he be helping her?"

"All I know is that they met at a coffee shop."

Zuza frowned. "There's got to be something else."

"Lena found out that the pipeline protests were arranged by someone using a false identity. She did a research project on energy in the Baltics. We posted it just before the outage. Then I posted an analysis of the organizations capable of orchestrating such a disaster. My apartment was searched, and Lena was held at knifepoint by a Russian. Maybe the same guy. That's it."

"Does Matas know what Lena was working on?"

Vit crossed his arms. "It wasn't a secret. He lives here. Maybe he heard something. I can't believe he knows anything significant or something that Lena doesn't already know."

"When you call me, I don't know whether to be glad, or leave town."

Vit winced. "If the simulation shows there are security problems, the people in Zug can fix them, and we can turn our attention to who's really behind this."

"People are already saying it was the Russians."

Vit rubbed his eyes. "Stop equating the Russian people with the Russian government. I have wonderful Russian friends. They're smart, creative, and intelligent. They're not responsible for any of this."

"You know what I mean."

His first time alone with Zuza in ages, and they were already bickering. Why hadn't he called her months ago and asked her to meet him for a drink? They could have talked. Maybe her feelings had changed. He could have asked whether she still felt she couldn't do her job and have a husband. Or whether something else going on. It felt like it was too late to ask any of those questions now.

CHAPTER 28

Vilnius, Lithuania—August 28

Matas watched Lena sitting at her table, staring at the laptop, looking a bit dazed. No doubt the events of the last twenty-six hours and lots of tea had affected her. As Matas fed her details about the computer and communications systems in the control room, Lena entered the information. Once he had decided to help her, he'd held nothing back.

"That's it. That's all I know," said Matas, glancing over his shoulder to Vit and Zuza sitting on the love seat behind them and across the room. Zuza was watching them. Vit was sound asleep, his head resting on Zuza's shoulder.

"That might do it," said Lena. "All we have to do is wait for the simulation to run."

She gazed at him, looking exhausted, hurt, angry; nothing like a woman in love. Maybe he'd misjudged her and she wasn't in love with him at all.

"Without Annie," whispered Lena, "I didn't believe I'd get anywhere, but this might be enough. You really were involved in this, weren't you?"

"There's a lot you don't know about me, but please don't say anything."

"More secrets? Every time you tell me something, it only leads to more secrets. All I care about is finishing this simulation, going home, and getting on with my life."

Matas closed his eyes and took a deep breath. He should have expected this. She was too smart, and had become too skeptical to believe anything he said. All she wanted to do was go home to America. There was nothing else he could do or say. She was lost to him. And he was just lost.

Lena went over to Vit and shook his shoulder. He awoke instantly.

"The simulation's done. Let's look at the results," she said.

Matas gave Vit his chair at the table and stood behind him. Zuza stood behind Lena. Lena pointed to the graphs, explaining each one, constantly making observations. She said the results were as Annie had predicted, showing exactly how an attack could have been carried out.

Vit looked at Matas. "This is great, but where did you get all the information for Lena to put into the simulation?"

Lena spoke up before Matas had the chance. "It was all Annie. I didn't realize that she had collected a great deal of information while she was running the simulation. Matas was helping me go through it."

Vit pulled out his phone and punched in a number. "Great job, you two. Really great job."

Matas let out a slow breath.

Vit put the phone on speaker. Harold Weber identified himself.

"We know how it could have happened," said Vit.

"Mr. Partenkas. I told you before that we're very busy. We don't have time for your amateur analysis. It will take us days to get through the log files alone."

"We created a simulation. We can tell you how it could have happened. You can use this as a starting point to find out what actually did happen."

"Our best cyberanalysts don't know exactly what happened yet. If you're looking for publicity or unauthorized information, you won't get it from me."

"Harold, you need to listen."

"Mr. Partenkas, you need to stop. Please don't bother me again. I'll contact you when we have some answers." Harold ended the call.

Vit looked dazed as he put his mobile phone down. "I don't want to give up. But what in hell can we do?"

"We can release the results we have anyway. We don't need Harold," said Lena.

"Wrong," said Zuza. "If you release your results, other pipelines could get hacked in the same way. It's too risky to make anything public at this stage. Cyberterrorists will gobble this up. I can get in touch with my boss and see if there's anything we can do in ARAS to help you, but the pipeline isn't our jurisdiction."

"So, it's all been for nothing," said Lena, gazing at Matas. "All this work, the break-in at Vit's apartment, destroying Annie, the assault on me—we'll probably never find the guy. All for nothing."

Matas felt like she had doused him with cold water.

Lena glanced at Vit, who had gotten up and was pacing the room.

"I'm going to lie down for a while. I'm really tired," she said.

~~

Matas knew that if he was going to fight for Lena, this was the time. The stakes were higher than he'd ever imagined—his life, his country, his very sanity. And above all, the woman he loved. He might not get another chance. He followed Lena into the bedroom. She lay down and pulled up the quilt, tucking it under her chin. Matas kicked off his shoes and lay down next to her, his back against the headboard. "I steal cars for a living. Well, I don't actually steal them. I find them so that other people can steal them. And it's not just cars. It's all sorts of high-end electronics."

She turned away from him. "I don't care, and I don't believe you."

He put his hands under his head and looked up at the ceiling. He told her about Peter from Boston, Matas's team, the job and its objective—reminding the world of what Russia is capable of doing. How good it was to finally do something meaningful. Lena was so still, he wasn't sure she was listening.

"It sounds foolish when I say this was a warning to pay attention to Russia and what she might do one day," said Matas. "I don't know if the world cares. God doesn't. We're born alone, and we die alone. All the rest is just surviving."

Lena finally turned toward him. "Do you really believe that?"

Matas took a deep breath. There was no reason to stop now. "I arranged our meeting in the coffee shop. I'd been watching you. I knew where you lived, where you worked, and your routine, before I met you."

"You were watching me?"

"Ever since you got to Lithuania. I knew your work would involve the pipeline, and I needed to know specifics. I had to keep you away from my team. The best way was to get to know you and gain your confidence."

"You used me."

Matas's heart raced. He wanted to stop talking, but couldn't. "Ramute isn't your cousin. She's a friend who I helped a long time ago. Sometimes she and Antanas work for me. They put on a show to convince you to trust me."

Lena sat up and turned to face him. Matas braced himself for the onslaught. She leaned over and slapped him hard on the face. The sting went right to his heart.

"You bastard!" she said. "All of that was a lie? Ramute isn't even related to me? Where's my real family and what happened to them? Do you even know? Did you even care enough to find out?"

"All I know is that Gerde was released from the camps in 1956. She came back to Lithuania, and never left. The only relatives we found were in America."

"But we sent packages and got letters in return, at least for a while. Why didn't she contact us?"

"Like Ramute said, people were afraid to have too much contact with America. Gerde might have been terrified that they'd deport her again. After the occupation ended, maybe she thought you were angry because she hadn't written in so long."

"I hope you were paid well, because you certainly fooled me."

"That's why I came back to find you. Ramute told me to listen to my heart. She said you don't have to share blood to be family."

In the quiet and dark room, Matas couldn't see Lena's expression. "You may hate me for what I did, but it was all for the right reasons."

"Were you paid?"

"Generously."

"Well, I think that was your reason for doing all this."

That made Matas angry. "I risked everything. My team risked everything. Don't you get it? Don't you see how important this was? We reminded the world of Russia's past so that might consider what Russia has in mind for the future. But what do you know? You Americans don't care about anything besides yourselves. And you call yourself a Lithuanian."

He waited for Lena to react, but she didn't, so he continued. "My fate is in your hands now. If you want to tell that ARAS agent who I am, I won't stop you."

"How do I know if any of this is the truth? You played me for a real sucker, and I guess I am one. For all I know, you just told me another raft of lies to hide something else. I don't trust you, Matas. I don't think I ever will."

Matas glanced at the door. "Are you going to tell the Lithuanian police about me?"

"I'll let you know." She turned her back to him.

He sat on the side of the bed, feeling overwhelmed. He wished he had never met Peter, had never taken the job, and had stayed clear of this entire mess. He wasn't a hero—he was a failure. He never thought he'd fall in love, but he'd found Lena and God had snatched her away. He should have known it would end this way.

He picked up his shoes and went to the door. He glanced back at her lying on the bed, and then left the room.

~~

When Lena awoke, she felt like hell. She was alone. Her head was sore, and her neck stiff. She remembered the Russian and breathed in sharply. She heard voices in the next room. It must be Vit and Zuza. And Matas. Then she remembered what Matas had told her last night and felt even worse.

She went to the bathroom and washed her face. Running her fingers through her hair, she looked at herself in the mirror. The bruises on her neck looked like splotches of purple watercolor. Her eyes were red-rimmed. She looked like she hadn't slept in a week. But she didn't care. She'd made the mistake of falling in love with a con man and a criminal. At least it was over. Lena took a deep breath and went out into the living room.

Zuza and Vit were watching TV—another news broadcast. Matas wasn't there.

A female CNN reporter was speaking from outside the Kremlin, its onion-shaped towers clearly visible in the background. "While an international team of cyberexperts continues to analyze yesterday's outage of the new Baltic pipeline, there's been a public outcry among European Union members against Russia. Some blame the president of the Russian Federation, Vera Koslova, for ordering the shutdown, in retaliation for anti-Russian protests in Greifswald, Germany last month. The Kremlin has denied this and issued a report condemning Ukraine for the attack."

Another face came on screen, an older man with thick glasses speaking from an office with a view of the London Eye Ferris Wheel. The caption listing his name mentioned he was from the University of London. "Having analyzed Russian politics for decades, I can say that the possibility remains that Russia eventually plans to hold Europe hostage for their shipments of gas. What happened this week may be a dress rehearsal for something far more dire in the future."

Another face came on the screen, this time a younger woman economist. "It makes no sense that Russia would sabotage their own pipeline. They need the hydrocarbon sales to Europe to pay off debt. Without this money, their economic future is tenuous at best."

Zuza turned the sound down.

"Did you get any sleep at all?" said Lena.

"Sleep's overrated," said Zuza.

"Where's Matas?" Lena tried to sound casual. It had been cruel to make Matas think she might repeat last night's conversation to Zuza. But he deserved it for deceiving her. Maybe he was hiding, thinking he was going to be arrested. Whatever he was doing, it was over.

Vit shrugged. "He left a few hours ago. Said he had something to do. He didn't say when he'll be back."

Matas isn't coming back. Still, the thought of never seeing him again made her shake.

"I know how to reach him," said Zuza, handing her a slip of paper with a phone number on it. "He gave it to me before he left."

Lena handed it back. "There's nothing more for us to do, is there Vit?"

"We need to find out who did this," said Vit.

"The authorities will do that, with the help of Harold's people," said Lena.

Zuza spoke. "I want you to help us catch that guy who broke into your apartment and held you at knifepoint."

"I don't care about him. I just want to go home," said Lena. "Back to Virginia. I don't want to be in Lithuania anymore."

"Sure, if that's what you want," said Vit. "I was hoping you'd stay for a few more weeks. There's plenty to write about these days, and traffic to our website is way up."

"I'm going to pack." Lena glanced at her laptop, still on the table. "You can keep my laptop for a few weeks if you'd like, then ship it back to me. I don't care if you clone it. There might be some files and data you need. I'll let you know where you can send it." Lena hugged Vit. "Thanks for everything."

"This seems very sudden, Lena. I wish you'd stay for a few more days. Or at least think about it when you're rested and your head is clear."

"My head's just fine." *Crystal clear now that Matas has told me the truth.*

"Just keep your phone with you. Okay? I thought of a way to get Harold Weber's attention. This isn't over."

~~

Seated in his car in an alleyway off Pylimo Street, Bok was more than a little annoyed. He had gotten out of the apartment building fast, and had escaped to his car. That damn Lena Markus had been lucky. He, unfortunately, had been unlucky. Sofia's phone call had warned him that the boyfriend was coming back. Bok had considered staying and dealing with the boyfriend once and for all. But it was unplanned and risky. Bok hated to take chances. He could always come back for Lena Markus. This country was no good for him, but he was stuck here. It could be worse. He could be dead.

A police officer, a policewoman, and another woman arrived shortly after Bok had moved his car. Bok could still see the apartment building, and the alleyway provided better cover than a spot on the street.

An hour or so later, the woman came out with the officer. They stood together talking. She showed him her phone. Bok's recollection of the sodyba or guesthouse outside Utena where he'd seen that woman came back. He'd been trying to get Vit Partenkas to answer some questions when she'd interrupted them. She had a gun. He had to jump out the window to escape, badly twisting his ankle. Then she chased and shot at him. He attacked her with his car, but that hadn't gone well, either.

He sank down in his seat. If he recognized her, it was possible she could recognize *him*. Bok put on sunglasses and another cap from the glove compartment. Even if she caught a quick glimpse, it might be enough.

Never in a million years had he believed he'd see her again, although he'd dreamed of teaching her a lesson. He imagined cutting her face until blood trickled down her cheek like tears. Then he'd kill her and put her where no one could find her. He was an expert when it came to making bodies disappear. But he was a practical man, and was only being paid to take care of Lena Markus. He enjoyed his dreams, though.

Being here was dangerous now that police were involved. Stefan and Sofia were nowhere in sight. They should be watching the building instead of him. He took out his mobile phone and dialed Sofia's number.

She answered. "What?"

"Where the hell are you? I need you."

"I saved your ass last night. What more do you want? Besides, we've been sent home." Sofia hung up.

Something was going on, although he didn't know what. His phone buzzed. He answered; Orlov.

"We're pulling you," said Orlov. "Get the hell out of there."

"Does Vera Koslova know about this?"

"Of course she knows." Orlov had answered too quickly, and Bok didn't believe a word of it.

Bok spoke. "We in the SVR aren't accustomed to taking orders from the FSB."

"I want you home by tomorrow." Orlov hung up.

With all three of them being sent back before the job was done, something had changed. But what? What was Orlov hiding? Bok knew Orlov had been sleeping with Vera Koslova for some time, something he'd learned from his connections. Nothing had been said outright—no one would dare. A hint and gesture were enough to imply that their liaisons had been of a romantic nature. While Nina usually spoke to Bok, he knew Vera, and knew that she ran things when it mattered. That he was here meant the work mattered.

Bok considered that Orlov might just be asserting his power, showing that he was still in control. It made Orlov an irritant who inserted himself into situations that didn't really involve him, but Bok didn't know for certain. He'd contact Nina Ditlova when he got back to Russia. If anything had gone wrong causing Orlov to act independently, Bok wasn't going to bear any blame. He'd go to Moscow as ordered, and find out why he'd been taken off the case.

He glanced at his watch, and then at the woman and the police officer still standing outside Lena's building. Both were gazing in his direction. Bok waited until a car was about to pass the alleyway. He started the engine and pulled out, turning onto the first side street. There was a morning Aeroflot flight from Vilnius to Moscow, but he didn't dare take it. He'd drive to Belarus and fly home from Minsk. It was safer. He could probably be in Nina Ditlova's office sometime tonight.

In the meanwhile, it would be good to get out of Lithuania for even a little while.

CHAPTER 29

Vilnius, Lithuania—August 29

Still reeling from Matas's news last night that Ramute and Antanas were not her cousins, Lena tossed her clothes into the suitcases. She'd expected to go back to the US refreshed, but she was exhausted, sad, defeated. She felt like hell. At least she was going home. Soon, Matas would just be a bad memory. She sat on the last suitcase to close it, and then dragged it into the living room, placing it by the front door. She went back for the other two pieces, and once more for her shoulder bag.

Standing by the window, Zuza watched.

"I'll be done soon," said Lena as she went through the room, picking up items scattered here and there and putting them into the bag. "I was just subletting, so most of this stuff isn't mine."

Zuza smiled.

"Where's Vit?" said Lena.

"He went to his apartment to change."

"Is he safe going there alone?"

"An officer is escorting him."

Lena put down the bag and sat at the table in front of her computer. "I need to make a plane reservation. I know there's a SAS flight every evening to DC. I'll have to see if there's a seat on tonight's plane."

"And what about Matas?"

Lena bit her lip. He was the last person she wanted to talk about right now. It was over. There was nothing to say, nothing to do.

She started when her phone rang. She couldn't see the number—it was blocked. Thinking it might be Matas, she was about to ignore it. Then something told her this might be important. She answered.

A woman from the US Department of Homeland Security, a Mrs. Brown, introduced herself. "I know Vit. My team at DHS bought his Annie program. I don't know if Vit told you about Annie, but she's quite something."

"I'm familiar with Annie," said Lena. "In fact, she's helped me with several important projects."

"Really? We'll have to talk about that sometime. Vit called me today with information about a simulation you worked up testing the security of the control room for the Baltic pipeline."

Lena was stunned.

Mrs. Brown continued. "In anticipation of this conversation, we checked up on you. Hope you don't mind."

"Of course not, but why . . ."

"Vit said I can trust you. He was right. You have a flawless record."

"Thanks?"

"This whole thing's a political powder keg. You never know what the Russians are up to. My people are already headed to Zug to help out where they can. It's not our rodeo, but I think it's good for everyone if we get a handle on this right away. We're only sending our best people. I'd like you to meet my team there tomorrow. I'll be along in a few days. Do you think you can manage it?"

"I'm not sure . . ."

"Why don't you talk it over with Vit and let me know. I could really use your help."

After Mrs. Brown hung up, Lena was simply too astonished to speak. When she collected her wits, she said, "Zuza, I need to talk to Vit right away."

~~

The Wilson Blade 104 tennis racket felt like an extension of her arm as Vera prepared to receive Rozoff's serve. The new grip tape felt secure, and the racket was perfectly balanced. The warm sun felt good on her legs—playing tennis was the only time she wore shorts.

She'd broken Rozoff's serve seven times in the match so far, and needed just one more point to win. Normally, a match took hours, but not so when playing with Yuri Rozoff. *It was like taking candy from a baby.* He tossed the ball into the air, looking ridiculous in his Lacoste polo shirt—the hem flipping up to reveal his navel and the flesh around it. Vera considered letting the poor bastard win the point if he could get the ball over the net in one try. He managed to hit it well, which was a shock. He'd gone to second serve eleven times. *But who's counting?* As the ball came toward her, she moved into position and straightened, while pulling the racket head back with her left hand. At the perfect moment, she let her backhand unwind, spinning the ball over the net toward the right side of the baseline. It dropped like a rock just within bounds.

From his mid-baseline stance, Rozoff gawked.

"One more match?" called Vera, knowing Rozoff would decline the invitation. She wanted to get back to the Kremlin, but she had to keep up the appearance that she could afford to take the time for another game; that everything was under control. Rozoff shook his head.

They retired to white, wrought-iron chairs on the patio. The servant, dressed in a white shirt and white trousers, brought over glasses of kvas from the refrigerator bar setup on the edge of the courtyard. Rozoff drank his straight down. The servant poured him another, and then went into the residence.

"What do you make of all this pipeline business?" said Vera. The tennis match had been her first distraction since the crisis began. For a moment, she'd actually forgotten about the turmoil. She took a deep breath. Her gaze fixed upon Yuri like hot glue.

Rozoff wiped his forehead with the towel he had slung around his neck. *Probably a mix of sweat and nerves.* He seemed to be thinking about his response.

"The problem," Rozoff said, "is that the world isn't interested in evidence. They've already made up their minds that Russia is guilty. If and when the truth is discovered, it will fall on deaf ears."

"So, there's nothing to be done?" Vera had expected some helpful advice, not that she would follow it. He was merely saying the obvious.

"I think that if you find the truth, you're better off keeping it to yourself," said Rozoff. "Outside Russia, people will see it as a weak attempt to lay blame," said Rozoff.

"And inside Russia?"

"Our people think it was the Ukrainians."

"And you? What do you and your business associates think?"

Rozoff appeared decidedly uncomfortable. Maybe it was the heat, the physical exertion, or perhaps it was the question. "Once the money starts coming in, all will be forgiven."

"Are you saying they blame me for this fiasco?"

"Absolutely not. They blame the guilty party, whomever that may be."

"And what if Europe decides to substantially reduce their purchases of gas?"

"They need our fuel. In a worst case, they'll look for other sources of gas, but it will take time. The money will keep coming in. It's just a question of when revenues will drop off and how badly."

The servant came back, rolling a tea cart laden with plates and platters of food. He ladled out bowls of *okroshka*, a cold cream-based soup made from potatoes, cucumbers, and eggs. It was one of Vera's summertime favorites. But today, she had no appetite for it.

Vera sipped her kvas as Rozoff ate. She gave him credit for telling the truth, albeit in a way that could easily be misconstrued. That his business associates would forgive the culprit when the money came in meant they were probably as angry as she was. But right now, they were angry at *her*.

Rozoff had already revealed his true intentions by not phoning her the day of the outage. A mistake, perhaps? Or was he busy celebrating her failure? Katharina Becker had called, expressing her condolences in a way that actually brought a tear to Vera's eyes. Joe Day from Britain-Energy had phoned, too. While his tone was reserved and even off-putting, he said that the most capable engineers in Great Britain were at her disposal, to help her get to the bottom of this. Even Grinsky had phoned, offering his assistance in a conversation that she had found preposterous. Grinsky never helped anyone with anything.

Rozoff's failure had been a tiny one, so small that most people would have ignored it. Except for the fact that he had phoned Grinsky the night of the outage. The person in charge of recording it, one of Orlov's people, had failed to do his job. Oddly, the operator shared a surname with a man who had done some work for Fedov years ago, but it was a common name. Vera didn't think anything of it—Orlov would have checked the man's loyalties before hiring him, but loyalties changed. The operator would be spending the next several years in Siberia, honing his surveillance craft. But the call itself had been noted, along with its duration: four minutes and forty-six seconds. Just long enough to say Vera's head was on the chopping block and to have a good laugh about it. In Russia, men have been killed for less.

Despite this, she had to keep up appearances, which meant a tennis match and lunch with an old acquaintance was in order. Otherwise, all her energy and effort went to obsessing over how she could possibly recover from this political disaster that remained fresh in everyone's minds. It looked like her enemies had won.

She didn't want to believe it, but in truth, she'd half expected something dastardly from Rozoff ever since the oligarch meeting last winter. His people could have caused the outage or hired experts to do it for them. Grinsky could have been behind it, too. Still, doing harm to Russia's future financial interests didn't seem a likely course of action for them. In any case, whether or not they were involved, she was sure they were preparing to seize the government from her. She hoped she was wrong. Unfortunately, in such matters she was never wrong.

~~

Vit knocked on the door of Lena's apartment. Zuza let him in. His instinct was to hug her again, but he refrained.

Lena rushed over to him, looking excited. "Mrs. Brown from DHS called."

They discussed the phone conversation with Mrs. Brown. Vit had called the woman himself earlier. He convinced Mrs. Brown of the merits of the simulation and the value Lena could provide. It was relatively easy for him to convince Lena to accept Mrs. Brown's invitation to Zug.

"I need to change and pack an overnight case." Lena went to the front door and dragged her suitcases into the bedroom, closing the door behind her.

Zuza read something on her phone and said, "Did you know Matas was a priest?"

"Hell no."

"He's never had a job, from what we can tell." Zuza moved her index finger over the phone's screen. "He's been linked to a number of Ukrainian businessmen, some running legitimate enterprises, and some not. The questions are, who is this guy? How does he make his living, and was he involved with the pipeline outage?"

Vit felt a chill on his spine. He knew what was coming. Zuza had been angry with him before, and it had always taken a toll.

"You never had Annie check him out, did you?" said Zuza.

Vit shook his head.

"Lena works for you. She's young and probably a little naive. It's your responsibility to keep her safe, yet you did nothing. Did it ever occur to you that Matas might be involved in the pipeline failure?"

"If he's involved, then why didn't you arrest him?"

"I may. A team is following him right now. He said he was going to the apartment where he's staying for a shower and a change of clothes."

"If he's guilty of something, why did he come back looking for Lena? He saved her life. If he were involved in something illegal, he would have run. He wouldn't have bothered to look back."

"That doesn't absolve him. He might be in love with her. People do stupid things when they're in love."

"I know." Vit searched Zuza's eyes for a softness, a hint of the love they'd shared.

Zuza glared at him. "If anything happens to Lena, I will hold you personally responsible. By the way, you're flying to Zurich with her this afternoon."

"I am? Why?"

"Two reasons: to keep her safe, and because I told you to. We'll stop at your apartment on the way to the airport so you can pack an overnight bag."

"And what will you be doing while we're gone?"

"My job. By the way, you'd better tell Lena what we know about her boyfriend. It'll be easier if it comes from you."

CHAPTER 30

Zug, Switzerland—September 1

Three days later, Lena glanced up from her newspaper and checked her watch: ten minutes past the hour. Vit sat next to her on a brown leather sofa in front of a round coffee table. They were in the Starbucks on Baarerstrasse, a few blocks from the Baltic Pipeline AG headquarters in the city of Zug. With its roots in medieval times, the old fishing village was now host to many corporate headquarters in shiny new structures.

They were waiting for Harold Weber, who had broken their appointment yesterday, the day before, and the day before that, claiming he was too busy to see them. Vit had used the unexpected free time for some sightseeing, but Lena's heart hadn't been in it. She'd spent a few lonely afternoons in her hotel room trying to forget about Matas.

As she reread the same article for the third time, she returned to thoughts of him. He had used her, deceived her, outright lied to her. But had it been for the right reasons? Had his confession proved that he trusted her? What did it matter? He had *lied* to her.

Harold Weber burst through the door.

"Here we go," said Vit, standing.

Lena gave him a wry smile before putting the newspaper down. "He's only three days and ten minutes late."

Harold came over. He shook hands with them both.

"You're alone?" said Vit, glancing at the door.

Harold's left eye twitched so many times Lena lost count. "I'm not going to waste my team's time. I'm here only because of some woman from your Homeland Security department who insisted I speak to you. Her people are already here, taking up my valuable time, and she'll be flying in tomorrow. It's a wonder I get anything done with so many interruptions. You Americans shouldn't even be involved with this. It's none of your business, but you've inserted yourselves as usual. I have more important things to do than chat over a latte. Now hurry up and show me the results from your silly little simulation, so I can get back to doing real work."

"Sure thing," said Lena. She wanted to slap Harold. She turned her laptop to him before continuing. "It would be easier if we could plug into a larger screen. You must have one in the control room. You'd be able to see better."

Harold gave her a blistering look, his eyes slits. "The control room is a secure facility. We don't let just anyone in."

"Especially us riff raff," Lena muttered, as she displayed on her laptop the parameter values and list of the assumptions the simulation used. She discussed the possibility of undetected viruses on control room computers transmitting important information to the hacker over the network. As Harold's look became more focused, Lena's self-confidence grew. She spoke with authority, tapping all her knowledge about computer security learned at school and at her job in Virginia in her explanations. She even offered the history of specific hacks that had been used in the energy industry over the last few years.

"How would viruses get on our computers?" Harold said, raising his eyebrows. "It's a secure facility. We have nothing but state of the art . . ."

"There are several ways—phishing is one possibility," said Lena. She glanced at Vit who was sitting back, a whisper of a smile on his face.

"Our systems are secure," said Harold.

Lena shook her head. "All it takes is one email with a link to an infected website. If anyone goes to that website, their computer will be infected."

"Do you think we're amateurs? Our people are trained to delete emails from unfamiliar addresses." Harold's face turned red.

"No," said Lena. "I think your people are human. And it's not just your people. It's everyone in all of the businesses that have a need to connect into the control room. Phishing emails can look very authentic."

Harold squinted at her. "That was our conclusion, too. Our analysis showed spikes in outgoing network traffic at the same time every day up to the day of the outage."

"I would suspect that the virus was sending out information."

"Yes, that's what we suspect as well."

Lena proceeded to review other assumptions, some involving programs and hardware in the control room—information Matas had provided. Harold grew quiet.

"How do you know all that?" he said.

This was the moment. She could tell Harold and Vit about Matas, or protect the man she once loved. She remembered that Ramute and Antanas were frauds, and that Matas had followed her when she first arrived. The lies still hurt—a knife to her heart. Now was the time to take revenge, but her words surprised her. "I worked in computer security for years, and know what to look for."

Harold looked like he expected more, so Lena continued. "I researched the pipeline and control room operation for a report I was doing for Vit. Many of the companies involved are known to the public. Once I had a list of companies, I had a good idea about the products selected. It would be the best each company has to offer in their field of expertise. Many of the specifications are available for download from corporate websites."

"If you know all this, what's to make me think you're not the hacker?" Harold said, eyeing her suspiciously.

Lena felt her face grow hot. "I'm not the hacker. You have a lot of nerve talking to me like I'm a damned idiot. Take my computer and see for yourself." She shoved her laptop at him.

She got to her feet and was about to walk away when Vit stopped her.

"Harold," said Vit. "Don't you think we should go somewhere a little more private to talk?"

~~

Two weeks later in her Kremlin office, Vera finished reading the memorandum, and went back to read it again. "This is official?"

Orlov, Rozoff, and Krum, the accountant, were in her office at the Kremlin sitting across from her desk.

Rozoff spoke up. "The EU just concluded their meetings and came up with a decision to curb the shipment of Russian gas by putting a cap on the amount we can send into the European pipelines. That effectively limits the amount of gas we can ship through the Baltic pipeline. That they were able to do anything in such a short time is amazing to me, but there you have it."

"Did you have anything to do with this?" said Vera.

Rozoff flushed. "Absolutely not. I wasn't there, and neither was Nina Ditlova. Only the non-Russian members of the Baltic Pipeline AG were involved. They even excluded your friend, Katharina Becker."

"This is outrageous."

"We have no choice but to concede."

Vera almost spat the words, "There is always a choice."

Rozoff pulled out a handkerchief and wiped his brow. "In terms of money lost to Russia, it's substantial. The agreement comes with assurances that Europe will continue to buy our fuel—just not as much of it through the Baltic pipelines. Europe will probably want more gas through the legacy pipelines traversing Ukraine and Poland. They're already threatening to increase their transit fees."

"I don't want to lose anything!"

Krum spoke up. "Over time, we stand to lose close to a billion rubles. We'll have to get creative to recoup the money."

Vera watched the men for any sign that they appreciated how dire this was. The data they gathered from the sensor equipment could be analyzed for intelligence purposes. It could tell them of a threat. Then, because they controlled the pipeline and provided most of the gas, they could remove that threat, even if it meant toppling governments and stepping in to control people, resources, everything. No one would object because they were protecting a valuable resource. The EU decision diminished that possibility. Russia would have to join with other countries to quell any threat instead of acting unilaterally. Vera didn't like working with other countries. Then there was the new mandate that operating the Baltic pipeline would be done by a coalition led by Germany. *She* wanted to operate the pipeline. It gave her the best opportunity to do what was right for Russia. But all that has changed. No one in the room seemed to react.

No one seemed to care. No one seemed to understand. All they showed was barely concealed anger.

Krum readjusted the wire-rimmed glasses balancing on his nose. "In terms of pure accounting, we can gradually increase the price of gas to make up for our losses. The EU will complain, but a modest cost increase should be tolerable. On the other hand, our business associates won't be very happy, especially if Ukraine demands additional tariff fees. Our businessmen are never happy with any delay in profit. In the short term, it may affect our ability to get new investors for the Power of Siberia pipeline, because we'll be in a less powerful position."

Vera slammed her palm on the desk. "We shouldn't have to recoup anything. We did nothing wrong. We didn't cause the outage."

"The universe can be unkind," said Rozoff.

Vera skewered him with a look. "Colonel Orlov, what did Bok find?"

"Nothing, so I brought him in."

Vera recalled her brief chat with Nina relaying the information Bok had provided upon returning from Vilnius. At least this detail was consistent in their stories. At the time, Vera had been angrier than she'd been in years—she had wanted Bok to stay and finish the job. That Orlov had brought Bok back to Russia was an affront. Angry as she was, Vera forced herself to take a deep breath and calm down. Anger doesn't solve problems. Orlov had done this without consulting her. Did he assume her power was already waning? Or did he know something?

She would send Bok back to Lithuania, but not yet. Orlov needed some time to believe he was still in control. She clenched her jaw. *Maybe he really is in control, and I'm the one who's not.*

"Did you really think that Bok was going to be caught?" she said.

Orlov continued. "I felt that with the high-profile nature of the case, it was a real risk if any of our agents were found in Lithuania. It would lead to conclusions that were bad for us."

Vera glowered. Orlov cleared his throat before speaking. "ARAS issued another alert for Bok. They knew he was in the country, so I called everyone back. It's just too risky to keep our agents there."

"It's your job to take risks!" Vera didn't have time for a fight, at least not now. She abruptly waved the men off. They glanced at each other before standing and exiting the room.

When she was alone, she poured a cup of tea from the samovar and thought of Babushka. Vera had loved her grandmother very much, but inevitably, she died. Things changed. Good people left us, sometimes all too soon.

She went back to her desk and read the memo again. It was the worst possible news; absolutely the worst. She felt like she had been personally violated.

The concessions forced upon Russia by the EU were substantial, and they had no choice but to agree. Contesting the proposal meant heavy sanctions against Russia. Agreeing meant some money would come in from sales of gas to the EU, but far less than she had expected and far less than what others had expected. It would take longer to pay off construction debt. Looking to the future, it would give China the upper hand when it came to negotiating a fuel price. That's when this fiasco of an agreement would really hurt, but Vera was relatively certain few people were thinking about the future right now.

She went to the wall switch and turned on all the lights in the room, casting away the shadows. She took a piece of the tea cake that was laid out for her every afternoon, and put it on a plate. She set it on the floor for the Domovoy—maybe the house spirits would help her.

Time was running out. The end could come at any moment. The road might explode under her on the way home tonight. A well-aimed missile might destroy her lovely residencia as she lay in bed. A gunman might come into her office and shoot her dead, although that was highly unlikely, given the raft of bodyguards paid to give up their lives for her. Either way, blood was a bitch to get out of a light blue rug.

She expected the oligarchs to summon her to a meeting—they might even wait until January. If she were arranging things, she'd let her victim suffer for a few months. The oligarchs might do the same thing. They'd want to see how far she deteriorated after feeling hunted for months. They'd tell her she'd been stripped of power. Orlov would probably be there, but in support of someone else. She might bring a gun and shoot anyone who smirked.

An interim president would be introduced. Probably Grinsky. He'd appoint whomever he wanted as prime minister. How ironic if it were Rozoff. The next election would be discussed. Then she would be escorted out of the room to an uncertain fate.

Nina's future was over, too. Russia held nothing but darkness for them now. No hope, no joy, no families. Just each other, and whatever money Nina had been able to hide from prying Russian eyes. If they were able to escape, life abroad would be precarious: they'd be hunted and when found, slaughtered. Vera didn't know if she had the energy to fight for that kind of life.

She imagined the headlines announcing her demise would be something like *Vera Koslova, Known for the Baltic Pipeline Debacle, Dead of Natural Causes*. If they didn't kill her, she'd undoubtedly be held under house arrest in some remote dacha, where she'd probably be controlled by drugs. If that was her end, Nina was bound to be executed and tossed into an anonymous grave.

If the oligarchs were charitable, they'd allow her and Nina to live out their lives in Siberia. It was where they grew up. Dying there would lend a certain symmetry to her life. But Vera didn't think she'd be allowed this luxury.

In the end, her childhood friend, a sister in her heart, would be dead because of her. Vera brushed away a tear. Perhaps they could have a last meal together. She picked up the phone and went to the window, dialing Nina's number one last time, wondering how she was going to say goodbye to her dear friend.

As she listened to the phone ring, Vera went to Babushka's samovar, touched the silver, and closed her eyes. She pictured her grandmother's deep wrinkles and thin smile, feeling strength through the cool metal. Babushka never gave up.

Nina answered. Upon hearing the concern in her friend's voice, Vera's despair lifted a little, and it was enough. She thought of the injustice perpetrated upon her, and raw anger took hold. Anger was something she could always rely on.

"Nina," said Vera. "We're not going to just sit back and let those bastards get the best of us."

CHAPTER 31

Zurich—September 28

Baltic Watch Issue 33724: Breaking News. *Yielding to pressure from the EU, Russia has curbed its shipments of gas through the Baltic Sea pipelines to comply with new regulations limiting the amount of Russian gas allowed to enter the European pipeline grid through Germany. The EU decision balances German interests against potential negative impact to other EU states. Additional gas is available to European homes in shipments of Russian gas through legacy pipelines in Ukraine and Poland. Both countries have already increased their gas transit fees to Russia. The EU decision specifies that Baltic pipeline maintenance and oversight will be performed by an international coalition of EU members led by Germany.*

"Good summary, Vit," said Lena, looking past Vit's shoulder to the laptop screen. They were waiting with Mrs. Brown at the Flughafen Zurich airport in a corner by themselves. The massive walls of windows flooded the area with natural light as Vit and Lena waited for their flight to Vilnius. Mrs. Brown was headed for DC.

Vit grinned. "I can't believe the way people have been responding to our analysis. Subscriptions are up two hundred percent. For the first time in Baltic Watch history, we have subscribers from twenty-three countries. We may stay in business for a while longer. I'll be in need of full-time help, preferably a reporter. Any interest, Lena?"

Lena's mobile phone rang. She held up a finger. It was Harold Weber. She put the phone on speaker.

Harold's unctuous voice came from the phone. "Thank you again for your help, Ms. Markus. I wish you had told us about your simulation earlier. It would have saved us a tremendous amount of work. I can't tell you the stress we've been under."

"But I told you about it right away . . ." Lena rolled her eyes. "You're welcome, Harold."

After hanging up, Lena said, "I won't miss him one bit."

"The last month has been outstanding," said Mrs. Brown. Even in the nondescript dark suit, wearing glasses and with her hair pulled back, she gave off a sexy government bureaucrat vibe. "When you called me, Vit, I got the wheels turning. The early results of your simulation, Lena, were enough to get the US government to contact the EU with a damn good working theory as to how the break-in occurred. That got their attention. The EU got the Russians to agree to give up controlling votes in the Baltic Pipeline AG Corporation. The EU still wants the gas, but at least they have some assurance that Russia won't use it to sway political decisions."

"But another outage could occur," said Vit.

Mrs. Brown nodded. "Yes, it could. But not this particular outage. In fact, DHS and the FBI got word out through our security channels to all pipeline companies worldwide with instructions on how to prevent this particular scenario from ever happening again. I can say with confidence that this actually made the world a safer place."

"It really was the Russians, then?" said Lena. She knew the truth, but couldn't help asking one last time to check that her deceptions had been enough to keep Matas's role a secret. *Why am I still protecting him? He doesn't deserve it.*

Mrs. Brown looked over her shoulder. "Dunno. And it doesn't matter. Shared control of the pipeline monitoring and maintenance should have been part of the agreements in the first place. At least they have it now. And there'll be a lot more interest in building LNG terminals in Europe."

Mrs. Brown smiled at Lena. "I'm glad you accepted my offer. I can't give you stock options or a stupendous salary like you can get in the private sector—one drawback in working for the government. But on the positive side, it's very important and rewarding work."

"What offer?" said Vit.

"I asked Lena to come to Washington and work at DHS. What she did at Zug was amazing. She explained the simulation and results so clearly that even Harold Weber understood. Her additions to the simulation were flawless and showed a fundamental understanding of computers and computer security that I rarely see, especially in a person her age. I want her on my staff."

Lena smiled. "The people at Zug offered me a job, too. I turned them down, mostly because I couldn't bear working with Harold. But if you want me, Mrs. Brown, I'm all yours. Sorry Vit. If you had predicted this outcome when I first got to Lithuania, I'd have called you crazy."

"You needed confidence, Lena," said Vit. "And a massive problem to solve to show off your skills."

Lena stared at Vit. "It wasn't only that. When I realized how dearly Lithuanians cherished their independence, I had to ask myself what I was doing to help my own country. It was nothing. At DHS, I have a chance to do something significant. Money isn't everything."

"You've changed, Lena," said Vit.

Mrs. Brown glanced at Vit. "You're not getting off so easy, Mr. Partenkas. I know you had to destroy Annie. You changed her configuration, didn't you?"

Vit nodded sheepishly.

"I told you not to, remember?" Mrs. Brown looked downright angry.

He nodded again.

"Your actions show me you can't be trusted. Don't even consider asking me for another copy of Annie. The answer will be unequivocally no. You are a threat to national security."

Vit held out his hands as if he were about to be handcuffed.

Mrs. Brown grimaced. "I want you in DC next month to brief my team. They need to know how you reconfigured Annie, because we thought we'd locked her down so no changes were possible. That's the only reason we allowed you to have a copy of her in the first place. Apparently, we missed something."

"You need me to consult? For how long?" Vit deadpanned.

"Plan to be in DC for a month at least. Let's say you'll be doing this work for me in lieu of a prison sentence."

"In that case, I'm sure I can manage some time away. I'll have to make temporary arrangements to keep Baltic Watch going while I'm in the US. Fortunately, I can do a lot of work remotely. I'll see you in DC."

Mrs. Brown stood, placing a hand on Lena's shoulder. "For your personal safety, I think it would be good if you got out of Europe. I think the Russians did this, but if they didn't, they'll search for the culprit who did. You could be on their short list."

Lena shivered, remembering the Russian who had tied her to a chair and had held a knife to her neck. "I'm confused. Now you think it wasn't the Russians?"

"We just don't have any concrete evidence, yet. Take a day or two to get your things together, but it's time for you to come home. In the meanwhile, Zuza told me she pulled in a few favors and will have an agent keeping an eye on you until you leave Lithuania. Just as a precaution."

Vit looked surprised. "How do you know Zuza?"

Mrs. Brown glanced at her watch. "We talked by phone a few times. We women have to stick together." She winked at Lena. "Have a safe flight to Vilnius. I'd better get to my gate. I'll see you both soon."

Lena stood and gave Mrs. Brown a hug, whispering, "Thank you."

Mrs. Brown shook hands with Vit. "Whenever you phone me, I know it's going to be interesting."

Vit gave her a peck on the cheek and she walked away, wheeling her carryon bag behind her.

Lena spoke first. "I think the financial agreement with Russia was the best one possible. Russia had their leash shortened, and Europe gets their fuel."

"We'll see if Vera Koslova survives. Russians don't like failure, and they don't like to lose money."

"I read the analysis you posted about her. It had most of my original material, but you backed up every sentence with real data. It was beautiful. Thanks for including my name in the byline."

Vit nodded. "You gave me a good basic piece to work with. I had to fill in material, but your conjectures were all justified. I had to tone down your venom, though. You don't like that woman, do you?"

"Not a bit, but I guess as a political analyst, I have a lot to learn."

"What about Matas?"

Lena felt hot under Vit's gaze. "I haven't heard from him, and I don't expect to."

"He's led an interesting life from priest to . . ."

"Say it. Thief."

"You knew?"

"He told me."

Vit sighed. "Zuza had her people dig into his past. They weren't sure about the thief part."

"Are you going to tell her?"

"There's no evidence against him." Vit shrugged. "As far as Zuza's concerned, he didn't do anything other than orchestrate a meeting with a pretty young woman from the US. Morally unethical, but not illegal."

Vit gazed at her. "What did he know about the hack?"

Lena considered telling him every sordid detail about Ramute, the hack, Peter—all of it. Vit had been good to her. She felt she owed him something, but she couldn't tell him the truth. He was too close to Zuza and might tell her everything. Lena shouldn't care what happened to Matas. But once again, her heart ruled her head. "He had nothing to do with it, as far as I know."

"You should call him." Vit sighed. "Don't make the same mistakes I've made."

"Are you talking about me and Matas or you and Zuza?"

"People like Matas who survived the occupation went through a lot. When freedom finally came, things changed for the good, but it took time. Jobs were hard to find, services were inadequate, medicine was scarce. It took time for the government to be able to step in and help in a significant way. Until they did, people had to survive. That's what Matas did. It would have been nice if he'd taken up a trade like baker or carpenter, but he didn't."

"Even if I wanted to contact him, I don't have his number. And I don't think he wants to talk to me."

Vit handed her a slip of paper. "You won't know for sure unless you try. Zuza's compliments."

"How do I know this number is still good?"

"It is."

"Are you going to call Zuza when we get back to Vilnius?"

Vit gave her a rueful smile. "And the student becomes the teacher. I guess I'll have to."

CHAPTER 32

Moscow—September 30

The Channel One TV crew had overrun Vera's office with a staggering amount of equipment. Cameras were in position. Technicians bustled about checking microphones. Lighting experts adjusted the high intensity lamps. Vera sat at her massive desk as a makeup artist put the final touches of powder on her nose.

When Nina Ditlova entered the room, Vera waved off the cosmetician and went to her friend. The women embraced.

"Is it done?" said Vera.

Nina nodded, handing Vera a copy of *Rossiyskaya Gazeta*. The newspaper smelled of fresh ink.

Feeling relieved, Vera glanced at the headline. "Do I need to change anything in the story we rehearsed?"

"Not a word."

"All I have to do is sell it to the entire world."

Nina put a hand on Vera's shoulder. "It gives us time to find out who really screwed up the pipeline."

"There's no other way?"

"The plan is already in motion."

"Then let's get on with it." Vera went back to her chair while Nina remained in the shadows.

Trying not to think of Orlov made his image all the more vivid. Vera lay the newspaper down on her desk. The producer motioned her to begin. She took a deep breath, folded her hands, and looked into the camera.

"Good citizens of Russia, we have weathered many storms together. Each time, I emerged stronger and more resolved to provide you and your children with opportunity for a good and meaningful life.

"The storm we weather now is one of the worst we've ever seen. Weeks ago, our cyberexperts, the best in the world, linked the Baltic pipeline outage to Ukrainian hackers. Shocked as we were to find little brother engaged in such heinous activity, we found it wasn't the entire story."

She held up the newspaper while flexing her arm muscles to keep them from shaking. The headline read *FSB Head Orlov Accused of Treason.*

"Recently, the GRU Main Center for Special Technology discovered that the pipeline outage had been orchestrated by one of our very own, Colonel Orlov, head of the FSB. An incontrovertible trail linked Orlov to the Ukrainian hackers he had hired. Believing it was a means to overturn our government and oust me from office, Colonel Orlov engaged these hackers in a first step to take over the government. When the time was right, this team perpetrated a complex and extremely well-coordinated act of cyberterrorism designed specifically to discredit me and Russia in the eyes of the world." Vera touched the corner of her eye—a gesture she had planned with Nina, but it felt real.

"In this detestable act, we found a co-conspirator. Yuri Rozoff, a Russian businessman, helped plan and orchestrate these actions. While Colonel Orlov was meeting with his team of cyberexperts, Yuri Rozoff was working behind the scenes to provide that team with the information they needed to plan the outage. Thanks to Rozoff's trusted position in the Baltic Pipeline AG, he provided technical details, specifications, and more. He had access to everything the hackers could possibly need, and they were almost successful.

"Despite the truths we uncovered, the result of the pipeline sabotage was that a EU coalition forced Russia to accept terms limiting the amount of gas we can ship into the European pipeline grid. This means we will get less money from our gas sales. It also limits my ability to provide you with more hospitals, schools, and better living conditions."

She gazed into the camera, remembering Nina's coaching: *Make everyone feel like you're speaking just to them.* "The West is not our friend.

Unfortunately, the damage has been done, and there is little we can do beyond punishing the guilty parties to the fullest extent of Russian law. Orlov has been stripped of his rank, and is being questioned in Lubyanka prison.

"When investigators went to Yuri Rozoff's apartment last night to arrest him, they found his body hanging from rafters, in an apparent suicide." Vera paused for a sip of water. She cleared her throat, forcing her voice to remain steady.

"All of the substantial assets of these two traitors will be liquidated and donated to the newly formed Center for Morality and Justice at Moscow State University.

"Thanks to the hard work of many dedicated people, we have found the cancer, and I have cut it out. Russia is healthy once again. Your government is strong and I am here to continue protecting you. I have saved you from the enemies within our ranks.

"Orlov and Rozoff damaged the integrity of Mother Russia. Our EU gas customers no longer trust us, but I will work tirelessly to regain that trust. I will personally be involved with all negotiations for future fuel prices, and I will make sure your financial needs are well represented. As long as I live and serve you as President of the Russian Federation, I personally guarantee the integrity of the Baltic pipeline, and any other pipeline Russia builds. I personally promise successful and prosperous lives for you and your children.

"Our gas and oil reserves have already saved the world from its next energy crisis. With my guidance and your support, we are on the road to making Russia the greatest nation on earth."

When Vera finished speaking, the high intensity lights went dark and the room immediately felt cooler. The crew applauded as she detached the microphone from her lapel and pulled off the tape that hid the wire going to the body-pack transmitter hidden in an inside pocket of her jacket. She handed the equipment to a technician, trying to read his face. The man smiled and nodded. Vera relaxed. At least one person had believed her.

She led Nina into the privacy of the sitting room next to her office while the film crew packed up.

The first phone call came in just as Vera was settling into her favorite spot on the sofa. She put it on speaker.

"Madame President, it's Stas."

Vera had to think for a moment. *Grinsky.* She waited for him to speak.

"Our nation is grateful that you found the culprits and dealt with them so swiftly."

Did you have a role in this, Grinsky?

"With you leading us, we're sure to have a great future," he said.

"I assume," said Vera, "that I can rely on your support in all of my future projects?"

"Certainly, and with pleasure, Madame President."

Vera ended the call. Grinsky gave hollow promises. Still, he had sounded convinced that she had told the truth. *If Grinsky believes me, everyone else probably does, too.* She should feel relieved, happy with her success. All she felt was exhaustion.

The phone rang again. Vera waved it off. "Let my secretary handle it. He's been hovering in the outer office all day no doubt wondering what's going on. I'm off for the night, as much as it's possible."

Nina poured out two tumblers of vodka. Vera took one. Her eyes misted as her thoughts went to Orlov in Lubyanka, painfully waiting out what little time he had left.

"It had to be done," said Nina. "Orlov broke your trust. He knew what you wanted, and yet he took it upon himself to bring Bok home. Who knows what other things Orlov might have done given the time and opportunity?"

"Yes. He had to be punished, but it doesn't make this easier." Vera pictured the crescent shaped scar on Orlov's back. She drank the vodka and held out the glass. Nina filled it again.

"No one can do what you do," said Nina. "No one thinks like you do. No one makes the sacrifices you do. Russian is lucky to have you as her leader."

"Have them end it quickly for Orlov. There's no need for him to suffer."

"He's already dead."

Vera gazed into her glass. Dwelling on her old lover could doom her, and still . . .

Nina spoke. "There'll be an announcement tomorrow that his heart gave out, or something of the sort. He signed a full confession."

"It's too bad about Rozoff. I warned him to stay away from Grinsky. I couldn't risk the two of them plotting against me, could I?" said Vera. She remembered Rozoff's feeble tennis serve.

"Of course not. He was a schemer who took credit for things he didn't do."

"Maybe he was a politician after all. What are we going to do about finding the people who really did this?" said Vera.

"We know what happened. We just don't know who did it. We know that Lena Markus is going back to the US soon. I'm not convinced she was smart enough to do this, even though she had computer security training."

"Keep our best people working on this, but do it quietly. No one can know we're still searching. Hopefully, the hackers left something behind."

"And if we find nothing?"

"Then get that other man involved—that hacker we hear about from time to time. But only use him as a last resort. I don't know if we can trust him."

"Yes. Wizard. Volshebnik."

"That's him. He's supposed to be the best."

~~

In the book-lined office in his home, Grinsky hung up his phone, feeling ill from his show of support for Vera Koslova. *The woman has as many lives as a cat.*

The TV was on. Channel One commentators were reviewing the president's brief speech. He had muted the sound to make his phone call. A practice Fedov had taught him—always be the first to congratulate your enemy.

Grinsky had almost felt the brush from the white-robed woman of death, but she had come for Rozoff instead. He wasn't sure Koslova had discovered their plot against her, because they didn't really have one yet. That Grinsky was still alive meant Rozoff had either kept silent, or Koslova wasn't sure Grinsky was involved. For now.

Poor Yuri. He would never commit suicide. He was too fat and happy with his creature comforts to even think about death. It had to have been a staged suicide ordered by her, that bitch. Yuri's cold-blooded murder was another example of the swift hand of Koslovian justice.

Grinsky and his cronies had no plan to cause any disruption to the pipeline. They were only interested in discrediting her by leveraging opportunity presented them by chance. Orlov hadn't even been part of their scheming.

Orlov couldn't have attempted a coup—Grinsky would have known about it. Either Orlov was a master of discretion, or this was a Koslovian-manufactured fable to rid her of an enemy. Grinsky suspected the latter.

Shivering, he got up and went to the fire roaring in the fireplace. He filled a glass with vodka from the mantle and drank it down. His instinct was to contact Fedov right away to get the elder statesman's perspective. Grinsky dialed the number he knew by heart, but instead of completing the call, he ended it. He'd do absolutely nothing to garner suspicion. At this point, he had only one goal—to survive the reign of Tsarina Koslova.

~~

A few days after returning from Zug, Lena sat in the coffee shop across from her apartment on Pylimo Street trying to warm her hands on the double latte. The leader of the FSB, a Colonel Orlov, had been charged with orchestrating the pipeline outage by hiring Ukrainian hackers. She pictured Vit, undoubtedly still at the office, happily analyzing the turn of events for his subscribers. One good thing from all this mess was that it appeared to have saved Baltic Watch. Vit was still in business, and money from new subscribers was pouring in.

Still, Lena knew the headlines to be false—absolutely untrue, based on what Matas had told her. Matas's story made sense: a wealthy Lithuanian had funded a team to hack the pipeline and blame Russia, causing her political damage in the international sphere. They had been tremendously successful.

She had to admit that Vera Koslova was brilliant and ruthless, no doubt the most capable person to lead Russia in decades. Fingering Orlov as the culprit allowed her to remain in office, absolve herself of any involvement, maintain power, and use her influence to build another pipeline, this time to China.

Lena's gaze went to the few people in the coffee shop—any of them could be the Russian who had held her at knifepoint. The police had been watching her, but it wasn't enough to settle her nerves.

She looked through the window to her apartment. The memory of being tied to a chair by that Russian was too fresh. Here in Lithuania, she was constantly nervous, constantly distressed, thinking he was going to appear again and this time do even more damage. She had gotten a room in a hotel on the other side of town, hoping she would feel safe enough to get some sleep. It hadn't worked, but that's where she was staying anyway.

Despite Mrs. Brown's warning, she couldn't bear to leave Vit alone with so much work. She'd lied to him about Matas, so helping out was the least she could do. Yesterday she'd assisted Vit with more analyses and handling the new subscribers at Baltic Watch. Last night, she had lain awake in her hotel room, waiting for that Russian to burst in through the door. It didn't matter that he couldn't possibly know where she was, and might not be in the country anymore. She had to tolerate this fear until she left the day after tomorrow. But fear might follow her wherever she went. She wondered if it would be with her for the rest of her life.

Every day, she visited the coffee shop. It wasn't the closest one to the office, but here, she felt closer to Matas. In the last few weeks, she'd gone from hating him for deceiving her, to realizing he had helped his country and all of Europe for that matter. Despite the danger, he'd shown a dedication to his country that put her to shame.

But did she love him? She'd protected him to the very best of her ability. Was that because he was a patriot or because she still felt something for him? Damnit! Falling in love wasn't part of her plan.

She pulled the slip of paper from her pocket that Vit had given her holding Matas's number. Lena dialed it, and he answered. She said they should talk. He said he'd be there in thirty minutes. The coffee shop where they had first met seemed a fitting place.

She had said some horrible things to Matas. She'd let him believe she might tell the police about him. As she waited, she wondered if he was going to show up. She wondered what she would say when he did. When her latte had turned cold, a voice spoke from behind her. "It's good to see you."

CHAPTER 33

Vilnius, Lithuania—October 1

Lena watched Matas sit down across from her. No one was near them in the coffee shop's front corner by the window—their usual spot.

Lena folded her hands and rested them on her lap. "Do you have any idea how bizarre this entire incident has been? I don't know truth anymore. I read the headlines in the newspaper, and I think they're all lies. I think everything *you* tell me is a lie."

Matas looked down at the table, appearing contrite, but she couldn't stop. She took a breath, ready to cast more daggers. "You told Ramute to fool me into believing she was my cousin. How could you do that to me? Even the letter she showed me was fake, wasn't it? Did you tell Ramute to tie it in a ribbon, kiss it, and hold it to her breast? Or was that her idea? It was a nice touch. I believed every word of it. I certainly made it easy for you to trick me, didn't I? That will never happen again."

Matas hung his head. "I'm sorry. I owe my freedom to you."

An apology was important, but still, Lena scoffed. "How do I know your involvement wasn't just some story you made up? Besides, what could the authorities prove? Nobody knows anything about you. And what you did left no trace on the computers. They have no idea who did it."

"Except for you. You know everything."

"Do I? Or do I just know what you've decided to tell me?"

Matas looked up at her. "You know everything because I trust you."

"What's supposed to make me trust *you*?"

"If you say anything, they'll put me away for a long time, not to mention what the Russians would do to us in retaliation."

"Don't put it on me that I have to keep my mouth shut to save Lithuania. You deserve to be punished for what you did. Just because I could put you in jail doesn't mean I can trust you."

"I can't argue with that. You already saved me once. I can't expect you to save me again."

Was this just another story to divert her attention? "I don't know what you're talking about."

"I hated the Soviets for this terrible lack of ethics they instilled in my father. I hated the church because I thought I was a failure. A woman pregnant by a Russian came to me for help. As a man, I was jealous. As a priest, I was useless. I drifted into a world where life had little purpose, and all I cared about was myself, my team, and what rich people paid me to do."

His gaze was on her face—his expression serious. Lena calmed down. She knew this was the truth, and that she had brought him to tell it.

Matas continued. "Peter gave me the chance to be a hero and use everything I learned from years of living in the darkness to actually help my country. Everything was going well until I met you. I had a lot to lose, so I had to know what you were doing. I had no choice but to get close to you. When I saw what Ramute meant to you, it broke my heart. You woke me up from a trance. You showed me that I could love and care. You saved me."

It wasn't nearly enough, but words might never be.

Gazing into her eyes, Matas said, "You're the real hero here. I was able to embarrass Russia, but without you, she would still control the pipeline. You sped up the investigation. Without your simulation, it might have taken months and by then, who knows what Russia would have said to defuse the situation?"

Lena pursed her lips. *Just another lie?* "By giving me the information I needed to run the simulation, you got the result you wanted—Russia shipping far less gas to Europe. That must have been part of your plan, too."

Matas vigorously shook his head. "No. After the hack, we posted a few messages to various social media sites blaming Russia. We expected an avalanche of comments and got it. But that was supposed to be the end of it. My team was supposed to disappear. I was supposed to disappear, too. The morning of the hack, I left your apartment after you did, planning to drive to Utena and never come back. Instead, I went to Ramute, told her I loved you, and asked her what I should do."

Lena sat up straighter. It was too late to talk of love, but she wanted to hear the rest of the story.

Matas continued. "She asked me if I thought you loved me. I told her you did. She told me to find you and tell you how I feel. That's why I came back."

Lena thought of Matas breaking into her apartment to save her from that psychotic Russian. *If it weren't for Matas, who knows what would have happened to me?* "It's been weeks. A lot has changed."

"I want to spend the rest of my life proving to you that I'm a good man. If you give me the chance."

"Why should I?" Lena waited for a reason she could live with.

Matas rested a hand on the table. "Because I risked everything to come back to you."

Lena didn't move. "Who's to say that Russian thug isn't going to put a bullet in my head when I walk out into the street?"

"I won't let him."

She lifted her hands from her lap to cradle her cup. Her fingers were inches from his. "And the Russians. Do you still hate them?"

"They're just people—probably a lot like us. The Russian government, well, I don't trust them. I don't think many people here do. I don't think that will change, at least not in my lifetime. Before I met you, I dreamed of a life of solitude where I couldn't hurt anyone, and no one could hurt me. I still want a place in the woods, but I don't want to be alone anymore. I want to be with you."

Lena shook her head. "I've already made my plans. I'm going to Washington, DC to work for the US government." *A few months ago, my plan was to get rich and travel the world.* So much for plans.

"I know. Vit told me."

I should have expected as much. "No one will ever know what happened. Not even Vit. You can trust me." She bit her tongue at the irony of telling Matas that *he* could trust *her*. *That wasn't the issue here, was it?*

"I do trust you." Matas gave her a weak smile—an expression of hope perhaps? "We pulled off probably the biggest deception of the 21st century. I think we can figure out how to make a long-distance relationship work, if you're willing to try."

"You think everything's all right now? Well, it's not."

"Then let's keep talking until it is, even if it takes years—a lifetime."

~~

Zuza glanced up from her book at the sound of a knock on the door. She wasn't expecting anyone, and it was late. She looked through the peephole and grinned. Vit. Who else?

"Would you be interested in a late-night snack?" Vit handed her a bag. "Mexican burritos from *No Forks*."

"Food—the key to my heart." Zuza brought the bag to the living room and set it down on the coffee table. After a quick trip to the kitchen, she came out with plates, napkins, two glasses, and a bottle of wine.

Zuza sat on the sofa with Vit next to her. It felt good having him here—more like home.

She opened the carryout bag and took out a burrito wrapped in foil. She pulled back the covering and took a bite.

"You have a knack for saving me," said Vit, pouring out the wine.

"I didn't save you, but you have a way of finding trouble."

"We have a relatively happy ending here, which is good. I happen to know that Matas talked to Lena. She's already in the US, and he's planning to visit her."

Zuza smiled. "I knew they were in love the first time I saw them together. I hope it works out for them."

"Their love endured through the pipeline crisis. That's saying a lot."

"Some people are lucky that way." Zuza gazed up at him, wondering what was next. If she and Vit get back together, would he propose again and would she have to choose between him and her job again? The last time, it had torn her apart.

"The important thing is that Lena's safe." Zuza raised an eyebrow. "Are you sure Matas had nothing to do with the pipeline failure?"

"Vera Koslova is the obvious culprit."

Zuza smiled. "And Vera Koslova is paying dearly whether she did anything or not. I don't think she'll be making any big moves, although you can never tell with her."

"Europe has fuel for the foreseeable future."

"All the countries who fear Russia feel safer."

"There's only one issue unresolved."

"I know. Who gets the last burrito?" Zuza pulled another package from the bag, drew back the foil and took a bite. At least Vit was with her in her apartment, and they were talking again. For now, it was enough.

"I think you like food better than you like me." Vit smiled.

"There's no doubt about it. Food wins."

Vit took the burrito from her and set it down. "We're good together. Can't you see that? Your job is dangerous. I know. But some would say that anyone who lives within a stone's throw of Russia lives dangerously."

"You know what my job is like. When we were chasing Darius Artis, you saw for yourself. I can't expose you to that kind of risk."

"How would you be exposing me to anything? I'd be at home taking care of our kids."

Zuza glared at him, and then her expression softened. As an ARAS agent, she knew how fickle life could be. Agents were killed in the line of duty. It was something she accepted. It made her appreciate the anticipation of a future as much as life itself.

"I have to admit," said Zuza, "I'd been hoping something would bring us back together. But it would have been easier if you had just called me."

He leaned in and kissed her. "I'd invite you to my apartment, but we're already here."

Zuza put her arms around his neck and kissed him back, full on the lips, yielding to his arms and his scent and to him. After a long delicious moment, she stood and pulled Vit to his feet. Taking his hand, she led him into the bedroom.

"Let's see if we remember how this goes," she said.

THE END

ABOUT THE AUTHOR

Ursula Wong writes gripping stories about strong women who struggle against impossible odds to achieve their dreams. Her work has appeared in *Everyday Fiction, Spinetingler Magazine, Mystery Reader's Journal,* and the *Insanity Tales* anthologies. She is a professional speaker appearing regularly on TV and radio.

Wong's debut novel, *Purple Trees*, the enchanting Peruvian folk tale, *The Baby Who Fell From the Sky*, and *Finding my Father: A Story of Vietnam* are available on Amazon and other online retailers.

Her World War II historical fiction thriller *Amber Wolf*, the first in the Amber War series, is about a young Lithuanian woman who joins resistance fighters. *Amber War*, the second in the series, tells a little-known story of post-World War II Eastern Europe and the continuing fight against the Soviet occupation. *Amber Widow*, third book in the series, matches Eastern European radicals against Russia in a vicious game of nuclear chess. *Black Amber*, fourth book, has cyberterrorists attack the pipeline bringing natural gas from Russia into Germany. In *Gypsy Amber*, fifth book, Russia unleashes a devious plot to thwart China's territorial expansion into Central Asia.

Ursula is available for speaking events and lectures on writing and publishing. For more information, contact her at urslwng@gmail.com and sign up for her popular Reaching Readers newsletter at http://ursulawong.wordpress.com.

Finally, reviews are more important than you might think. If you enjoyed *Black Amber*, please consider leaving a review on Amazon.com or sending Ursula your thoughts.

Connect Online:
Website: http://ursulawong.wordpress.com
Email: urslwng@gmail.com

Books by Ursula Wong

Amber Wolf (The Amber War Series Book 1)

Amber War (The Amber War Series Book 2)

Amber Widow (The Amber War Series Book 3)

Black Amber (The Amber War Series Book 4)

Gypsy Amber (The Amber War Series Book 5)

Purple Trees

The Baby Who Fell From the Sky

Finding my Father: A Story of Vietnam

Ursula is available for speaking events and lectures on writing and publishing. For more information, contact her at urslwng@gmail.com and sign up for her popular Reaching Readers newsletter at http://ursulawong.wordpress.com.

LIST OF CHARACTERS

Annie – Sagus computer program and Vit's personal assistant.
Antanas – Friend of Matas, son of Ramute.
Arkady – Hacker from Belarus. Works for Matas.
Zuza Bartus – ARAS agent.
Alexy Bok – Contract killer for the Russian SVR.
Dalia – Ramute's friend who had been deported to Camp Userda, Siberia.
Mrs. Brown – IT Manager from the US Department of Homeland Security.
Katharina Becker – CEO of Baltic Pipeline AG.
Joe Day – CEO of Britain-Energy.
Nina Ditlova – Special assistant to Vera Koslova, and her friend.
Igor Fedov – Former president of the Russian Federation.
Stas Grinsky – Prime Minister of Russia.
Rina Kleptys – Simona's sister. Car thief.
Simona Kleptys – Rina's sister. Car thief.
Michael Koslov – Vera Koslova's husband.
Vera Yaroslavna Koslova – President of the Russian Federation.
Krum – Russian accountant.
Peter Landus – Wealthy Lithuanian-American funding the cyberattack on the Baltic pipeline. Shares his name with an uncle who was executed by the Soviets in 1946.
Aldona Markus – Lena's grandmother. Sister to Gerde.
Lena Markus – American of Lithuanian descent working as an intern at Baltic Watch. Computer expert.
Gerde Markus – Lena's great aunt. Sister to Aldona. Married into Simoliunas family.
Matas Nortas – Team lead for the cyberattack on the Baltic pipeline.
Colonel Orlov – Director of the FSB.
Vit Partenkas – Tilda Partenkas's grandson. IT expert. Former owner of Sagus Corporation.
Tilda Partenkas – Nuclear physicist, co-inventor of the anti-radiation drug Z-109.
Ramute – Friend of Matas, mother of Antanas.
Yuri Rozoff – Russian oligarch and oil millionaire.
Sofia – SVR agent sent to Lithuania by Orlov. Stefan's partner.
Stefan – SVR agent sent to Lithuania by Orlov. Sofia's partner.
Volshebnik – Russian hacker and Arkady's teacher.

Harold Weber – Engineer and public liaison to the control room in Zug, Switzerland.

Zeitzev – Russian oligarch.

READING LIST

"Leave your Tears in Moscow," Barbara Armonas, J.B. Lippincott Company, NY, 1961.

"Michael Strogoff: A Courier of the Czar," Jules Verne, Charles Scribner's Sons, NY, NY, 1927.

"Siberian Dawn: A Journey Across the New Russia," Jeffrey Taylor, Hungry Mind Press, 1999.

"Siberian Light," Robin White, Delacorte Press, NY, NY, 1997.

"The Quest: Energy, Security, and the Remaking of the Modern World," Daniel Yergin, The Penguin Group, NY, NY, 2011.

"The Bear and the Dragon," Tom Clancy, G. P. Putnam's Sons, NY, NY, 2000.

"Tom Clancy: Commander in Chief," Mark Greaney, G. P. Putnam Son's, NY, NY, 2015.

"Titania," Martin Cruz smith, Simon & Schuster, NY, NY, 2013.

"The New Great Game," Lutz Kleveman, Atlantic Monthly Press, NY, NY, 2003.

Made in the USA
Middletown, DE
02 October 2023

39994563R00146